Praise for
Repairing the World

"In *Repairing the World*, Epstein has created a story that acknowledges the little miracles of building new friendships and surviving grief. It is a story sprinkled with moments of unthinkable heartache, but also moments of extraordinary healing and glimpses into a world of bright magic. This book itself is a gift of healing—a lyrical story so filled with hope and light it will show you the brilliance coming through your own cracked places."

—Sarah Allen, author of *What Stars Are Made Of* and *Breathing Underwater*

"A moving and many-layered tale about what it means to navigate the complexities of friendship and loss—and the power of believing in the possibilities life holds for renewal. This is a stirring debut, a book that will be a consolation and a joy to many young readers."

—Ben Guterson, author of *The Winterhouse Mysteries*

"When eleven-year-old Daisy loses her best friend her world breaks, and my heart broke along with it. But as Daisy discovers the way through her grief is to connect, to create, to repair, I felt my own heart knitting itself back together, right along with Daisy's. This is a profound and lovely book about loss, grace, and the beauty and magic that is all around us."

—Gayle Forman, author of *Frankie & Bug*

Repairing the World

Linda Epstein

ALADDIN

New York London Toronto Sydney New Delhi

ALADDIN

An imprint of Simon & Schuster Children's Publishing Division

1230 Avenue of the Americas, New York, New York 10020

First Aladdin hardcover edition July 2022

For information about special discounts for bulk purchases, please contact Simon & Schuster Special Sales at 1-866-506-1949 or business@simonandschuster.com.

The Simon & Schuster Speakers Bureau can bring authors to your live event. For more information or to book an event contact the Simon & Schuster Speakers Bureau at 1-866-248-3049 or visit our website at www.simonspeakers.com.

Book designed by Heather Palisi

The text of this book was set in Griffo Classico.

Manufactured in the United States of America 0522 FFG

2 4 6 8 10 9 7 5 3 1

Library of Congress Cataloging-in-Publication Data

Names: Epstein, Linda, author.

Title: Repairing the world / by Linda Epstein.

Description: New York : Aladdin, 2022. | Audience: Ages 8-12. |

Summary: Grieving over the sudden death of her best friend, eleven-year-old Daisy finds it hard to get excited about things like her new baby sister and her community service project for Hebrew school, but new middle school friends and supportive family members help Daisy discover a way to move forward.

Identifiers: LCCN 2021045088 (print) | LCCN 2021045089 (ebook) |

ISBN 9781534498556 (hardcover) | ISBN 9781534498570 (ebook)

Subjects: CYAC: Friendship—Fiction. | Grief—Fiction. | Middle schools—Fiction. | Schools—Fiction. | Jews—New York (State)—Fiction. | Long Island (N.Y.)—Fiction. | LCGFT: Novels.

Classification: LCC PZ7.1.E625 Re 2022 (print) | LCC PZ7.1.E625 (ebook) | DDC [Fic]—dc23

LC record available at https://lccn.loc.gov/2021045088

LC ebook record available at https://lccn.loc.gov/2021045089

Excerpt on page vii: "The World I Live In" from *Felicity* by Mary Oliver, published by The Penguin Press New York. Copyright © 2015 by Mary Oliver. Reprinted by permission of The Charlotte Sheedy Literary Agency Inc.

Excerpts on pages 225–227 and 307: "Mi Shebeirach"

Words and Music by Deborah Lynn Friedman

All rights on behalf of The Farf, Inc.

Administered by The Farf, Inc.,

30300 Agoura Rd., Suite 250, Agoura Hills, CA 91301

International Copyright Secured All Rights Reserved

Reprinted by Permission of The Farf, Inc.

For my parents,
Sandi and Lee Epstein,
and for my children,
Anna, Rayna, and Spencer Weingord

I have refused to live
locked in the orderly house of
reasons and proofs.
The world I live in and believe in
is wider than that. And anyway,
what's wrong with *Maybe*?

You wouldn't believe what once or
twice I have seen. I'll just
tell you this:
only if there are angels in your head will you
ever, possibly, see one.

—Mary Oliver

Finding Magic

Ruby let go of the swing; her arms flung out, hair flying behind her. "I'm jumping!" she yelled as she flew through the air. Daisy watched as her best friend soared, then landed on both feet with a satisfying thump. Ruby had looked magical for a moment— like a small, fearless fairy who might sprout wings at any moment and flutter straight up into the trees.

"Now you!" Ruby said breathlessly, turning toward Daisy with an expectant smile. Daisy scraped both feet along the ground, slowing her swing until she could hop off.

"Nah," Daisy said. "I can't fly like you."

"You could," Ruby said. "If you wanted to. You never even try."

"Your hair tie's coming out," Daisy said, ignoring her comment.

Ruby pulled the band through her wispy brown hair and messily retied her ponytail.

"What do you think we should do now?" Daisy said, pushing her own curly hair behind her ears.

Daisy looked around the yard. Ruby scrunched her face up, thinking.

"Raspberries!" they said at the same time.

"Perfect," Ruby said, flinging her arm over Daisy's shoulder.

They walked away from Daisy's house, past her dad's herb garden. As she always did, Daisy let her fingertips brush along the top of the rosemary to release its lemony, woody scent. Then they passed the honeysuckle that was blooming along the chain-link fence that separated their property from Dower Nature Preserve, and both girls breathed deeply in.

"Yum," Ruby said.

"I know," Daisy replied. "Honeysuckle."

"I always think about Winnie the Pooh when I hear the word 'honeysuckle.'"

"Me too," Daisy said.

Finally they reached the bramble of raspberry bushes.

"It was so windy yesterday, half the berries have fallen," Daisy said.

"We can eat ones from the ground, right?" Ruby said, picking up a slightly bruised berry. "These still look okay."

"You always ask me that," Daisy said, "and you know I always say yuck. It's so gross."

"But it *looks* fine," Ruby said.

Daisy made a face. "Does it have bugs on it?"

Ruby tossed it up in the air and caught it in her mouth. "Nope," she said.

"Gross," Daisy repeated, picking one carefully from the bush so she didn't get scratched by the prickles.

"Well, I don't care. The ground ones look fine to me." Ruby popped three more into her mouth as Daisy picked two more from the bush.

"Let's go see the horses," Daisy said. The neighbors had a barn near the fence that separated the two properties.

"Nah," Ruby said. "I'm bored of those horses. They never come close enough to pet."

Daisy shrugged. "They're still fun to look at."

"Then let's go down to the stone wall," Ruby said. "If we're going to look at something, looking at the water is prettier than those dumb horses." She started skipping away.

"I guess so," Daisy said as she ate another raspberry, savoring the tartness as the tiny globes of fruit burst in her mouth.

"Come on!" Ruby said, smiling over her shoulder. So Daisy followed, skipping to catch up.

When they reached the stone wall at the end of the property, overlooking the Long Island Sound, they saw that a huge oak tree from the nature preserve had fallen. The whole top of the tree was on their side of the fence, resting on the low wall. A breeze blew in off the water, and the leaves rippled, whispering in the wind.

"Let's climb it," Ruby said, scrambling onto the flat top of the stone wall and poking her head into the branches.

"I don't know," Daisy said.

Ruby said, "But this is so cool!" and disappeared into the canopy of leaves.

Daisy could hear her father's voice in her head, telling her to be careful. She remembered him telling her some fact about how fallen trees were dangerous. Maybe? Or was it only *falling* trees?

"It doesn't look safe," Daisy said. "It might not be stable."

The breeze blew again, and now it sounded like the tree was saying, *shush shush shush.*

"I can't even budge it," Ruby said, her voice slightly muffled by the foliage. "I'm pushing on a branch super hard, and it's not moving at all."

That wasn't reassuring to Daisy. If the branch could have been moved by the power of Ruby's personality alone, it might have budged. But even though Ruby was technically older than Daisy by six months, she was tiny, almost half a head shorter than Daisy.

She heard Ruby rustling from inside the branches. "I'm sure it's fine," Ruby said, popping her head out of the greenery. Daisy wasn't sure, though. "I'm going to climb it!" Ruby disappeared back into the leaves.

Daisy clambered onto the wall, pushed a branch aside, and carefully stepped inside the shade of the treetop. Ruby had already started to climb onto a big branch, grabbing at the limb and pulling herself up and onto it. Daisy took a step forward, feet still planted on the stone wall, her hand clutching a nearby limb for balance. She watched as Ruby scooted on her stomach until she reached a fork in the branches.

"Come on!" Ruby called to her as she sat up and perched in a nook.

The way Ruby had done it had looked pretty easy,

like she was climbing the monkey bars in the playground at school. Daisy pulled herself up, like Ruby had, and began to scoot her way over. A slight breeze rippled through the leaves, and Daisy closed her eyes and hugged the branch she was on, her heart thumping in her chest.

"You're okay," Ruby said.

Daisy opened her eyes and gazed at Ruby.

"You are," Ruby said. "Promise."

But doing it was scarier than watching Ruby do it. "Rube, I don't like this," she said in a small voice.

The wind fluttered through the leaves again. Daisy chewed her bottom lip and scooted another couple of inches. The bark of the tree felt rough under her hands, and it was hard to get a good grip. Every time the wind blew, the whole tree rustled, the leaves catching even the smallest breeze, and Daisy's heart sped up.

"Just keep going, Daze," Ruby said.

Hand over hand, little by little, she made her way toward Ruby. When she finally got to the fork where Ruby was perched, they sat together for a moment, leaning into each other among the leafy green foliage, like two birds in a nest. Daisy took a deep, relieved breath.

"See?" Ruby said. "I knew you could do it." She smiled at Daisy, her eyes crinkling in the corners.

Ruby slipped off her hair tie and fixed her pony-tail again, smoothing her hair back to get the escaped bits off her face. Sitting in the branches like this, she looked like a tree sprite or wood elf, Daisy thought, or some kind of magical creature from a fairy tale, with her olive-toned skin, wispy hair, and moss-colored T-shirt. A mosquito buzzed, and Ruby swatted it away. "Let's keep going," she said.

On her butt, bit by bit, Ruby scooched her way over to the main part of the trunk and out of the crown.

"Careful," Daisy said, still perched between the fork in the branches, waiting to see what Ruby did. Ruby inched herself out of the greenery, her legs hanging down on either side of the trunk. She pulled her feet up, crouched, got her balance, and stood up. Daisy looked over at her from where she was still sitting in the shade of the branches. Ruby had turned and was standing with the sun at her back. Daisy couldn't see her face because it was cast in shadow. All she could see was the outline of her best friend, hand outstretched, beckoning.

"Come on!" Ruby said. "This is ah-mazing!" she sang.

Daisy held her breath and inched her way over just the way Ruby had. The bark of the tree scratched at the backs of her thighs below her shorts. When she got near Ruby's feet, Ruby leaned down, offering a hand to help her up. Daisy grabbed it and stood. She got her balance and looked at Ruby, who threw her head back and yelled, "Woo-hoo!" The words punched their way into the sky. Daisy was smiling so hard, her cheeks hurt. She'd done it, and it really *was* amazing!

She didn't let go of Ruby's hand, though. She took a deep breath. It smelled very green where they were standing, like it does after it rains.

Together the two friends looked out at the Long Island Sound. It was the same view as from the stone wall, but they were a little higher up here. The sun glittered and sparkled on the water, dots of small whitecaps dancing across the surface. Standing atop the tree trunk, with the slight breeze stirring the air, it felt like the sky was bigger, the view more sweeping. It also felt like they were breaking some kind of rule, climbing up on a fallen tree. Her dad definitely would have said it was dangerous, Daisy thought, but that made it kind of more fun because she felt daring. The view from where they stood was spectacular. A big bird flew overhead, its wingspan huge, even from far away.

"I think that's an osprey," Daisy said.

"It's tremendous!" Ruby said.

The bird let out a long, keening screechlike tweet. The girls eeeeeee-ed back.

Ruby said, "I think he knows we're talking about him," and they giggled.

"Look!" Daisy said, pointing down the length of the trunk. The tree had crashed through the chain-link fence, crushing it, and had formed a perfect bridge into Dower Nature Preserve. The actual entrance with the parking lot was at the other end of the forty-two-acre preserve property, near the old mansion that people rented out for fancy parties. The preserve was also the home of the Long Island Wildlife Sanctuary, where rescued birds and animals lived. There had once been a wooden donation box near the entrance, but you didn't have to pay to get into the preserve or the wildlife sanctuary. When Daisy was little and went with her parents, they'd give her a few dollars to put into it. But the donation box had rotted and fallen down a few years before.

"Oh, we have to go in!" Ruby said.

"Do you think we should?" Daisy said.

"Daisy, it's like it's an invitation from the Universe," Ruby said.

Walking into the preserve on a tree bridge, over a squashed fence, nowhere near the entrance, felt like they were doing something wrong.

Daisy said, "But I don't want to get in trouble."

"Why would we get in trouble?"

"I don't know," Daisy said, "I mean, we've never been in the preserve without our parents."

"We won't get in trouble," Ruby said, "because we won't get caught!" She laughed, and her whole face lit up with mischief, so Daisy laughed too, even though she was still a little bit uncertain.

"Okay," Daisy said. "I guess we can."

"Yay," Ruby said as she carefully turned to keep walking down the trunk. For a split second she lost her footing and slipped. Daisy grabbed her arm, and both girls got their balance.

"You all right?" Daisy asked, her stomach fluttering.

"Yep," Ruby said. "Yeesh! Thanks for catching me."

"Of course," Daisy replied. They took turns being the faller and the catcher in different situations. Sometimes Ruby's fearlessness was what was needed, and other times, like now, Daisy's caution saved the day. Daisy always felt good when she was the one catching instead of the one falling.

"Let's keep going," Daisy said.

She held on to Ruby's shoulders from behind, her fingers pressing into the soft cotton of her friend's T-shirt. They took tiny steps, moving slowly and carefully in sync, wobbling their way over the tree bridge toward the preserve—Ruby leading the way.

Ruby's tan arms were stretched out to the sides, like an acrobat on a tightrope. Walking behind her, Daisy saw that her hair had slipped out of the ponytail again. Daisy smiled. Her own thick curly hair stayed put no matter what she did with it.

When they got to where the fence was crushed, they stopped for a minute. It wasn't like her parents had made a specific rule about not climbing over fallen trees into the preserve, Daisy thought to herself, but she knew that if she'd asked if she could do it, they probably would have said no. So it felt like a big deal when they stepped through the fence, like she was more grown up, conscious that she had made a choice to do something daring.

It felt darker on the other side, like a cloud had covered the sun, although when she looked up, it hadn't. There were acres and acres of trees in the preserve, with paths winding this way and that all through it, and it was particularly dense where they were.

Ruby jumped off the huge oak onto the soft mulch below. Daisy watched from atop the trunk. For a second her vision blurred, and she couldn't see Ruby, who had blended into the earth tones of the fallen leaves.

Her stomach clenched. Then her vision cleared, and there Ruby was, as always. It wasn't really that high up, it just felt that way. And it wasn't that Daisy didn't like adventure, but she got scared. It was a lot easier to push through her fear when Ruby was there with her. Daisy didn't know why she felt scared so much, but she did know she was grateful for Ruby's confidence and bravery.

"Jump down!" Ruby said.

Daisy crouched. "I don't think I can," she said. "Is there a way to climb?" Her heart skipped a beat as she looked for another way to get down.

Ruby looked up at her. "Just jump. It's not far," she said. "It's like jumping off the swings!" But Daisy had been too scared to do that, too. She felt like such a baby.

"Come on!" Ruby said, grinning up expectantly at her. "Magic 8 Ball says, 'Outlook Good'!"

Daisy took a deep breath and jumped. She couldn't help the small scream that escaped, but Ruby was right; it really wasn't far down at all. She surprised herself when she landed as nimbly as her friend.

Ruby gave her a quick one-armed hug. "See?" she said. "Magic 8 Ball doesn't lie." Daisy nodded. Then they walked on, arms over each other's shoulders, like nothing had happened. Ruby was the best kind of best friend, who knew when to not make a whole big deal out of something. Daisy really appreciated that.

There were some small branches down from the previous day's storm, but the oak was the only serious damage they could see. As they walked in the direction of the path, Daisy thought how perfect the day was turning out to be. It had gone from regular and boring, same old same old in her yard, to an unexpected adventure.

"Let's look at the bottom!" Daisy said, shrugging Ruby's arm off her shoulder. Ruby stopped for a second to push her hair back off her face.

She caught up to Daisy, staring up at the bottom of the fallen oak. "Oh wow," Ruby whispered.

From where they stood, they could see the torn-up roots of the tree. It was at least fourteen feet high. On the tree side—the top side that they had seen from the trunk when they were walking over it—there had been grass and soft green moss and stones and dirt. On this side, though, the part that had been beneath the ground was dark and moist, with reddish brown soil and gnarly, twisted roots poking out. The roots had been ripped from the earth and were pale and torn.

"They look like broken bones," Daisy said.

"Look," Ruby said, pointing. "That looks like a magic window."

Toward the top of the wall of gnarly roots, some had grown in an oval. The soil in the middle had fallen away, leaving a hole. It looked like the sun shone brighter on the other side.

Then the light shifted, and something sparkled through the gap. It was a small something, and it looked like it was fluttering. Ruby grabbed Daisy's arm. Neither girl moved, as if they had silently agreed to hold their breath. Daisy squinted, trying to see better.

"What is that?" Daisy whispered.

All around them the woods grew quiet. No cracking twigs or rustling leaves. No birds chirping or mosquitoes buzzing or squirrels chittering.

"I don't know," Ruby softly said back. "I think it must be something magical, though."

Ruby squeezed Daisy's arm, and then all of a sudden the thing flitted away.

"That was a hummingbird or something, right?" Daisy said.

"It was too tiny to be a hummingbird."

The girls hadn't moved. Ruby finally let go of Daisy's arm.

"Maybe it was some kind of bug?" Daisy said.

"Or maybe the hole is a way into a magic place," Ruby said with a grin. "Like the rabbit hole to Wonderland or the wardrobe to Narnia!" Daisy and Ruby had had tons of conversations, late into the night of many sleepovers, about how cool it would be if they could really go to Narnia or Wonderland or Oz. Ruby took a step closer to the underside of the fallen tree, trying to get a better look.

Daisy didn't answer.

"Come closer," Ruby said, gazing up at the wall of dirt. But they didn't see anything through the hole anymore. Whatever they had seen was gone.

"I think we just saw a fairy," Ruby said breathlessly.

Daisy didn't say anything; she kept looking up, wide-eyed, at the tree roots.

"Daisy," Ruby said, turning toward her and grabbing her arms, "that was a fairy, right?" It was a question this time.

That was impossible, wasn't it? Daisy wanted it to be true, but she couldn't be *sure* of what they'd seen. She didn't know what else it could have been, so she said, "I think so?"

"It was *definitely* some kind of magical something," Ruby said.

Daisy looked up at the wall of earth again, like the answer might be there. She wanted to see magic in the world the way Ruby did, but her brain always turned practical on her. It felt like Ruby could find magic in everything. It was another reason she was grateful she had a friend like Ruby. She said, "Maybe you're right. Maybe it was."

Ruby's face broke into a huge smile. "Come on," she said. "Let's see what else there is in these magical woods!"

Daisy had never thought of Dower Nature Preserve as magical woods before. But whatever they'd just seen had changed everything. Like maybe there really was magic here, things that were beyond what she thought, beyond what she already knew about the world. Maybe it was as simple as being able to believe, like Ruby did, and if Daisy kept her eyes and heart open, she would be able to see magic everywhere too.

"Okay!" she called to Ruby, who was already striding through the woods ahead of her. "Let's go!"

Imaginary Friends

The next morning it was raining. The *pit, pit, pit* sound on the roof was soothing, and Daisy burrowed more deeply into the couch, looking over at her friend as she did and sighing with contentment. *Captain Marvel* was playing on the big TV over the fireplace, but she and Ruby had seen it so many times, they'd stopped paying attention. Whenever Ruby slept over, they stayed up so late, they ended up sleeping away half the next day curled up on the couch together like puppies.

Ruby yawned and said, "I watched a video the other day about a British guy who was talking about 'unexplainable' findings in a forest in Cornwall. That's part of England." She made air quotes on the unexplainable part. "Which means magic or fairies, you know," she said.

Chewbacca, Daisy's big curly brown dog, was on the couch with them, squished between the girls, running after squirrels in his sleep. The tips of his hairy brown paws twitched, and his eyebrows quivered. Daisy reached out and rubbed his side.

"I don't know if I believe in real magic," Daisy said. It was uncharacteristically cold in the house, even for a rainy June day, and the girls were cuddled up under blankets. Daisy's purple afghan was draped over her head like a hood, one little curl peeking out the front. She was cocooned under the rest of the blanket, her bare feet stuck between the velvety couch cushions. Ruby had pulled her own afghan up under her chin, stretching the soft pink wool over her body, which left her toes uncovered. She tucked her cold, bare feet between the cushions on her end of the couch, snuggling them against Daisy's warm ones. Ruby pushed a wisp of her hair out of her eyes and yawned again.

"Well, I definitely believe in magic," Ruby said.

"I want to believe, but I'm just not sure," Daisy said.

"Well, what do *you* think we saw in the woods yesterday?" Ruby asked.

Daisy said, "Shhh, I don't want my mom to hear." She continued in a quieter voice. "I don't know. We can ask my aunt Toby. She knows about things like that. Plus, she won't tell my mom that we went into the preserve."

"Your aunt Toby's so cool," Ruby said. The music boomed from the television as Carol Danvers turned into Captain Marvel. Chewbacca picked his head up and looked around, the sound waking him from a deep sleep. Ruby reached out and tickled him behind his ear, and he put his head back down. "You're lucky you have an aunt like that."

"I know," Daisy said. "I wish she still lived here, though." She sighed. "We could try texting her, but she's still got, like, a flip phone or something."

"It's so funny that she's your mom's twin," Ruby said. "They're so different, but also not."

"To me they're totally different, even though they look a lot alike," Daisy said. "Anyway, we talk every Friday, so I'll ask her what she thinks it was when I talk to her."

The smell of cinnamon wafted into the family room, and Ruby's stomach grumbled. "I'm hungry," she said.

"Me too," Daisy replied.

"I don't feel like getting up, though," Ruby said, burrowing further into the couch.

"Me either," Daisy said.

She looked toward the kitchen. She could see her mom making French toast, the bump of her belly sticking out, occasionally talking to herself as she cooked. Daisy could see her dad out the back slider, puttering about in the rain.

"There has to be some *logical* explanation for what we saw," Daisy whispered.

"Ugh! The explanation is, *it was a fairy*," Ruby whispered back. "Why do you even *want* to find another explanation?"

"I don't know. I thought it might be possible when we saw it, but it doesn't seem like it could really be true now," Daisy said. "What if it was just a dragonfly? Or a hummingbird?"

Ruby shook her head.

"It was not a hummingbird, and it definitely wasn't a dragonfly," she whisper-shouted.

Daisy thought about it. "Well," she said, "*maybe* it was a fairy."

When they'd been standing there, side by side, actually seeing it, Daisy had definitely felt something. Maybe it had been magic? She couldn't imagine what else it could have been.

"I mean, I guess it *was* too big to be a dragonfly. And

I suppose hummingbirds *don't* hover in the same way that it hovered." Daisy liked to pick a problem apart. It wasn't that she didn't believe at all, but she wanted to think the whole thing out before committing to an answer.

Ruby pushed her hair out of her eyes and turned toward Daisy. "I'm telling you, it was a fairy. And I bet there's other magic things in there, too." She said it like she knew for sure, her dark brown eyes wide open. "We've got to go back."

"French toast is ready, girls!" Daisy's mom called from the kitchen.

"Coming!" Daisy called back, still settled into the couch. "Well, that's something we agree on, at least. We definitely have to go back."

"Come now," her mom said. "Not in five minutes, when it's cold."

Daisy whispered to Ruby, "She's been *so* annoying."

Ruby patted her stomach. "My mom said pregnant ladies get cranky."

"She's only a little bit pregnant," Daisy said. "You can hardly even see the bump."

"Girls?" Mom called.

"Let's go," Ruby said. "My stomach's rumbling."

They paused the movie and padded into the kitchen. The hems of Ruby's purple pajama pants were ripped in the back where she walked on them. Daisy's orange ones had a tear in the knee. They'd bought the same pajamas in different colors the previous summer and had worn them to death.

Daisy's dad came in from the yard, dripping from the rain and holding a big wet bunch of weeds.

"Check it out, Lori," he said, showing it to Daisy's mom. "I was weeding between the flagstones, and I think this is purslane! We can eat this stuff!" He plopped the muddy clump on the granite counter and sat down at the table with the girls.

"You want us to eat weeds?" Daisy said.

"Weeds are just plants, Buddy-Girl. Plants growing where you'd rather they didn't."

"If you say so, Dad." Daisy rolled her eyes at Ruby. Ruby grinned.

"Will, you're getting mud all over the kitchen," her mom said in an irritated voice.

But Dad ignored it. "You making coffee, Lore?" he said. He took off his wet hat. Mom threw him a kitchen towel, and he dried his bald head.

"It's brewing," she said.

Daisy said, "Can we have some hot chocolate?"

Mom sighed a big exaggerated sigh, like Daisy had asked her to bake a cake or something.

"I think you know how to make your own hot chocolate," Mom said.

"But I like how you make it. Please please please?" Daisy begged, making what she hoped looked like puppy-dog eyes to match her pleading smile.

Mom said, "Fine." But she still looked a little irritated. Daisy knew her mom wasn't really annoyed, though. Ruby was right. Being pregnant was making her mom crabby, even if she was only five months along.

Ruby poked at the clump of purslane. "How do you eat these weeds, Will?" she asked.

Ruby and Daisy had been friends since they were babies, so her parents had always been Lori and Will to Ruby. Just like Ruby's parents had always been Leo and Maria to Daisy, never Mr. and Dr. Affini.

"I guess you can make a purslane salad or something," Dad said.

"Actually, I think I have a recipe somewhere for a curried soup that uses purslane," Mom said. It was like her mood could shift in a nanosecond.

"That sounds good!" Daisy said. "I like curry. What does purslane taste like, Dad?"

He put a sprig in his mouth. "It tastes peppery, and kind of like arugula," he said, chewing thoughtfully.

"Yum. Make that curried purslane soup, Mom," Daisy said, nodding to her. "Will you?" Daisy pinched two little leaves off. She put one in her mouth and gave one to Ruby.

"That's not bad," Ruby said.

"Not bad," Daisy echoed.

Dad said, "Google says you can use it in salad, soup, smoothies." He took another nibble and kept scrolling through his phone. Chewbacca came into the kitchen, toenails tapping on the wood floor, and plopped down underneath Daisy's chair. Daisy slipped her bare feet under him, and he turned his head and licked her ankle before settling down.

"Can you eat curry, Lori?" Ruby said. "Daisy said you couldn't eat the carrot soup my dad sent over."

"And he was so thoughtful to send that over," Mom said. She tipped her head, thinking. "I'm not sure yet what this bump will let me eat." She rubbed her hand on her belly.

"That's what I'm going to call the baby from now on," said Daisy. "The bump!"

"Hmm . . . I can't tell if the thought of curried *any-thing* sounds appealing or disgusting," Mom said.

"Well, I like curried *everything*," Daisy said. "You could just make it for me!"

took a sip of his coffee, and said, "What are we talking about?"

"Writer's block," Daisy and Ruby said at the same time. Ruby raised her mug and pointed.

"Righty-o, Ruby McDooby," he said. He stood up. "I'm going to go pick the last of the raspberries before the wind or the birds get the rest of them."

"Some of the ground ones are fine," Ruby said. Daisy rolled her eyes.

Mom handed Dad a metal bowl for the berries. He put his hat back on and went out into the drizzle. Daisy's mom turned to the sink to wash the skillet. Ruby nudged Daisy, grinned, and began to lick the leftover syrup off her plate. Making sure her mother didn't catch her and yell about manners, Daisy picked up her plate too and licked it clean. Then the sticky girls cleared their dishes into the dishwasher, gave their hands a quick rinse, and went back to the couch.

Daisy turned the movie back on, and it covered their quiet conversation.

"She's not *totally* cranky," Ruby said, wrapping herself in the afghan again. "She made us hot chocolate."

"She's okay right now," Daisy said, wrapping herself up too. "But she keeps complaining about how tired she is, and how she can't wait for my aunt Toby to be here

Mom sighed again, but smiled. "You want more French toast, girls?"

"No, thanks," Daisy and Ruby said in unison.

"Apparently purslane is a nutritional powerhouse," Dad said, still looking at his phone.

Mom put Daisy's hot chocolate, in the mug with a big *D* and a sketch of a daisy on it, on the table in front of her.

"Here, you get my mug today," she said to Ruby. "Yours is in the dishwasher." Ruby usually used the mug with a unicorn farting rainbows on it. Instead Lori handed her a mug with writing on it that said WRITER'S BLOCK: WHEN YOUR IMAGINARY FRIENDS WON'T TALK TO YOU.

"Is that a real thing, Lori?" Ruby asked, taking a sip of her hot chocolate. "Writer's block?"

"I don't write fiction anymore," Mom answered. "So I'm not talking to my imaginary friends." The girls laughed. "Magazine articles are different."

"We had to write a story for homework the oth day, and I sat looking at the blank computer screen f ever. I couldn't think of anything to write," Daisy sai

"We had to write a poem in class, and the same tl happened to me," Ruby said.

Dad said, "The official name for purslane is *Por oleracea*. It's also called little hogweed, red root pursley." Finally he put down his phone, look to help when the baby comes. And my dad keeps telling me I have to be nicer to her because she's pregnant." She shrugged. "I'm nice. And I'm happy we're having a baby and all, but I wish they hadn't waited so long." Chewbacca jumped back onto the couch between the girls, and they adjusted their positions.

"Why *did* they wait so long?" Ruby asked.

"She got pregnant a few times, but Mom said they didn't stick. She had three miscarriages. After that they stopped trying for a while."

"I didn't know that," Ruby said. "That's sad."

"I guess," Daisy said. "But they were all in the very beginning, like the first month or something."

"But still," Ruby said. "Aren't you afraid something bad is going to happen again?"

"Nah," Daisy said. "My dad said most miscarriages happen in the first three months. She's past that time, so it's unlikely anything bad will happen again. That's what he told me."

They quietly watched *Captain Marvel*, and Goose the cat, who was really a Flerken, scratched Fury in the face. "He told me that after three months there's only a five percent chance that she'd have a miscarriage. That means a ninety-five percent chance of everything being okay. He told me there's more chance that I'd get appendicitis than something happening to the bump."

"The bump," Ruby repeated, and giggled. She rubbed Chewie's head with her foot. They both smiled about the new nickname.

"By the time my brother or sister is our age, you and me are both going to be grown-ups already."

Neither one of them said anything for a second, and then they said, "Grown-ups!" at the same time and giggled again.

"My cousin Sonya's brother, Vincent, is eight years older than her," Ruby said. "He just graduated from college." She thought for a minute. "I mean, he's my cousin too, but he's a lot older."

"Well, when I grow up, I want to have two kids two years apart. A boy and a girl," Daisy said.

"I want to have three girls," Ruby said. "Because girls are better than boys, and I don't want my daughters to have an annoying brother like Luca."

"Luca's all right," Daisy said.

Ruby said. "You just think that because he's not *your* brother."

"I hope our baby's a girl."

"Can't your mom find out?" Ruby asked.

"She doesn't want to," Daisy said. "And my dad said it's up to her."

The movie ended, and Daisy flipped through some other shows. A cartoon. A war movie. A sports show. "Not only that, but my mom asked me if I want to *be there* when the baby's born."

"What do you mean?"

"She's having the baby here—at home—and she told me I could be there, if I want, to see it when it happens."

"At home?" Ruby sat up. "Are you even allowed to do that?"

"You can do whatever you want," Daisy said. "She's having a midwife, like when I was born, only this time she's having the baby at home instead of at the hospital."

"Wow." Ruby's eyes were wide. "Are you going to do it? Be there when, you know . . ."

"I don't think so," Daisy said. "The other day she started explaining exactly what happens. . . ."

Ruby snuggled back into the couch. "Well, we *know* what happens."

Daisy shook her head. "Right, but I asked her *one* question about one little part of it, and then—you know my mom—she told me *way* more than I wanted to hear. She wouldn't stop talking."

"Ew," Ruby said.

"I know, right?" Daisy said, still flipping through shows on the television.

Then Ruby said, "Only your mom and my mom talk to kids about stuff like that. Other kids' moms *never* tell them anything like that. My mom has the excuse of being a doctor. What's *your* mom's excuse?"

Daisy laughed. "Maybe her imaginary friends tell her to do it."

Ruby laughed too. "As Magic 8 Ball says, 'Without a Doubt,'" Ruby said.

Magic 8 Ball

That afternoon the two girls were hanging out at Ruby's house. It was still raining, and Leo had plopped a pile of clothing onto Ruby's bed and told her to go through it to see what still fit. Now that Luca and Ruby were done with school, the Affinis would be going back and forth from Roosevelt Cove to their beach house in the Hamptons all summer. Half of Ruby's clothing usually stayed out there, but there was no point in taking anything that had gotten too small.

Ruby was sitting cross-legged on her bed, and Daisy was squished into a big fuzzy pink chenille beanbag chair, nibbling on a pretzel rod and holding Ruby's Magic 8 Ball in her other hand.

"Is this going to be a good summer?" Daisy asked, shaking the ball. She looked in the plastic window on the ball and through the murky purple liquid. "It says, 'Reply Hazy, Try Again.'" She rolled her eyes. "Un. Cool. 8 Ball."

Ruby said, "Of course it's going to be a good summer." She grinned at Daisy. "Because it's summer! Summer is summer, and summer is good!"

Daisy shook it again. "Ugh," she said. "It says, 'Concentrate and Ask Again.' You ask it something."

Ruby held up a blue-green one-piece bathing suit that looked like fish scales.

"I love that bathing suit," Daisy said, taking another small bite of her pretzel.

"Me too," Ruby said, "but it's too small. It kind of inches up my butt now." She scrunched up her face. "It came with a towel that looked like a mermaid tail, remember?"

"I love that towel, too," Daisy said.

"Yeah, I lost it last summer," Ruby said. She tossed the bathing suit onto the get-rid-of pile on the floor. "Ask it if I'm always going to be short. . . . No, ask it if I'm going to grow *this summer*!" Daisy shook the ball. "No! I know! Ask it if I'm going to get my period this summer! Yeah, that."

"It says, 'Outlook Not So Good.'" Daisy said.

"Wait, to which thing?" Ruby asked.

In the past year both girls' bodies had started changing. Even though Ruby was older than Daisy—Ruby would turn twelve in August, and Daisy's birthday wasn't until February—Daisy had already gotten her period and was physically maturing quicker than Ruby.

"I think it's about growing and getting your period," Daisy said.

"Un. Cool," Ruby said.

"But if the Magic 8 Ball thinks you're not going to get your period this summer, then you still have time to get taller," Daisy said. Ruby's mom had told them that girls usually only grow a couple of inches after they start menstruating, and Ruby was barely five feet tall.

Ruby held up another bathing suit. "I hate this one," she said.

Both girls said, "Donate pile," at the same time.

"You ask it something," Ruby said.

"Okay, how do I ask it if the baby's a boy or a girl?" Daisy said as she started shaking the ball. "I know. 'Will I have a brother?' That should do it." She stopped shaking. "It says, 'Better Not Tell You Now.'"

"The Magic 8 Ball is being a jerk today," Ruby said.

Daisy laughed.

"My mom ordered me a bunch of new bathing suits."

"I still fit in most of last year's," Daisy said. "I had to get some in the middle of the summer because I grew out of everything by the end of July." She took a tiny bite of her pretzel. "It was so annoying because there was nothing good left, so now I have a bunch of *meh* bathing suits."

Ruby pulled a T-shirt on over her tank top. "This still fits," she said.

"For now," Daisy said. She popped the last bite of pretzel into her mouth. "But if you grow even a little, that's going to be tight on your . . ." Daisy waved her hands in front of her T-shirt. "You know, where your boobs are."

Ruby laughed. "Boobs. Ha!" She put her hands on her T-shirt over the place where there were barely two knobs. "I can't imagine having *actual* boobs."

Daisy giggled. "Mine aren't anything much more," she said. "But they're still boobs. . . ."

"I guess," Ruby said. "Ask it if I'm going to have big boobs."

Daisy smiled, her eyes crinkling up, as she gave the Magic 8 Ball a big shake. "Will Ruby have big boobs?"

"Let me see!" Ruby said, jumping off the bed and grabbing the ball. "It says, 'Very Doubtful.'"

Both girls laughed.

"Good!" Ruby said, plopping down next to Daisy in the beanbag chair. "I don't want big boobs anyway."

Daisy took the ball from Ruby and shook it with both hands. Daisy said, "Will Ruby and I always be best friends?"

And Ruby added, "For the rest of our lives?"

The girls leaned their heads together to see what the Magic 8 Ball predicted. It said, *You May Rely on It.*

Only a Week

The next day Ruby and Daisy were in Daisy's family room, which was strewn with camping gear—a tent, sleeping bags, a propane lantern, a stove. Mom was going through everything. Chewbacca was chewing a dog toy, watching them all. Ruby was helping Daisy.

"Why can't we just go to Seattle to visit Aunt Toby, like last summer?" Daisy said, trying to squeeze a freshly washed sleeping bag back into the stuff sack Ruby was holding open for her. "Or stay home. Why can't we stay home so I can go out to the Hamptons with Ruby? And go camping another time?"

"I don't want to keep having the same conversation

with you," Mom said. "Aunt Toby will be here in the fall when the baby comes, and you'll see her then. And I probably won't want to go camping for a while after the baby comes."

"But why do we even have to go camping?" Daisy said.

Ruby whispered so only Daisy heard. "I know my mom would let you come with us, if I asked."

"Maria already said if I want to go with them to the Hamptons, I can," Daisy said.

"Adirondack camping is fun," Mom said. "We're going to have a whole island in the middle of a lake to ourselves for a week."

"No offense, Mom, but it's going to be *boring* being there with just the three of us."

"Give it a break, Daisy. I know this isn't your ideal vacation," Mom said.

"Well, then why do we have to go?" she whined. "Can Ruby come with us?" she said, changing tactics.

"I can't," Ruby said. "My cousins are coming from California."

Daisy blew air out of her mouth, making a *pffffft* sound. "Mom," she moaned, saying it like it had two syllables, "I don't want to go camping."

"Just stop," Mom said, starting to get a little snippy.

"Consider yourself lucky. Some families don't get to go on vacation at all."

Daisy looked at Ruby, who didn't say anything. Mom was shaking a propane tank for the camping stove, trying to figure out if it was empty. Ruby nudged her and started rubbing her stomach, making wide eyes until Daisy shook her head and giggled. They pulled the cord tight on the stuff sack they were holding.

"Stuff the other two sleeping bags too, please," Mom said in a nicer voice. "When are you guys leaving for Westhampton, Ruby?" She placed the tent poles on top of the tent bag and started poking through a plastic box of fishing tackle.

"Me and Dad and Luca are going out on Thursday," Ruby said. "My mom's got to work, though, so I think she's coming Saturday. And my cousins are going to meet us out there."

Daisy stuffed the next sleeping bag into the sack Ruby was holding open, the slippery material sliding through her hands as she tried to push it in.

"Can Daisy come out to the beach when you get back from camping?" Ruby asked. "We're going to be there for two weekends." She said to Daisy, "You remember my cousin Sonya, from California, right?"

"I'll talk to your mom about it when we get back

from camping. We don't want to intrude when you have family visiting." Mom poked at a box with her foot. "Bring these camping dishes into the kitchen, girls. I want to run them through the dishwasher. They're a little gross."

Daisy and Ruby each took an end of the big plastic box of dishes and silverware and brought it into the kitchen. Chewbacca followed them. They plunked the box down, and Ruby jumped up and sat on a stool at the counter. Daisy opened the dishwasher and leaned against the sink next to it. Chewie nosed his way in, looking for dirty dishes to lick.

"Last year when we went to visit Aunt Toby, we took a ferry from near where she lives in Seattle to Orcas Island," Daisy said.

"That's when you saw real whales, right?" Ruby said.

"Yeah, it was so cool. That was a good vacation. Camping upstate is going to stink. What am I going to see there?"

"You can look for fairies," Ruby said with a twinkle in her eye. "You're going to be on an island! Maybe it will be magical, like Neverland."

"I guess," Daisy said.

"Or maybe it's like Themyscira, where Wonder Woman's from!" Ruby said.

Daisy lowered her voice. "We have to go over the fence to the woods *here* and see if we can find whatever that was again." She opened the cabinet, took out a bag of cookies, and handed it to Ruby.

"It was a fairy," Ruby said. "But yeah, I hope we can go before you leave."

"Me too. But we can't climb on the tree or over the fence if it's still raining," Daisy said. She got some milk out of the refrigerator and poured two glasses.

"Westhampton's not going to be so fun either," Ruby said. "I wish you could come with me instead of going camping." She took a sip of milk. "My cousin Sonya's great, but she thinks she's *so* mature now. It's annoying." She tried to open the cookie bag, but it wouldn't rip. Chewie heard the crinkle of the bag and sat up, like a good boy, hoping something was coming his way. "She told me she *likes* some boy."

Daisy asked, "*Likes* him, likes him?"

"Yeah, *likes* him," Ruby answered, rolling her eyes. "Like crushing on him."

She handed the cookie bag to Daisy. Chewie followed the bag with his eyes, and the tip of his tail wagged.

"And she said he likes her *back*."

Neither of them said anything for a minute, and then they both said, "Yuck," and Daisy wrinkled her nose.

"But she's only a year older than us," Daisy said. She ripped the bag open with her teeth and handed a cookie to Ruby, who shoved the whole thing in her mouth. Chewie snuffled at the floor, licking up the falling crumbs.

"Right? We were video-chatting on my computer last weekend," Ruby said. Cookie crumbs spewed out of her mouth when she said "computer." "She called me from SeaWorld. She was showing off, because she knows I don't have a phone yet."

"She video-called you from SeaWorld? God, I can't wait to get a phone," Daisy said, taking a nibble off the side of her cookie. "It's so *stupid* to have to wait until we start middle school. Everyone has a phone."

Ruby nodded, shoving a second cookie into her mouth. "I think waiting until middle school was *my* mom's idea. Sorry about that," she said, more crumbs popping out. Chewie snuffled those up too.

Daisy took a sip of her milk. "I don't know," she replied. "I think my mom wrote an article for some parenting website about kids and technology, or something dumb like that. It might be *her* fault."

"Girls! Is all that stuff in the dishwasher?" Daisy's mom called from the family room.

"We're doing it!" Daisy called back, leaning on the counter and nibbling her cookie and not doing it at all.

Ruby said, "Sonya told me *all* the kids in her school have had phones forever."

"A lot of kids already have them here, too," Daisy said. Slowly she started putting the dishes into the dishwasher. Ruby hopped down and helped. Chewie nosed his way in again, hoping this time there was lickable silverware in the dishwasher.

"Sonya wasn't boy crazy when she came last Christmas. That happened fast."

"A lot of girls are getting boy crazy," Ruby said, "even here." She dug in the bag for another cookie. They sat down on the kitchen floor, cross-legged, hidden from Daisy's mom's view by the counter, the dishwasher forgotten again.

"Are you getting boy crazy?" Daisy asked. "Do you like somebody?"

"Me? Nah," Ruby replied. "I only like boys as friends."

Daisy didn't say anything. Ruby stuffed another cookie into her mouth and started chewing loudly.

Daisy said, "Do you like girls?"

Ruby looked at her with a blank face.

"What do you mean? Of course I like girls," she said, and took a sip of her milk to wash down the cookie.

"No, I mean, are you maybe getting *girl* crazy?"

But Ruby just stared at her.

"You know, like how my aunt Toby likes girls?"

Then Ruby understood what Daisy was asking. "Nah," she said. "I'm nothing crazy. I mean, I don't want a boyfriend or a girlfriend or anyone yet."

She broke a cookie in half, and Chewie sat expectantly in front of her.

Ruby had a huge milk mustache, there were cookie crumbs all over her chin and shirt, and her hair had slipped out of her ponytail again and was in her eyes. She looked so very Ruby. Then she said to Daisy, "What about you? Do you like anybody?"

"Nah," Daisy said. "I don't want to *like* like anyone yet either. Maybe it's babyish, but I don't care. I don't want to be more grown-up or a teenager or whatever yet."

"Me neither," Ruby said. Then she shoved half the cookie into her mouth and gave the other half to Chewie.

Mom came into the kitchen carrying the propane lantern and saw the girls sitting on the floor eating cookies.

"Daisy, I really need you to finish loading this stuff into the dishwasher!" she said with exasperation.

"I'm *doing* it," she said, and stood up. To push the point, and perhaps steer the conversation away from the fact that she hadn't been doing it at all, she said, "But I still wish we didn't have to go camping upstate."

"I wish I didn't have to go to Westhampton," Ruby said under her breath.

"Oh, girls, it's only a little bit more than a week," Mom said. "It's not that long to be apart."

But to Daisy and Ruby, even a week seemed like it would last forever.

A Space between Then and Now

The first day of vacation was long. After being in the car for six hours, it was a relief to be out on the water in the pontoon boat that was carrying Daisy and her parents and all their gear from the marina to the island campsite. The guy driving the boat had laughed at how much they'd brought with them. Mom had no commitment to roughing it, and Daisy insisted they have their usual first night of camping meal—chicken-and-vegetable shish kebabs, which had been skewered at home, with corn on the cob pre-slathered in butter and wrapped in foil, which got cooked right in the fire. Dad prepared food like mad before they went camping. The three of them liked to eat well, no matter where they were. As the boat dropped them off at the island, Daisy thought maybe camping wouldn't be too bad after all.

The second day, after breakfast, Daisy and her dad went out in a kayak for a few hours, paddling around the islands. They saw an eagle, two hawks, some wood ducks, and lots of what Dad called LBJs—little brown jobs—small brownish birds that could be any of a variety of species. When they got back to their island, they ate hot dogs and baked beans for lunch, followed by a very cold, very quick swim in the lake. She played cards with Mom, then some backgammon with Dad, and then she read her book. After that was a dinner of steak and baked potatoes, followed by s'mores around the campfire.

By the third day Daisy was getting bored. The campsite was starting to feel pretty small. She'd poked around in all the trees, looking for anything that might be the least bit magical. No Neverland and Tinker Bell. No rabbit hole to Wonderland. She'd rooted about in the rocks and crevices and crannies at the shoreline, wading into the chilly water, looking for anything that might be remotely fairylike. She caught a frog, which she held in her hands and peered closely at. It was the furthest thing from a fairy she could imagine. She was pretty sure it wasn't a magical prince, either. *I bet Ruby would try giving you a kiss, just in case,* she told it, before she opened her hands and let it hop away. She finished reading *Ghost Girl* and started reading *Aru Shah and the End of Time.* She and Ruby were both reading *Aru Shah* this week so they could at least feel like they were doing *something* together. She went for another paddle in the kayak, this time with her mom, and they saw another eagle and lots more LBJs. They ate more things. They ended the day with s'mores again, like they had every night so far.

On the fourth day it was overcast. Dad had taken a fishing pole and was on the far side of the island, where the water was deeper. Mom was grilling hamburgers and onions on the grate over the fire pit, and the delicious, mouthwatering smell of it was everywhere. "Why don't you jump in the lake?" she called to Daisy.

"It's too cold," Daisy replied, slouching down in the camp chair and going back to her book. She wore a long-sleeved shirt over a T-shirt, plus a hoodie and sweat-pants. Her bare feet were dirty, and she lazily kicked one foot back and forth in the dust.

"The guy from the marina is picking us up to go to town right after lunch," Mom said. "Dad's got to get to some cell service for his conference call, and you and I can get ice cream."

Daisy didn't even look up from her book. "Why does he even have to be on a conference call when we're on vacation?" she asked.

"Because he's got seven people who report to him, and nobody else on his team is on vacation," Mom said. "Just because the senior sustainability director goes camping doesn't mean everyone else stops working on energy efficiency."

"Whatever," Daisy said, continuing to read.

"Lovie, you're three days dirty, and you've got marshmallow in your hair from last night," Mom said as she put plates and napkins on the picnic table. "Just jump in to get clean."

"I'm clean enough," Daisy said. "We don't know anybody in this town anyway. What difference does it make?"

Mom was riffling through the cooler. "Did you and Daddy eat all the cherry tomatoes? Let's pick up some cherry tomatoes when we're in town," she said.

Daisy sighed a big exaggerated sigh. "We're leaving in two days," she said sullenly. "Who even cares about tomatoes?"

She was so done with camping. She'd made the best of it, and it hadn't been too bad. But now she was ready to go home, to television and the internet, to her dog, and hopefully out to the Hamptons to hang out with Ruby and her cousin. But if that didn't work out, at least Ruby would be home a couple of days later, and they'd finally get to go back into the preserve.

The more she thought about that day, the more convinced Daisy was becoming that it really had been a fairy . . . or at least something magical. She couldn't wait to tell Ruby that she'd thought it all the way through, and that they'd have to do some research, because it might have been a pixie or a sprite, which are specific kinds of fairies. When they got to town later, back to civilization, and finally had cell service again, she'd be able to call Ruby with her mom's phone.

The pontoon boat pulled up to the marina, and Daisy and her parents walked to where they'd left their car. "God, I can't wait to get a decaf chai latte," Mom said. "There's got to be a place in Saranac."

Dad turned on his phone, but they still didn't have cell service. "Hey, Buddy-Girl," Dad said, "Roy told me there's an ice cream place called The Big Dipper."

"Who's Roy?" Daisy said.

"The guy who just drove our boat," Dad said. "And there's a coffee shop near there too. Maybe they have chai, Lore." He looked pleased with himself. But Mom wasn't listening to him. They got in the car and pulled out of the marina parking lot.

"My phone's totally dead," she said. "Where's the cord?"

Daisy fished the cord out from between the seats, and Mom plugged it in.

They drove the winding road through the trees toward town, and Dad punched in a Beatles playlist. Daisy rolled her window down and hung her arm out the side of the car, letting the wind catch her palm. The song that sounded like a lullaby came on when the Bluetooth finally connected, and her hand moved slowly up and down in the breeze in sync with the music. It took her a minute to remember the name of it. *"Golden Slumbers,"* she thought. Her hand moved all by itself, like it was dancing in the wind to the sweet, gentle melody, like she had no control of it.

Then the song segued to "Carry That Weight," and the electric guitars came in and started rocking. Daisy loved this song. She pulled her hand in and leaned forward. "Turn it up," she said. Dad turned the volume all the way up, and Mom looked back at her and winked. They started to sing together at the top of their lungs, and then Dad joined in with his off-key baritone.

They were laughing and singing when they pulled into Saranac and found a place to park. Dad turned the car off, and Mom's phone started buzzing and dinging like it was possessed by a demon now that it was charged and they were in town with cell service.

"Geez," Mom said, picking up the phone. "You'd think we'd been gone a month instead of a few days." Daisy got out of the car. She looked through the window. Mom had the phone up to her ear now and was shaking her head.

She saw her put her hand to her mouth.

Dad came around to their side of the car, opened the passenger door, and said, "Lori, what's up?" He leaned into the car. "Are you okay? You're shaking."

"Oh, Will," Mom said, her eyes brimming with tears. She looked quickly at Daisy, and then away. Daisy's pulse quickened, and her stomach clenched.

"Mom?" Daisy said. Mom was shaking her head. "What's going on?"

"I, um . . . ," Daisy's mom said. "Oh, Will, I can't . . ." She put a hand on the bump of her belly and handed Dad the phone.

"Lori, what is it? Take a breath," Dad said. He took the phone and started scrolling through it. Daisy's mom was crying, but she closed her eyes, leaned her head back on the seat, and tried to take a deep breath, both hands on the top of her stomach.

"Mommy, what?" Daisy said, looking from her mom to her dad. Dad had the phone to his ear now. A muscle in his jaw twitched. He looked at Daisy with the phone to his ear and reached out and pulled her into a side hug. When he was done listening, he shoved the phone into the back pocket of his shorts and put both arms around her.

"Daddy? What's happening?" Daisy said. Her heart thumped hard in her chest, and her pulse raced. The sun had come out and was beating down on her now. A family walked by, the mom yelling at one of the kids, whose ice cream cone was dripping all over the place. Dad released her from his hug but held on to her hand as he leaned into the car to quietly say something to her mom. Daisy stood next to the car, awkwardly holding her father's hand and not knowing what to do. She scuffed her sneaker back and forth on the sidewalk.

She'd never seen her parents like this. Her dad pulled his head out of the car, took a deep breath in through his nose, and held it for a moment, chewing on his bottom lip. Then he squared his shoulders, and it looked like he'd decided something.

"Oh my god," Daisy said loudly. "What's going on? Tell me!"

"Let's sit in the car for a minute, Buddy-Girl," Daisy's dad said gently. "Something's happened, and we need to talk about it."

Daisy was about to argue, to say, *Geez! Talk about what?* when he gave her a look that stopped her. Daisy's dad never did that. Then he leaned down into the car and murmured something else to her mom.

Daisy opened the car door and got back into the back seat. Her dad went around to the driver's side, but instead of getting in the front, behind the wheel, he got in back with her. Daisy had never seen her father in the back seat of the car before. She frowned. None of this made sense.

Daisy thought about all the bad things that could have happened. Maybe something had happened to Grandma. She was old. Or Chewbacca? *Oh god, I hope Chewbacca's okay,* she thought. Or maybe something had happened to Aunt Toby. The thought of that made her stomach ache. Whatever it was, though, was really, really bad, she could tell. Her mouth felt dry, and it was hard to swallow.

Then Daisy's mom got out of the car and got in next to Daisy on the other side.

This is so weird, she thought. *What are they doing?*

She was squished in the middle, between her parents,

her knees sticking up a bit because she was sitting on the hump.

"Tell me," Daisy said. She braced herself and said in a lower voice, "Is it Aunt Toby?" Her head felt tight, like something was squeezing it.

Daisy's mom said softly, "Aunt Toby's okay, lovie." Then she looked down. Her dad put his hand on her knee and squeezed.

He said, "It's Ruby, Daisy."

"What?" Daisy said.

That didn't make any sense. Ruby? What did that mean?

Out loud she said, "What do you mean?"

Daisy's mom opened the car door to let some air in, because it had almost immediately gotten too warm. A lady with a dog walked by on the sidewalk. A car playing music, way too loud, drove slowly by, and Daisy felt the booming bass until it passed and faded away.

Her mom said, "There was an accident." She took Daisy's hand in her own two hands, opening Daisy's fingers one by one because they were clenched so tightly.

"An accident?" Daisy stared at their intertwined hands. Her mom gently squeezed. Daisy looked up at her mom, her gaze following a tear as it slowly made its way down her mother's cheek until it dripped off her chin, and then was followed by another.

Her dad said, "Breathe, Buddy-Girl." She gasped as the air rushed back into her lungs. She hadn't realized she was holding her breath, as if it could stop whatever was happening from happening.

"Come here," Daisy's mom said, pulling her in close. Her dad fidgeted in the seat next to her. He reached over and stroked her hair, placing a curl behind her ear, off her face.

An accident? What kind of accident? What did her mom mean?

In a small voice she asked, "Is she okay?" But she didn't want to hear the answer.

"Oh, lovie," her mom said, and her dad leaned over now and was awkwardly hugging her from the other side.

Daisy's mom tried to go on talking.

"She's . . . She . . . ," her mom coughed.

She felt her dad swipe at his eyes, and she turned, burrowing her face into her mother's hug.

"She got hit by a car," her mom said softly, whispering it into Daisy's ear and hugging her tighter. Her mom kind of hiccupped when she said, "And she . . . she died."

Daisy felt the air pressing in on them from all sides. For a minute she didn't move, as if staying perfectly still might freeze this moment in time. Her mom's words would freeze too, never leading to anything in real life, never leading to a time after right now. Her heart was thumping so loudly in her chest, pounding in her ears, hammering in her head. It felt like nothing existed outside the boundary of her own skin—until her mom, hugging her tighter, coughed again.

Then the world started up once more. She heard a truck drive by, making a rattling sound as it went over a bump in the street. Some teenagers walked past the car on the sidewalk, laughing. A horn honked somewhere. She sat up and took a deep breath, crossing her arms over her chest. She was crushed between her parents. They both leaned away a little, giving her some room.

In her mind she heard the words again. *An accident. Ruby.* Blackness was creeping into the periphery of her vision. The last thing her mom had said played back in her head. *Died.*

"I don't feel well, Mommy," Daisy said, resting her head back on the seat.

She was gasping, and her dad said, "Breathe, Buddy-Girl. Take a deep breath."

Why did he keep telling everyone to breathe?

What her mom said couldn't be true.

"I don't . . . ," she said, and gasped again. Nobody

was saying anything, and she could hear her mom crying. She made an effort to take a regular breath.

The words that came out of her mouth were "I don't understand." But she had understood her mom's words. *Died.* It just couldn't possibly be true. It had to be a mistake.

"Are you sure that's what they said?" Daisy asked. "Maybe you didn't hear it right."

"Oh, lovie," her mom said again.

"But what happened?" she asked. She needed to understand. Daisy's mom stroked her hair, and after a moment she finally caught her breath—slowly in, slowly out. She felt like she was in a movie, like this was happening to someone else and she was watching it, like she wasn't in her body.

They told her that Ruby had been hit by a car walking across the street in Westhampton. An old woman had gone through the stop sign. They told her that this had happened three days ago, that Maria and Leo had tried to get in touch with them while they were on the island. There were texts and emails, and finally a voice mail, letting them know.

A darkness—murky brown, empty and awful—overcame Daisy. It was as if it came from the center of the earth, through the seat of the car, up into her torso, out into her whole body, to the ends of her very finger-tips, filling up her skull. The darkness was in her chest like it might stop her heart; it filled her throat until she felt like she might drown. Sadness like she'd never experienced before. And finally tears came. And when they came, it felt as if they'd never stop.

Daze

It was like Daisy was moving through a dream. Her mom hadn't left her side, staying in the back seat of the car with her on the drive back to the marina. She felt like she was losing time. One minute they were in Saranac, and the next minute they were getting back onto the pontoon boat. Daisy's mom sat close to her on the bench seat of the boat, her arm protectively around Daisy's shoulders. Her dad was standing next to the boat driver, talking softly to him. When they got to the island, the guy said he'd come right back to pick them up. Daisy's cheeks were tight and salty with dried tears. Her mom led her to the picnic table at their campsite and sat her down, then plopped heavily down next to her.

"We've got to pack up," she said softly. Daisy nodded her head. "Can you get your stuff together?"

Daisy didn't say anything. She just looked at her mom and felt her chin quiver. Tears leaked from her eyes and started dripping down her cheeks. Her mom wiped them away with her thumbs and kissed Daisy softly on the forehead.

"Never mind. I'll do it. You stay here."

Her dad had gone into full-on packing mode. In what seemed like minutes he'd stuffed the sleeping bags into their stuff sacks, folded the huge tarp, and taken the tent down. He'd packed the poles away in their bag. Daisy's mom went over to him, and Daisy watched as they folded up the tent, working in the synchronized way that two people who have been married a long time can take care of a task without words. She pulled her hoodie up and stuffed her hands in her sweatshirt pockets. She was cold. So cold. She'd started crying again, and her teeth were chattering. But inside, her emotions felt muffled, like they were wrapped up in cotton deep within her. She could barely feel anything. Her brain kept saying the words inside her skull, though, over and over.

There was an accident.

She got hit by a car.

She died.

She lost time again. Somehow everything was packed up and loaded, and they were back on the pontoon boat. Then her dad was helping her into the car. She couldn't even remember the boat ride from the island to the marina. The next thing she knew, it was dark out, and they were driving. She must have fallen asleep. She didn't know how long they'd been driving, and looking out the window, she couldn't tell where they were. The Thruway or something. A folded beach towel was pressed into her cheek, a makeshift pillow that one of her parents had put there. She watched the reflection of lights on the car window and fell back asleep.

Her parents had somehow gotten her into the house, carried her like when she was a little kid, because the next thing she knew, she was waking up in her own bed. The light outside the window was that yellow gray that happens before sunup, when it's no longer night but not fully morning yet either. She was on top of the blankets and still in her clothing from the day before, and the purple afghan from the family room was on top of her. For a moment everything felt normal and regular, and she just lay there in her bed, watching it get lighter and lighter outside. And then she remembered.

There was an accident.

She got hit by a car.

She died.

Daisy felt so empty. She curled up, pulled the afghan tight around herself, and burrowed her face into her pillow. And cried and cried and cried.

Eternal Tissues

*D*aisy's dad handed Daisy a tissue. It had been an endless handing of tissues for the past twenty-four hours. Tissues as they'd gone through her closet that morning to find a dark dress that fit. She'd never been to a funeral before. Tissues driving to the church. This would be her first time at church. She'd had Christmas dinner and Easter lunch with the Affinis but had never gone to church with them. Ruby's whole family would be at the church today, but not her. Not really. So many balled-up tissues.

Her dad leaned over and kissed the top of Daisy's head. She hiccupped a little, trying to stop crying. She dabbed at her eyes. Her eyelids were puffy and tender, and her nose was sore from wiping it. The smell of incense wafted over her as a priest, or whoever the guy was, swung a brass incense burner from a chain, back and forth, back and forth. The smell tickled her nose, and she thought she might sneeze.

She was glad to be wedged between her parents. It made the light-headed feeling subside a little. As Daisy had walked from the car into the church, the sky had felt enormous, too open, too blue. A man, maybe it was another priest, had pressed some kind of card into her hand when they'd gone to sit in one of the pews toward the back.

The tag on her dress was sticking her in the back of her neck. She licked her finger and rubbed at the irritated spot. She kept her head bowed and her eyes looking down. Her fingernail picked at the edge of the card. She didn't want to look at the coffin. She couldn't believe Ruby's body was in it. It didn't feel like it could possibly be *her*. Just having that thought made Daisy's eyes overflow again.

She heard organ music. The grown-ups at the front of the church were talking or singing. Saying things. Maybe it was prayers. None of it made any sense. It was all just sounds. Maybe they were speaking another language, like at synagogue. The words coming from the front couldn't get past the whooshing sound in her ears, past the sound of her own heart thump thump thumping. She thought about hearts thumping and then not ever thumping again. More tears.

She pushed the toe of her shoe into the worn fabric on the low bench attached to the seats in front of her. *That must be the thing they kneel on,* she thought. Jewish people don't kneel, though, and she wondered if she and her parents would be the only ones in the church who stayed in their seats when the priest told everyone else to kneel.

She hiccupped again and sniffed. Another tissue appeared. There were so many people here. She could feel them in the room, sense their beings, feel their small movements. She noticed a cough, a sniffle, a whisper, even though her brain wouldn't let her hear what was happening at the front. She peeked up a teeny-tiny bit and saw stands holding giant flower arrangements on them up near the altar.

She could see the backs of Leo and Maria sitting in the front row, on the other side of the church, and the top of Luca's head, his hair sticking up like he'd slept on it. She looked away, afraid she'd see the coffin. A few rows back from them she saw Mr. Spencer, their third-grade teacher, sitting next to Mrs. Gilson, their principal. She saw Amanda and Caitlin, who she and Ruby sometimes ate lunch with at school. She looked down, not wanting them to notice her. She and Ruby had known Amanda and Caitlin since first grade. Their town was like that. Everyone was friendly with everyone else, but they also knew that Ruby and Daisy were a twosome. They always had been. But now Daisy was alone. She didn't want to see the look on Amanda's and Caitlin's faces when they looked at her.

The priest said something, and everyone stood up, so Daisy stood up too, but she kept her eyes on the floor. Her mom held her hand. After a few moments everyone sat down. More people said more things, and there was more organ music. Then everyone in the church kneeled on that low bench. She saw the backs of the people in the seats in front of them doing it and looked up at her mom. "It's okay," Daisy's mom whispered, and the three of them sat there, not kneeling. Daisy was pretty sure they were the only ones not kneeling, but she couldn't make herself lift her head enough to check. She really didn't want to see the coffin. Even thinking about it, more tears rolled down her cheeks. Daisy's dad gently kissed the top of her head. Again.

After what felt like forever, the service ended, and everyone stood up. People were moving around her.

As they walked out of the pew, she glanced up, and there it was. Ruby's dad, Leo; her brother, Luca; and some other men—they looked sort of familiar, maybe Ruby's uncles—were carrying the coffin out of the church. It was so small. She hadn't thought about that part. It made sense, though. Ruby's body was in that box, and her body wasn't very big. Daisy looked away but couldn't unsee the coffin. How could Ruby just be gone? How would it be possible for Daisy to live in a Ruby-less world? She swiped at her nose with the soggy tissue balled up in her hand.

Daisy's mom held her arm on one side, and her dad was on the other, his hand reassuringly on her shoulder. "We're going to pay our respects to Leo and Maria and Luca," her mom whispered.

Daisy looked up at her and pushed the wet tissue into the corner of one of her eyes, trying to stop the flow of tears. She shook her head the tiniest bit. She wanted to say, *I can't, I don't want to,* but she couldn't make the words come out.

"You'll be okay, lovie," her mom said. "We're doing it together. Daddy and I are with you." Daisy swallowed, trying to make the lump in her throat disappear.

They shuffled their way out of the church. Daisy could hear her mom and dad greeting people they knew, people from Roosevelt Cove, other kids' parents. So many people. She stuck close to her mom's side. Her dad was guarding her on the other side, and that was good. She wanted to be guarded. She heard her name said a few times but didn't lift her eyes to see if someone was talking *to* her or *about* her. The crowd slowly made their way out of the church and into the parking lot. They saw Maria and Leo and Luca, who were standing near the limousine that would take them to the cemetery.

Daisy looked at Maria. Ruby's mom was usually very put together. She almost always wore lipstick and rarely had a hair out of place. She was small and dark like Ruby. She was a doctor, outspoken, kind of loud, someone who gestured a lot with her hands when she got excited. But today she looked like a broken little bird. Her hair looked wispy, and even though she was wearing lipstick, somehow it looked like the color had been bleached out of it. She was talking to someone, shaking their hand, with a frown on her face. Leo was clutching Maria by the arm, like he was holding her up. She saw Luca talking to one of the uncles, and Daisy saw Ruby's cousin Sonya farther away in the crowd. When Maria saw Daisy and her parents, she beckoned them over.

"Oh, Lori," she said, her eyes filling with tears, "we

tried so hard to get in touch with you." The two moms hugged, crying in each other's arms.

Ruby's dad and Daisy's dad stood close to each other, gripping each other's elbows, talking intimately. Leo said in a low voice, "We didn't know what to do. We didn't want to leave a voice mail, but in the end, we had no choice." Daisy was standing behind her dad, holding on to the back of his suit jacket like she was a little kid.

Maria came around to her. She was barely taller than Daisy, but she wrapped Daisy up in a tight hug. Daisy always called it a Maria Mom hug, because even though Maria was a small lady, hugging her was reassuring and calming in a big-hug kind of way. Standing there in the parking lot of the church, Daisy remembered so many other times she'd been hugged by Maria. The time she and Ruby were first learning how to ride bikes and she'd wiped out and scraped both hands. The time she'd woken up puking in the middle of the night during a sleepover at the Affini house and they couldn't reach her parents. And more recently the time she got to tell them her mom was pregnant. A Maria Mom hug was a real deal hug.

"She loved you so much," Maria said. She pulled away a little and put her strong, petite hands on either side of Daisy's face. She looked Daisy in the eyes and said, "You were her very best friend in the world." Daisy nodded her head and then ducked back into hugging Maria as more tears streamed down her face. "She was so lucky to have had you as a friend," Maria said into her hair.

Were. Was. Had.

All in the past.

Daisy knew she should say something back to Maria. She tried, but nothing came out. It was all too much. She cleared her throat and tried again. "I . . . ," she said.

The tears were flowing so hard, they were dripping into her mouth. A tissue appeared, and she looked up at her dad, who had tears on his face too, and who hadn't left her side. Her mom was talking to Leo now.

"I love her so much too," Daisy said in a small voice, sniffling.

Loved. She was supposed to have said *loved.*

But she couldn't make herself think of Ruby in the past tense. Even now, after seeing the coffin, smelling the incense in the church, and hearing them say Ruby's whole name, talking about heaven and Jesus and eternal rest, and the sound of the organ filling the air. None of it felt real. It didn't feel like it had anything to do with Ruby herself.

Daisy's mom and dad told her they didn't have to

go to the cemetery. Daisy didn't want to; she couldn't bear the thought of it. She wanted to go home. Thinking about watching the coffin being put into the ground, with Ruby in it—*it's not really Ruby*, she told herself. *It's Ruby's body, not really her*—it was too much to even think about.

When they left the church, Daisy sat in the back seat of their car and leaned her face against the coolness of the window. She opened her swollen eyes and looked down at the things clutched in her hands. In one hand there was a clump of soggy tissues, and in the other was the card that the priest had given her when they first went into the church. There was a picture on one side. A statue of an angel, with the sun shining brightly behind it. She turned the card over. There was a poem. Or maybe it was a prayer. Something about the mercy of God. And under that, Ruby's birthday and then a dash. And then another date. A whole lived life in one small dash. More tears streamed down Daisy's face, and she sniffed. A hand reached back from the front seat, and her dad handed her another tissue. She dabbed at her tender eyes and read her best friend's name—Ruby Maria Affini—and under that, the final line said, *Rest easy in grace and love.*

What the Storm Blows In

It had been four weeks and four days since it happened, and four weeks and one day since Daisy had found out about it. That's how she thought about Ruby's death in her head. *It.* She never thought the words "death" or "died." She thought *It,* as if by not calling what had happened by the actual word, she could somehow protect her heart from hurting. That didn't work, of course. Her heart always hurt now.

Her mom was blasting music, and Daisy couldn't take it. It was something classical—Beethoven, Bach, Brahms. Something beginning with a *B*. When she complained, Mom said, "It's for the baby. Dad read a study about how playing music can be beneficial, even when still in utero."

"Did you play music for *me* when I was 'in utero'?" Daisy asked sullenly, making air quotes on the *in utero* part.

Not looking up from her computer, tucked into the pillow nest she'd made for herself on the couch, her mom said, "Yes, I played music for you."

"Well, it didn't help," Daisy said. "I don't even *like* classical music."

"I didn't *play* classical music when I was pregnant with you," her mom said absently, still typing.

"What did you play, then?" Daisy asked.

Daisy's mom looked up at her. "The Beatles," she replied. "Lots and lots of Beatles."

Daisy frowned and went to get a peach out of the fridge. "Come on, Chewbacca," she said, calling the dog and going out to the backyard to eat the peach on the swing. It was hot out, and very humid. She loved the Beatles, and it was annoying to think that it might be because her mom had blasted "Yellow Submarine" or something so loudly before she was even born and that it hadn't been her own choice to love them. She frowned again, thinking about listening to "Golden Slumbers" in the car, and how now that song would forever be associated with *It*.

She could still hear the stupid classical music out in the yard, though. The air was so wet and heavy, it felt solid, like something you had to physically push through. Chewie was lying in the dirt in the shade of a shrub, panting in the heat. Daisy sat on the swing, eating the peach and kicking her foot into the ground. The swing's movement back and forth didn't stir the air even a little. There were menacing, dark clouds in the sky, stacking up over the Long Island Sound, and a low rumble of thunder in the distance. Chewbacca whined. Daisy said, "It's okay, Chewie." He looked at her but didn't seem convinced. When she first bit into the peach, it had tasted cool and refreshing, but now, four bites in, the momentary coolness was gone, like it had been sucked out by the oppressive heat, and it tasted too sweet.

She walked to the fence and tossed it over, into the preserve. Chewie came up next to her and sat, looking through the fence where she'd thrown the peach. Daisy stuck her fingers through the chain link and leaned her forehead on the metal, looking through to the other side. The hole in her heart felt raw—a painful, throbbing wound in her chest—as if something had torn inside of her. She thought about the fallen tree and the day she and Ruby saw the fairy. It felt like so long ago. It had probably just been a bird or a bug or something. And now that Ruby wasn't here to try to convince her otherwise, the thought of it being something magical seemed far-fetched. There was another rumble of thunder in the distance, a little closer this time. The air was charged and heavy, like something was about to happen. It felt like work just to walk across the yard through the thick air. Chewie went to the back slider and barked to be let in. He hated thunder.

Daisy reached the slider just as the first drops began to plop out of the sky, and she and Chewie hurried into the air-conditioned family room. Mom was still typing on her computer and didn't even look up. There was a flash and then a gigantic crack of thunder.

The rain started to come down for real then. Not a delicate pitter-patter. It was violent and fierce. Chewie started whining, the hair on the back of his neck all prickly. He leaned himself against her leg like she could protect him. He looked really scared.

"It's okay, Chewie," Daisy said, bending down and hugging him. She nuzzled her face into the spot right behind his ear, which was super soft, and wrapped her arms around him.

Daisy's mom closed her laptop and adjusted her position, moving a pillow behind her back, with one hand on the side of her bump, which was bigger now. "Wow, what a storm!" she calmly said. She looked tired. "Thank goodness," she said. "Something needed to give." There was still a charge in the air, though, and it had Daisy on edge. Her mom being so undisturbed by the storm or the dog's crying made her feel anxious, like they weren't in the same place experiencing the same thing.

Another clap of thunder boomed loudly, and Daisy jumped. Chewbacca leaped onto the couch next to Daisy's mom, who gently petted him behind his ears. It sounded like the rain was made of knives, hitting the tin roof of their house, trying to get in. Even though it had been threatening for hours, the quickness with which it went from a few drops to a torrential downpour was epic and monumental. Lightning lit up the room, and with the flash came another huge cracking sound, like the sky had been ripped apart.

The electricity cut off, and the classical music abruptly stopped playing. "Mom," Daisy said, reaching out to her.

"It's okay, lovie," her mom said. Daisy squished herself onto the couch between Chewie and her mom. She grabbed her mom's hand and held it tightly, even though it was silly and babyish to be scared of a thunderstorm. Then it stopped raining, all at once, as if someone had turned a faucet off in the sky. Chewie jumped off the couch and ran to the front door, tail wagging.

The door popped open, and in walked Aunt Toby, lugging multiple tote bags, a backpack, and a suitcase, which she dropped on the floor. Somehow, they were all totally dry. "Blessings!" Aunt Toby sang, opening her arms wide and smiling a big, toothy Aunt Toby smile. It was like a hippie Mary Poppins had arrived.

Daisy's mom's face lit up at the sight of her twin sister. "Tobes! What are you doing here?" she said. "You're not supposed to come for another month!"

Daisy jumped off the couch and ran to her aunt, almost knocking her down with a hug. Daisy held on to her so hard, breathing in deeply to take in her scent— like spices and flowers with a secret special ingredient. It smelled so good, so comforting. "I missed you, honeypot," her aunt whispered into her hair. Mom awkwardly pushed herself off the couch and joined in the hug. Daisy heard them talking to each other over her head.

"How did you get here?" Daisy's mom said.

"I took an Uber from the airport," Aunt Toby replied. "I wanted to surprise you guys."

"Such an amazing surprise!" her mom said, looking a little teary-eyed. "How long can you stay?"

Chewbacca was pushing his head between Daisy and Aunt Toby, trying to nose his way into the hug that the three of them still hadn't released.

"I shifted stuff around at work," Aunt Toby said. "I'm staying until after the baby's born."

"Oh, Toby," Daisy's mom said, and Daisy heard a hitch in her voice. "I didn't want to tell you how much I missed having you here."

"I'm *always* with you in spirit, sissy," Aunt Toby murmured. "And now I'm with you in body, too." Daisy's eyes filled with a different kind of tears than they'd been crying since Ruby died. She felt a wave of relief enveloping her in this hug.

Daisy's aunt Toby was like a second mom to her. Aunt Toby didn't have children of her own, and she poured all her love into her one niece. If you could have a mom who was more like a kid than a grown-up, who liked to have fun and didn't make or follow a lot of rules, that was Aunt Toby. Most people thought her mom and Aunt Toby looked identical, but Daisy knew the small differences—the wrinkles at the corners of her mom's eyes, Aunt Toby's slight overbite, her mom's squishiness and Aunt Toby's muscles, and now, of course, her mom's baby bump.

"Besides," Aunt Toby said, "I felt a disturbance in the Force." Daisy's mom laughed. It was one of their twinsider things; they said they always knew when the other needed them. Aunt Toby pulled away from the hug and held Daisy at arm's length, looking into her face like she was searching for something. The corner of Daisy's mouth twitched, and she felt almost able to smile, but not quite. She looked down.

"I couldn't wait another whole month," Aunt Toby said as Chewbacca jumped up on her with his front paws.

Aunt Toby released Daisy and said, "Oh hello, Chewie," and bent down to let the dog lick her face. "I got coverage for my yoga classes, and I can manage the other retreat center stuff remotely. It's one of the benefits of being a boss." Aunt Toby was a partner at a fancy holistic spa, where she also taught yoga to rich and famous people.

"Don't let Chewie do that," Daisy's mom said. "Then he'll think it's okay to lick everyone's faces."

"Isn't it, though?" Aunt Toby said, while Chewie licked her chin. Daisy's mom gave her a look. Aunt Toby tipped her chin up and raised her eyebrows at Chewbacca, who clearly understood that to mean "lie down and roll over." Aunt Toby sat down on the floor and began to rub his belly.

Daisy's mom put her arm around Daisy. "I'm so glad you're here, sissy," she said, sighing and giving Daisy a little squeeze. "We could all use some of your good energy."

Daisy still hadn't said a word, but she felt a kind of release or relief now that her aunt was here. Aunt Toby had that effect on her. They'd always had a special connection, from the time Daisy was a baby and Aunt Toby lived in New York. The last few years, though, with Aunt Toby living in Seattle, Daisy had missed her fiercely. Seeing her three or four times a year never felt like enough. And Daisy talked to her about things she could never talk to her own mom about. Aunt Toby was kind of like Ruby; she saw magic everywhere in the world. Aunt Toby had a sparkle to her that other people just didn't have. Compared to Aunt Toby, her mom was so mom-ish. Aunt Toby was one of those people who everyone loved, as if good luck flowed her way and just being near her made everything seem a little better.

All of a sudden, the electricity flickered back on, and the music started booming again. But instead of the classical music that had been playing before, "Here Comes the Sun" blasted out of the speakers. "And there we are!" Aunt Toby said with a smile, as if she'd put the song on herself. Almost on cue, the sun burst through the clouds outside, and a big double rainbow formed over Roosevelt Cove. But Daisy wasn't looking, so she missed it.

Only Human

Aunt Toby had only been there a week, but the guest room already looked like it had been hit by a tornado.

"Why does Mom laugh at how messy this room is, but when my room gets messy, she gets mad?"

"I don't know," Aunt Toby said. "When we were growing up, we were both messy, but now she's such a neatnik. Or at least, she's neater than me."

Daisy hadn't ever thought her mom, or her house, were overly neat. But Aunt Toby's room was pretty much a disaster.

"Maybe she learned it from your dad," Aunt Toby said.

Daisy and Aunt Toby were lying on Aunt Toby's bed,

reading. Daisy was reading *Anya and the Dragon*, and Aunt Toby was flipping through a *Yoga Journal* magazine. Chewbacca was sprawled full out next to Aunt Toby, sleeping.

"Maybe it's something that happens when you become a parent," Aunt Toby said. "Maybe there's a secret parent handbook that says one of the rules of parenting is to tell your kid to keep their room clean." Aunt Toby flipped another page, then said, "Okay, honeypot, I can't sit still any longer!" She sang out, "Let's do something!"

That was another thing about Aunt Toby and Mom that was different. Daisy and her mom could sit together reading for hours. At least before she was pregnant anyway. Aunt Toby had what she called shpilkes, which is Yiddish for "ants in your pants." Daisy sighed, burrowed deeper into the pillow, and stuck her nose in her book.

"Let's go for a walk," Aunt Toby suggested.

"I don't want to," Daisy answered. "It's too hot out."

It was the beginning of August, and it was one of those summer days where the sun shone brightly, not a cloud in the sky. The humidity wasn't too bad, but it was still ninety-five degrees out. Daisy liked being inside in the chill of the air-conditioning.

"We could go to the library," Aunt Toby said.

"I'm not done reading this," Daisy replied, lifting her book up. "And I have another one I haven't even started."

"Honeypot," Aunt Toby said, "you've got to get out of this house. I've been here a week, and I'm pretty sure you haven't left it once."

"It's too hot," Daisy said. "And I've got cramps." Daisy didn't want to do anything, and period cramps were something Aunt Toby couldn't argue with. It *had* been hot, and Daisy *did* have her period. But it wasn't really the reason.

"Let's go ice-skating, then," Aunt Toby said with a satisfied smile on her face. "Exercise helps cramps."

"It's August," Daisy said. "Why would we do that?"

"I need to move my body," Aunt Toby said. "And you don't want to be hot. We can go to that indoor rink near the synagogue!"

Daisy couldn't think of any way to get out of it. She never dug in or acted stubborn with Aunt Toby the way she sometimes did with her mom. So, they took her mom's car and drove to the rink. As they passed Mill Pond Road, where you turned to go to Ruby's house, Daisy leaned her forehead against the glass of the car window and closed her eyes. She didn't think passing Ruby's street would ever get any easier.

Daisy's mom had called Maria Affini the other day.

Daisy had heard her talking when she'd been on the phone, saying all the things people say. *Checking in with you. Hope you're doing okay. We're here if you need us. We miss her too.* And then *She's been taking it hard. My sister's here. She's a comfort for Daisy.*

As they entered the rink, they were hit with a blast of cold air, which felt even colder after the hot parking lot. Aunt Toby had a bag with sweatshirts and gloves. They got rental skates from an old man who worked there and who looked a little grumpy.

Once they got their skates on, Daisy stepped onto the ice and for a second almost slipped. She was a decent skater. Not excellent or anything, but it was one of the things she had been better at than Ruby, who never got past the *clutching the rail at the side of the rink* stage. Aunt Toby was a great skater, though. She was already speeding around, as if she couldn't wait to get rid of her excess energy. Daisy righted herself and started to glide. Aunt Toby came up next to her, hopped from one foot to the other, and started skating backward, talking to her.

"I'm heading out east tomorrow for a few days," she said. "There's a couple, Garry and Bill, who've stayed at the spa a bunch of times, and they have a house in Southampton."

"Okay," Daisy said, building up a little speed. She didn't want to admit it, but it did feel good to be moving. The sharp scraping sound of the skates on the ice was soothing. There were only a few other people at the rink. A little girl who looked like she was training for the Olympics or something was twirling and doing that sitting-down kind of spin, and then skating backward, foot over foot.

Aunt Toby hopped again to face forward and skate next to Daisy, continuing to talk. "I'm doing some one-on-one yoga classes for them."

"All right," Daisy said.

"It's one of the perks of owning the spa," she said. "Meeting wealthy people who like private yoga classes." Daisy turned her head and looked up at her aunt, whose curly brown hair was flowing out behind her. When she glanced down at Daisy and smiled, her eyes sparkled.

Daisy didn't say anything. She'd heard her mom say that Aunt Toby was one of those people that nice things always happened to. Not many people could support themselves only teaching yoga, and it was like the Universe just wanted Aunt Toby to spread her type of peace, love, and magic everywhere. Opportunities always opened up for her. It's how she ended up part owner of a spa. Although that hadn't been so great for Daisy, since that was when Aunt Toby moved away to Seattle.

"They have an extra car out there that they don't use," she said. "They want me to borrow it while I'm here." The little girl zipped past them and startled Daisy. She slipped again for a second and grabbed Aunt Toby's elbow to get her balance.

"They're giving you a car?" Daisy said, righting herself and letting go of Aunt Toby's arm.

"They're letting me *borrow* their car," Aunt Toby said. "They said it would make it easier for me to get to them. They love their private classes."

"But why do you have to work while you're here?" Daisy said. "Why can't you just hang out?"

They stopped skating and rested at the side of the rink, watching the little girl practice some kind of twirly jump.

"First of all, I love to teach," Aunt Toby said. "Second of all, I feel like bringing a yoga practice to other people is what I was put on the planet to do."

Daisy thought about that for a moment. She had no clue why she was on the planet.

It had a been a while since Daisy had last gone skating, and her ankles hurt a little. "I'm tired," she said. "Let's be done."

"All righty," Aunt Toby said. "But should we get hot chocolate before we go? There's a machine."

They walked on the cushiony floor over to a bench and took off their skates, then returned them to the grumpy old man. Then they put their shoes back on, got hot chocolate out of the machine, and sipped it while watching the little girl skate. She was trying and trying to do some kind of spinning jump, but it didn't seem to be working. She tried again and fell. Daisy thought she might have hurt herself because she sat there for a moment on the ice.

Then Daisy saw her take a deep breath and stand up. It was like the scene in *Captain Marvel* when the Supreme Intelligence says, *You're only human*, to Carol Danvers, and Carol remembers all the times she got back up after being knocked down. *Only human* can mean being strong, being able to get up again, being resilient. Carol Danvers got up, again and again and again. Daisy watched the girl. *She's only human too.* She attempted her jump once more and this time landed it. Daisy sighed because it felt like she'd need superhero strength to pick her own self up. Being *only human* wasn't working.

Have a Nice Day

*E*very day after Aunt Toby came back from South-ampton with her borrowed car, she would make suggestions about places to go. There were only so many times Daisy could say no before finally giving in. Aunt Toby was insistent like Ruby in that way. So, when Aunt Toby said, "You and I are going to the beach, honeypot," Daisy didn't fight it. She just put on her bathing suit and went.

At South Shore Beach, Daisy could breathe in a way that she hadn't been able to breathe at home. The sound of the waves crashing, the rhythmic shush of it, punctuated by tiny moments of quiet, was comforting and soothing. The ocean in Long Island isn't a beautiful turquoise blue like when Daisy and her family had gone to the Caribbean. The Caribbean water had screamed Fun! Sun! Vacation! This water was dark green and brownish blue, still beautiful, but serious-looking. And it was endless in a way that the Long Island Sound, near Daisy's house, wasn't. When she gazed out, there was nothing on the horizon but ocean and more ocean. She could imagine getting in a boat and sailing straight across the Atlantic and ending up in Ireland or England or someplace like that. She wasn't exactly sure about the geography.

Even though it wasn't even noon yet, it was already hot. They sat in the beach chairs Aunt Toby had brought, which were wood-framed with soft, sun-bleached orange canvas slung between the rods. Aunt Toby had spread a brightly colored blanket out next to them, and a cooler was tucked behind one of their chairs, taking advantage of a tiny square of shade.

They faced the ocean, eating egg salad sandwiches. Aunt Toby was digging a trench in the sand with her heel, absentmindedly moving her foot back and forth.

"How long do you think you're going to stay?" Daisy asked.

"I'm definitely going to stay at least until your mom gives birth," Aunt Toby said. "Then I'll figure out what's next." She paused. "I might be all done with my fancy-schmancy spa."

Daisy tipped her head to the side so she could see past the brim of her cap, which was pushed low on her forehead.

"Really?" Daisy asked. "What do you mean? Are you going to move back here?"

"I don't know," Aunt Toby said, taking another big bite of her sandwich and chewing. "I think about it sometimes."

Daisy looked at Aunt Toby, who was thinking and chewing and staring out at the ocean. If Aunt Toby moved back to New York, that would be the best thing ever. Neither of them said anything for a bit, though. That was a good thing about hanging out with Aunt Toby; Daisy could be quiet with her, and it was okay. It never felt awkward.

"If I sell my share . . . I could. . . . But then . . . Hmmm . . ." She was thinking aloud, not really talking to Daisy, and she wasn't really finishing any sentences. Daisy just listened. She was used to this. Eventually she'd find out what Aunt Toby was thinking about.

Aunt Toby gave Daisy the same kind of space to think and talk about things whenever she was ready. Daisy could tell her anything, and she was never all judgy like most grown-ups. And she wasn't the kind of person who told you what to do or not to do. She listened.

Aunt Toby licked the side of her sandwich, where the egg salad was poking out.

"What?" she said as she saw Daisy looking at her.

"What?" Daisy said.

Aunt Toby took another bite. "You're staring at me," she said, talking with her mouth full, like a little kid.

"No, I'm not," Daisy said, staring.

Aunt Toby raised her eyebrows and grinned, egg salad peeking out the side of her lips. "Okay," she said, finally closing her mouth and swallowing.

Daisy was thinking about whether to tell Aunt Toby about the thing she and Ruby had seen in the preserve. Aunt Toby hadn't said anything about Ruby yet. She hadn't brought her up, waiting for Daisy to be ready to talk about it. Daisy knew Aunt Toby wouldn't tell her parents about sneaking into the preserve. Although that part probably didn't matter anymore anyway. She wouldn't get in trouble for it now.

Still, seeing the fairy felt private in a way it hadn't been before. She hadn't talked to anyone about it. It was a secret only she and Ruby knew about, and now Ruby was gone, and only Daisy knew about it. If there were anyone she could share the secret with, it would be Aunt Toby.

Daisy looked down at her own egg salad sandwich. The knot in her stomach, which was always there now, pulled tighter. She took a bite. A big seagull landed near the blanket, ruffled its feathers, and stared at her. Or it could have been staring at the sandwich; it was hard to tell.

"Ugh! Go away!" she said, kicking sand in its direction and getting some on the blanket. The seagull squawked at her, making kind of a *Ha! Ha! Ha!* sound.

Aunt Toby stood up and walked toward the bird, making shooing motions with her hands. "Take to the skies, my friend," she said. "Leave my girl alone." The seagull ruffled its feathers again, and if seagulls had shoulders, it would have given a little shrug. Then with a flap and another squawk, it flew away. Daisy smiled and shook her head. Aunt Toby was *so* Aunt Toby.

And then there were the tears again, rolling down her cheeks. Out of nowhere. Aunt Toby was so Aunt Toby in a very similar way that Ruby had been so Ruby.

"Honeypot?" Aunt Toby said as she walked back toward Daisy.

Daisy shoved the last bit of her sandwich into her mouth so she could wipe both eyes with her hands.

"I know," Aunt Toby said. "Grief is like that." She didn't need to say any more. Daisy could feel that Aunt Toby just got it.

Aunt Toby stood behind Daisy's chair and gave her shoulders a squeeze. Then they both took a deep breath in. Daisy closed her eyes and leaned her head back on the chair. The air smelled salty, and funky, and slightly fishy, but not in a bad way. There was something about the smell that was why Daisy felt like she could breathe here. At home she couldn't get away from her sadness, but she hadn't been willing to go anywhere or do anything. The smell of the woods near her house and the green growing of summer things, which she usually loved, had started to press in on her. Maybe it was because when Daisy thought about the woods, she couldn't help thinking about Ruby. She thought about the day they saw the fairy. She thought about camping and then finding out what had happened. Now the smell of the woods was a reminder of everything she had lost.

This was the first time she had been to the beach all summer. This air smelled different, and she welcomed it. The occasional breeze blew the low-tide scent toward her and then away, toward her and away.

She took a deep breath and said, "Do you believe in real magic?"

Aunt Toby plopped down onto the blanket and said, "My first reaction is to just say yes, but what do you mean by *real* magic?"

"Like unexplainable things," Daisy said.

Aunt Toby tilted her head. "What's an unexplainable thing? Like an object in an unexpected place, or proof of a multiverse, or real-life doppelgängers? What are we talking about here?"

Conversations with Aunt Toby often went this way. They started in one place and drifted, sometimes digging into deep and meaningful questions about hidden feelings or the nature of existence, sometimes tripping down a path into silliness, and sometimes floating into the clouds with talk of goddesses and magic.

Daisy said, "Like fairies. Do you believe in fairies?" She got up and joined Aunt Toby on the blanket. They both stretched out, stomach down, chins propped on their hands as they watched the waves.

Aunt Toby didn't even pause. "Definitely," she said. "I believe in the power of the Universe. And my Universe includes fairies. Doesn't yours?"

Daisy swallowed, the lump in her throat making it

hard to continue. "I don't know," she said softly. "I think so." Then she was quiet. They lay next to each other, with her question, and why she'd asked it, hanging in the air between them, waiting.

Since it was low tide, there was a large swathe of hard-packed wet sand between the soft, dry spot where they sat and where the water started. A handful of sandpiper birds ran across the wet sand, speeding back and forth in a group, like someone had choreographed a dance for them. They looked for little bits to eat, all stopping at the same time to peck, then moving on as a group, leaving a web of small birdie footprints, which got wiped away whenever a lick of water edged in close enough to erase them.

Finally Daisy said, "Ruby and I thought we saw one in the preserve at the beginning of the summer." Daisy looked over, and Aunt Toby was still gazing out at the ocean. Daisy cleared her throat. It was weird to say Ruby's name out loud, even though she thought about her all the time.

"Cool," Aunt Toby said. "Was it beautiful?"

That wasn't the response Daisy had expected, but she replied, "We didn't get a close enough look. It was hovering and flew away pretty quickly. But yeah, I think it was beautiful."

Aunt Toby sat up and clapped sand off her hands, still looking at the water. She said, "I thought I saw one once, when I was a little younger than you."

Daisy sat up. She followed Aunt Toby's gaze. The waves were forming far off the shore, like an urge under the water that was building and building until it started to push up, gathering momentum, then finally turning into what was discernibly a wave. Then, instead of a long, luxurious crest that some surfer dude in Hawaii would be able to ride on, they curled in on themselves almost immediately and smashed close to the shore.

"Where were you when you saw it?" Daisy asked.

"Central Park," Aunt Toby said, and chuckled. She looked over at Daisy. "Of all the places! But we were both pretty sure it was a fairy."

"Who else saw it?"

"Well, your mom, of course," she said. "We went everywhere together when we were kids."

Her mom had never told her anything about seeing a fairy when she was little. She couldn't dream of her mom believing in fairies now. She was so practical and so . . . non-magical. So mom-ish. But then again, Daisy had never said anything to her mom about the fairy either.

"What did it look like?" Daisy asked. "How did you know it was a fairy?"

"I don't remember exactly what it looked like," Aunt Toby said, "because it happened so fast." Daisy nodded. "Though I remember thinking when we saw it that it must be impossible, but there it was anyway."

"Same," Daisy said. She *knew* Aunt Toby would get it. "We couldn't believe it when we were seeing it, but at the same time we both just *knew* what we were seeing was real."

"You must really miss her," Aunt Toby said.

Daisy didn't say anything, just swallowed hard, because the lump was back in her throat.

"You know," Aunt Toby said, nudging Daisy with her shoulder, "seeing something like that doesn't happen to everyone. I think you have to have some magic inside of you to see it."

Daisy didn't feel like she had magic in her anymore, if she ever had. People like Ruby and Aunt Toby had magic. She was magic-adjacent—the kind of person who hung out with magical people, like a sidekick. She looked back out at the water, watching as another wave started building up, following it until it broke on itself, then withdrew, sucked back into the ocean.

"Let's go in the water," Aunt Toby said.

"Okay," Daisy said. She threw off her baseball cap and started running toward the surf. If there was one place she was completely at ease, unafraid, content, it was the water. Aunt Toby said it was because she was a Pisces.

"Hey, wait for me, honeypot!" Aunt Toby shouted.

When Aunt Toby caught up, they pounced into the surf together. They dove under a wave at the same time, right before it broke, their faces simultaneously popping up on the other side. They hung out in the deeper water beyond where the waves were breaking, bobbing and ducking under when they needed to. Floating on her back when it was a bit calmer, Aunt Toby showed Daisy how to do some water-ballet moves, pointing her toe up to the sky and making small figure eights with her hands, which turned her body in a circle. When they finally got tired, they waited for a nice big wave, then bodysurfed back to shore.

They got Italian ices at the concession stand.

Then Aunt Toby did some yoga, and Daisy sat in her beach chair, reading. As the sun shone down on her, she read her book and listened to the sound of the crashing waves in the background. Aunt Toby did a headstand on the blanket. Then they both laughed at the disapproving looks of an old guy walking by, who was way too tan and who muttered something about *crazy hippie ladies*.

At the end of the day when they got home, Mom

said they'd gotten too much sun, and Aunt Toby should have been more responsible. Both of their faces were covered in freckles. Aunt Toby's back was sunburned, but she just laughed at Daisy's mom, not even a little bit bothered by the reprimand. She hugged her sister from behind, wrapping both of her hands around Mom's belly, and said, "Oh shush, grumpy lady. We had a nice day."

Daisy's curly hair was crunchy from the beach. She got in the shower and stood under the warm water, letting the sand and salt rinse off. She soaped up, and the fruity smell of the bodywash mixed with the coconut scent of sunscreen. It was the first day since *It* had happened that she'd smiled about anything. Or, like Aunt Toby had said, *had a nice day*. She squirted shampoo into her hand and began lathering her hair.

She tipped her head back and stood under the showerhead. How could she *have a nice day* when Ruby was gone? She combed conditioner through her hair with her fingers. She thought, *I'm going to keep getting older. And someday I'm even going to be a grown-up. But that's not going to happen for Ruby. She's never going to grow up. She never even got old enough to get her first period. There's never going to be a grown-up Ruby Affini. She won't have three daughters, like she'd hoped.* The thought made her stomach hurt. She didn't want to keep growing up and not have Ruby there. It wasn't fair. Then she remembered it was August. Ruby's birthday was at the end of the month. As tears coursed down her cheeks, they mixed with the hot water showering down on her.

Daisy turned the hot water down. She stood under the shower, and as the water cooled, she rinsed out the conditioner, pulling her fingers through the silky-smooth strands of her hair. She couldn't stop the thoughts now. She couldn't stop thinking that she shouldn't be able to *have a nice day* when Ruby would never make her laugh about something dumb again. Or Ruby wouldn't be there to encourage her to be brave when she was being a chicken, and then pretend Daisy had been brave all along, so she wouldn't feel bad. Ruby wouldn't be there interrupting her anymore either. Sometimes Daisy couldn't get a word in when they were talking about something. She felt bad remembering that. Or when Ruby insisted they do something her way, which she sometimes did.

The cool water ran over her whole body, and she put her face right under it. They'd been looking forward to starting middle school together since orientation last spring. Ruby had said that if you make a wish on the first star of the night on the summer solstice, that it would come true. Of course she knew to do something like that. So on the day they were pretty sure was the solstice, they'd held hands and wished that their lockers would be next to each other's, because they'd each get a locker in middle school. Now that wouldn't happen. None of it. Wishing hadn't done anything.

She hated that she'd *had a nice day*.

Moise Like Louise

Daisy couldn't stand the fact that the days just kept coming, like the endless waves on the beach. And that Ruby wasn't in them, would never be in them again. She dreaded the end of summer and starting middle school without her best friend. About a week before regular school started, Daisy went back to Hebrew school. No one there knew Ruby. Daisy's parents had wanted them to be in a Reconstructionist congregation, and the closest Reconstructionist synagogue was a half hour from where they lived. The kids at Hebrew school had no way of knowing that Daisy's summer had been the worst one of her life. They only knew that they were all back for their final year before b'nai mitzvah tutoring. Daisy was a little taller, tanner, and older, same as everyone else. But she didn't feel like everyone else anymore.

Morah Jill was standing in front of the classroom and kept talking and talking, going on and on about the meaning of becoming a bar or bat mitzvah, about the first girl to have a bat mitzvah, how Reconstructionist Judaism was at the forefront of gender inclusivity, blah blah blah, as if they hadn't heard the same speech at least a hundred times. Daisy sat at a desk next to Rachel, who was next to Hannah. They'd been Hebrew school friends since Grade Bet in second grade, when she'd first started. That was the Morah Cynthia year. Then they'd been in Grade Gimmel with Morah Tracy, and Morah Jennifer in Grade Dalet. And here they were in Grade Vav, their second year with Morah Jill and the last year before everyone started b'nai mitzvah tutoring.

It wasn't a big class. They were mostly the same twenty or so kids from towns all over the North Shore of Nassau County, moving together from year to year, from classroom to classroom in the synagogue school. Rachel and Hannah were nice enough, but she only ever saw them there. It wasn't like they were home friends who knew anything about her life in Roosevelt Cove. Rachel nudged Daisy with her foot and slipped a folded piece of paper under the table. Daisy unfolded it in her lap and took a quick look down. *Who's the new kid?* Daisy glanced at Rachel, who wiggled her eyebrows and gave a head nod to the left. There was a new boy with a notebook out on his desk. He was busily writing in it. It looked like he was taking notes or something. Daisy shrugged.

Morah Jill's voice got super sincere. "My friends! This is *such* an exciting time in your lives." She beamed a gigantic, toothy smile. "Next year will be your b'nai mitzvah year, an opportunity to step into the responsibilities of becoming an adult in the Jewish community." Daisy felt sleepy. It was the kind of sleepy that overtakes you when someone starts talking about growing up and having responsibilities, when all you want is to stay being a kid.

"This year, we start preparing you for that."

It was warm in the classroom. Daisy stifled a yawn. Morah Jill continued, "When you become b'nai mitzvah, you'll be able to participate in the life of our synagogue in new and powerful ways." Morah Jill actually wiped a tear from her eye. Daisy really liked the Hebrew school teacher, but she and Hannah always made bets as to how many times Morah Jill would cry. Today Daisy had said three; Hannah said four. Daisy looked at

Hannah, and they both quietly raised one finger. Hannah put her hand in front of her mouth, hiding a giggle.

Rachel slipped another piece of paper to Daisy. *He's so cute!* it said. Daisy glanced at the new kid. He just looked like a regular kid to her, like one of the skateboard kids from school. He had longish, sort of curly brown hair and looked tan. He was wearing a Lord of the Rings T-shirt, shorts, and Vans without socks. He wore glasses, which were black and square and on the large side. Daisy looked at Rachel and shrugged again. She guessed he was cute, but she didn't usually think about boys like that. Was Rachel going to start getting boy crazy? Was *everyone* going to start getting boy crazy or girl crazy now?

The boy looked like he was listening closely to Morah Jill. He frowned and had a worried look on his face. Now she was talking about Shabbat services. She said, "On the day you become a bat or bar mitzvah, you'll have the opportunity to lead the whole service for the congregation!" She said it with so much enthusiasm, you'd think she was saying they'd get to be ringmaster of a circus. "For today, let's look at which parts of the Shabbat service we find the most meaningful." Everyone was quiet. Daisy didn't know which part felt meaningful to her. Morah Jill scanned the class with an expectant look on her face. "I'd like some participation here, people!"

Finally a boy in the back shouted out, "Challah and grape juice!" and a few people laughed. The corner of Daisy's mouth twitched, daring her to smile. She actually did love the challah and grape juice after Shabbat services.

Morah Jill said, "That's a perfectly valid thing to appreciate, but let's dig deeper, shall we? What else do you find meaningful?"

"I mean, I guess I like that 'Shalom Rav' song," the boy said.

Morah Jill smiled. "Yes! 'Shalom Rav' is a lovely thing to appreciate. Praying for peace is a particularly beautiful part of the Shabbat service. Thank you for sharing that." She looked around the class, trying to make eye contact with as many kids as possible. Nobody was saying anything, so she tried changing gears. "Also, doing acts of *tikkun olam*, 'repairing the world,' is something we take particularly seriously here at B'nai Shalom. In a way it goes hand in hand with the prayer for peace. We'll be talking more about tikkun olam later in the year," she said, "and I'm *very* excited to talk to you all about your projects!"

Big surprise—nobody in the class looked quite as excited as Morah Jill.

"Now, who else would like to share a part of the

Shabbat service that they find meaningful?" Morah Jill asked again.

Hannah raised her hand, and Morah Jill called on her. "I like singing 'Mi Shebeirach,'" Hannah said. "Because when somebody's sick, it's like you can't really do anything about it, so singing 'Mi Shebeirach' feels like you're kind of doing something."

"Yes!" Morah Jill exclaimed, clutching her hands to her heart. "How many other people have felt that way at some point?" A couple of kids raised their hands.

Someone called out, "Yeah, whenever I sing that prayer, I think about my grandpa because he has Alzheimer's. I know he can't get better or anything, but I like to think of him during it anyway."

"That's very thoughtful," Morah Jill said. She wiped another tear away. "Very lovely." Daisy sneaked a glance at Hannah. They both put up another finger.

A girl said, "Last year whenever we sang 'Mi Shebeirach,' I thought about my sister's friend who had leukemia. She was in the hospital for a long time." Then she said, "But she died anyway." Daisy looked at her. "It made me feel a little better knowing I'd said the prayer for her, though, even if she wasn't Jewish. Like, maybe she didn't suffer as much because I kind of prayed for her or something?"

Hannah put up a third finger, because Morah Jill was wiping both eyes now. But Daisy wasn't paying attention. The hollow pit in her stomach expanded. She hadn't thought about suffering. When her parents had told her Ruby was gone, she hadn't thought about if Ruby had suffered at all. Just the possibility of it made her dizzy. She held her breath, trying to will away the building tears. *What if Ruby had suffered? What if she had been in pain or knew it was happening? What if she knew she was going to die? What if she had been scared?*

The new kid had his hand raised, and Morah Jill called on him. "Yes, Moise?"

Wait. Did Morah Jill just call the new boy Louise? Daisy's attention was drawn away from the downward spiral of her thoughts. She swallowed the lump in her throat and looked at the boy.

"Oh, nobody calls me Moise," he said. "Just Mo." He was writing something in his notebook. "Um, that prayer, Mish-a . . . How do you spell that?" He looked up. "It's what you say for sick people?"

"It's the prayer for healing," Morah Jill answered. "'Mi Shebeirach.'" She spelled it out for him in English, then said, "I will give you a copy of it, *Mo.*" She stressed the "Mo," and it was like you could hear her trying hard not to say the last part of his name. Morah Jill pursed her lips and put her hand on her heart, in a weirdly emotional way, but she didn't squeeze out a tear this time.

"Cool, thanks," he said, looking embarrassed. Then he wrote something else in his notebook.

What kind of a name is Moise Like Louise? Daisy thought.

When he looked up from writing, he caught Daisy staring at him. His face relaxed a little, and he grinned at her. One of his front teeth was slightly crooked, overlapping the other just a smidgen. His smile was a tiny bit crooked too, like his whole face was following the lead of the misaligned tooth. Daisy looked away, pretending she hadn't been caught staring at him. *Awkward.*

Rachel was right, Daisy thought. *This Mo kid is kind of cute.* Having that thought was super weird, though. She'd never really thought that about a boy or a girl before. It was confusing. She wished she could talk to Ruby about it. It was like she was on a roller coaster— one minute thinking maybe a boy was cute and the next feeling like she would drown in sadness that Ruby was gone.

"Okay, let's get into pairs now," Morah Jill said. "You can move your chairs around if you have to. Grab a partner and find a spot!"

The sound of chairs scraping and people talking, everyone pairing off, made it hard to hear what else

Morah Jill was saying. Hannah and Rachel had already pulled their chairs together near the window. Daisy looked around, crossing her fingers one of the Roth triplets didn't come over and ask to be her partner, when someone softly tapped her on the shoulder. Moise Like Louise said, "Hey."

"Oh hey," Daisy said.

"Morah Jill told me before class that you live in Roosevelt Cove too."

Daisy looked at him. *He lives in Roosevelt Cove?*

"Yeah," she said. "Do you?"

"Yeah, we moved there at the beginning of the summer," he said. "To Birch Court."

"Birch Court?"

He nodded back. "Yeah, it's right next to Dower Nature Preserve," he said.

"I know," Daisy said. "I live on the other side of the preserve." She swallowed. "On Cedar."

"Cool," he said, and nodded again. They were both quiet for a minute. Then he said, "So, like, can we be partners since we're kind of neighbors?"

"Sure," she said, clearing her throat and looking away. None of the other kids at Hebrew school were from Roosevelt Cove. There weren't a lot of Jewish kids in their town.

Morah Jill said, "Simmer down, people, and listen up!" Rachel started coughing, and Daisy looked over at her. Mo was listening to what Morah Jill was saying, writing it down in his notebook. Rachel winked at Daisy, then wiggled her eyebrows again, giving another nod toward Mo. Daisy shrugged, then looked away. Then she sighed and really wished she were home, or could just put her head down on her desk and go to sleep.

It was all too much. Being back at Hebrew school. Seeing Hannah and Rachel, who she hadn't seen since last school year. Meeting a new kid, who she should probably be nice to. Nobody here knew Ruby. They might not have even heard. Hebrew school wasn't very close to their town. There were a lot of families that didn't live near the synagogue, just like Daisy's. If any of the kids had even heard that an eleven-year-old girl from a few towns away had died, they wouldn't have known she was Daisy's best friend. It wasn't the kind of thing you go and tell somebody. Like, *Oh hi! How was your summer? Mine was the most horrible summer of my life because my best friend in the universe was killed, and the world should really just stop spinning, and I can't even get through a day without feeling absolutely awful.*

Morah Jill had been giving them instructions about

what they were supposed to do next, but Daisy was so busy in her thoughts, she hadn't been paying attention again. And now Mo looked kind of how she felt. Like maybe he was about two seconds away from tears.

"What are we supposed to be doing?" she whispered.

In a small voice he replied, "Morah Jill said becoming a b'nai mitzvah is one of the major life-cycle events." His eyes were downcast. He read from his notebook: "'Life-cycle events are happening all the time, not just during the b'nai mitzvah year. Things like birth, death, and marriage are all life-cycle events. Share about another event in your life that has made a big impact on you recently, and the things you've done in response to it.'" He looked up from the page. If she wasn't sure before, now it was certain. This kid looked like he was about to cry.

The lump came back into Daisy's throat, and she tried to swallow it down. Seeing somebody else cry always made her eyes tear up. It would be so embarrassing if she cried in Hebrew school.

Mo said, "I didn't know Hebrew school was going to be like this." His voice cracked a little. "I thought it was going to be about learning rules and prayers and things like that." He swallowed. "I didn't know we'd have to share feelings and stuff." Daisy hadn't said anything.

"This is my first time doing it." His eyebrows drew together, and he looked at her expectantly.

She stared at him, but all she could think about was Ruby, who would have loved doing an exercise like this. She would have thought of ten amazing things that had made an impact on her, and then told funny stories about the things she'd done in response to them, and would have probably even been excited about sharing it all with someone new.

Daisy blinked but still didn't say anything. Everyone was chattering around them. She heard some kids cracking up. She heard Hannah say, "Oh my god, me too!" to Rachel. Morah Jill had started putting out paper cups, and grape juice, and a plate of challah, which meant class was almost over. Thank god.

For an awkward minute she and Mo sat facing each other, neither of them saying anything. He had his hands on his knees and was looking down, frowning. Daisy's hands were clasped in front of her on her desk. She looked at how her fingers were intertwined, at the desk where someone had drawn a Star of David with a peace sign inside, toward the window, where it was still light out. If she looked at this sad boy in front of her, she would burst into tears.

He cleared his throat. Then he said, "The event that's

made the biggest impact on me recently is . . ." His voice cracked again, and Daisy couldn't help herself; she looked at him.

"Well, my mom is pretty sick. She has breast cancer." He said the word "breast" a little quieter, like he was embarrassed to say it out loud. "It's why we moved here. To live with my grandma and grandpa." He nodded a little. "And be near a special cancer hospital in the city."

He was still looking down at his knees. Daisy's eyes widened. He cleared his throat again.

"The thing I'm doing in response to it," he said, as if he were answering a question on a standardized test, "is going to Hebrew school, and hopefully becoming a bar mitzvah next year, even though I never went to Hebrew school before."

Then he looked up at her. She saw tears gathering in the corners of his eyes. Her own tears started to well up, and her chest got tight. She squeezed her hands together on the desk, trying to make her tears stop.

He said, "We've never really been so Jewish in my family. I figure, if I learn how to be better at it, maybe God will help her get well."

He blinked a few times. He took off his glasses and wiped at his eyes with the back of his hands. Then he put them back on and looked expectantly at her again.

She said softly, in a whisper, "My best friend died this summer."

Mo leaned closer to her, like he might not have heard her right. She couldn't stop the tears, which were rolling down her cheeks freely. She said, "I guess . . . in response to it . . . what I'm doing is trying not to feel sad all the time."

The Living Environment

The Roosevelt Cove school district had two elementary schools, which came together at sixth grade for middle school and then high school. So even though half the kids in the middle school hallway didn't know Daisy, half of them did. Daisy felt sick at the thought of anyone saying anything to her about Ruby and having to listen or think of something to say back. A couple of kids had tried to say hello when Daisy was walking down the hall, but she'd kept her eyes down so she hopefully wouldn't have to stop and talk to anyone.

It was easy enough to find her locker, but opening it was another thing altogether. Daisy twirled the dial to the right again, stopping at five. Once all the way around to the left, stop at thirteen. Twirl to the right; stop at six. But it wouldn't click open. She took a deep breath and started from the top. Five. Thirteen. Six. Why wouldn't it open? *I will not let the tears come out of my eyes. I will not cry.* She swung her backpack off her back, plopped it on the floor in front of her locker, and pulled the bottom of her T-shirt away from her waistband, letting some air in underneath. She was already sweating, and she hadn't even been to her first class yet. The sound of other people's lockers slamming and kids' voices greeting one another was overwhelming. She wanted to curl in on herself and disappear. The background noise didn't drown out her very loud thoughts, though. *Somebody's going to say something about Ruby. I don't want to be here without her. I want to go home.*

A voice near her said, "I couldn't open mine either at first." Daisy swallowed past the lump in her throat. She looked away from the locker to a tall girl wearing a blue T-shirt that said SMART GIRLS RULE! in bold letters. Daisy didn't say anything. Her glance moved from the girl's T-shirt up to her face. Daisy blinked. "You have to go straight to the last number, without twirling it around again," the girl said.

"Oh," Daisy said, and tried again. Five-thirteen-six. This time it clicked, and the door of her locker swung open. Finally. Daisy looked back at the girl. "Thanks," she said, and gave her a tiny smile.

"This one's mine," the girl said, tapping the next locker over. Daisy's heart pounded in her chest as she looked at the locker next to hers.

That should have been Ruby's locker. Daisy didn't say anything. *They'd both wished for it.* The girl stood there, awkwardly, expectantly. Daisy took a pencil and a notebook out of her backpack, then shoved it into the locker. This girl must have gone to the other elementary school in Roosevelt Cove. She didn't know her. A bell rang, and a kid with a huge backpack strapped to his back pushed past her. She heard someone shout, "Are we late?"

She looked at the locker that should have been Ruby's and sighed. *I will not let the tears come out of my eyes. I will not cry.*

"I think that's just the warning bell," the girl said. She looked at her phone. "We have five more minutes to get to first period."

Daisy cleared her throat.

"What homeroom are you in?" the girl asked.

She said, "219, Mr. Herman's." Her voice came out scratchy and broken-sounding.

"Me too," the girl said as they started to walk down the hall together. Then she said, "My name's Avery."

Daisy was so tired. She felt like she was walking in a bubble, and the frenetic busyness of the hallway was happening outside it. She said, "I'm Daisy," and then fell silent. A boy came barreling down the hall and knocked into Avery, who bumped into Daisy.

"Sorry," Avery said. Daisy nodded but didn't say anything back. She kept her eyes down as they wound their way through the loud, crowded hall together, then went upstairs to the second floor and Room 219. *I will not let the tears come out of my eyes. I will not cry.*

When they got to the classroom, Avery went right in and took a seat near the front, looking back to see if Daisy was going to sit near her. Daisy paused at the doorway before going in, afraid to catch anyone's eye, not wanting to see the kids she hadn't seen since last school year. She didn't want to even think about what they were thinking. Probably things like *Poor Daisy Rubens. She's the girl whose best friend died.* Or *Daisy minus Ruby.* Amanda, who she'd seen at the funeral with her parents, was sitting in the third row. Amanda made a tight smile, then quickly looked away. Daisy's eyebrows drew together in a frown.

She didn't know where else to go, so she took the open seat right behind Avery, which was closest and easiest. Another girl Daisy knew from volunteering at the library was sitting in the seat behind her. She leaned forward and touched Daisy on the shoulder. Daisy turned. "I heard about Ruby. I'm really sorry," the girl said. Daisy gave a weak smile and shrugged the hand off but didn't say anything. Then the girl made a little-kid pouting face, sticking her bottom lip out. Daisy looked at her fake pouting. What was she supposed to say? *Thank you?* Was she supposed to say it was okay? She made a tight smile like Amanda had just made at her and turned back to the front of the class where Mr. Herman was writing something on the whiteboard.

Daisy kept her eyes on him, praying nobody else would say anything and that she wouldn't catch anyone else's eye. When the bell rang, Mr. Herman went to close the classroom door, but a boy squeezed past him at the very last minute, his backpack catching on the doorframe.

"Sorry! Sorry!" the boy said. All eyes went to the kid. Mr. Herman shook his head. "Go find a seat."

It was him. The boy who had been *taking notes* at Hebrew school. The boy whose mom had cancer. The boy Daisy had cried in front of. Moise Like Louise. She was mortified. If he looked at her, was he going to think about her as the crying girl from Hebrew school? Would he be embarrassed because he'd told her about his mom and kind of cried too? And then there was the weirdness of having someone in regular school who was also in Hebrew school. It had never happened before, because Roosevelt Cove was so far from the synagogue and Hebrew school.

"Oh hey, Daisy," he said, nodding at her and taking the open seat next to hers. It was like his voice had exploded into the quiet of the room, although he'd probably said hello in a regular voice. She was positive every single person in the classroom was looking at her, and now they all knew that he knew her. She turned her face the tiniest bit toward him. He pushed up his glasses, which had slid down his nose. He raised his eyebrows and looked at her expectantly.

"Hi," she said, barely audible. She turned her gaze back to the front of the classroom, wishing so hard that she could magically transport herself home or just disappear.

Then, giving a big clap of his hands, Mr. Herman boomed out, "Welcome to homeroom, Living Environment, and your first day of middle school!"

Black Licorice

I don't even want to go to Hebrew school anymore," Daisy said with her head on her arms on the kitchen table.

"I know," her mom said. "I know how hard everything's been. I get it."

Mom was making grilled cheese. Daisy didn't think her mom really did get it, though. Daisy had trudged through the first four days of school, dodging conversations. Kids she and Ruby had never even talked to were saying stuff to her like *Sorry about your friend* or *I heard about Ruby. Are you all right?* One kid used the word "condolences." Ugh. She thought some of the kids that had gone to the other elementary school in Roosevelt Cove knew about it too. Knew about her. People were probably talking about it. Which meant people were talking about her. It made Daisy uncomfortable.

Now it was Tuesday, Hebrew school night, and the thought of being with more kids, and carpooling with the Moise Like Louise boy, felt like too much. Even though Hebrew school was only one night a week this year, she wished she didn't have to go at all.

"But why do we have to carpool?" Daisy asked. "We never carpooled before."

"It won't be so bad," her mom said. "I'm a million months pregnant, and Daddy won't be back from California until Sunday. This is helpful, lovie."

"I thought Daddy wasn't going to travel for work anymore until after the baby," Daisy said. She knew she was whining. Even though she could hear it in her own voice, she couldn't stop.

"There was a big sustainability conference he had to go to," her mom said.

"Then why can't Aunt Toby drive me?"

"She went out east to teach a yoga thing for that couple she knows," her mom said. "And besides, there's *finally* another Roosevelt Cove family that we can share the driving with." Daisy's mom put two plates of grilled cheese onto the table and sat down across from her. Daisy took a small bite of the warm, gooey sandwich. Mom had used Brie and put tiny, chopped-up pieces of a cornichon pickle into the sandwich before grilling it in butter. Even though it was just grilled cheese, really, it was delicious.

"Apparently one of the parents is ill, so we're helping them by carpooling," her mom said before biting into her own grilled cheese. "We'll be doing a mitzvah helping their family out." She put her fingers in front of her lips because she was talking with her mouth full. "Did you meet this boy already?"

"Yeah," Daisy said. "He's in my homeroom and a couple of my classes." She took another nibble of her sandwich as her mom took a huge bite of her own.

"Nice kid?" her mom asked, talking around the food in her mouth again.

"He's all right," Daisy said, sighing. She heard the *tap tap tap* of Chewie's nails on the floor. He nosed at her thigh, hoping she'd share her food with him. "Stop," Daisy whined at the dog. He sat expectantly near her chair, hoping she'd have a change of heart. Daisy reached out and scritched him behind his ear.

Daisy's mom ate the last of her own sandwich and wiped her buttery fingers on a napkin. She brought her plate to the sink, and when she came back to the table, she said, "I'm going to go lie down." She put her hand on Daisy's shoulder, and Daisy leaned her cheek into it. "Oh, come here," her mom said, pulling Daisy up.

She wrapped Daisy in a hug, which felt awkward because of her big belly but also like home because it was her mom. Daisy's shoulders relaxed, and she let herself be hugged. She nuzzled her face into the bony part of her mom's shoulder. For the longest time her nuzzle spot had been right *under* her mom's collarbone. The top of her shoulder wasn't as squishy, but she could still snuggle her face in and be held by her mom's comforting scent—like if a flower could somehow smell like butterscotch. Mom stroked Daisy's head, her fingers gently pulling through the curls, which would be annoying if anyone else did it but was soothing when her mom did it.

"Carpooling won't be so bad," her mom said again. Daisy's chin quivered, and her lips turned down, and she tried super hard to will the tears away. "They're going to be here soon. Finish your grilled cheese, lovie." Daisy leaned closer into the hug, though. She put her hand on her mom's belly, and the bump moved, which was the same kind of soothing as her mom's fingers through her curls. Mom kissed the top of her head. "It will be fine," she told Daisy, and started to go upstairs to nap.

"Yeah, fine," Daisy said to Chewie. She sat down to finish her grilled cheese, taking a bite and pulling off a bite for Chewie, who had been waiting like a very good boy. The sound of wheels on the gravel in the driveway was followed by the doorbell, which was followed by Chewie running into the foyer and barking madly. Nobody ever rang the doorbell. Daisy opened the door, holding Chewie by the collar so he didn't bolt, and there was Mo—Moise Like Louise—standing on her front steps.

"Hey," he said, and grinned his crooked grin.

"Hi," she said, still chewing her sandwich. Even though she'd seen him at regular school, she'd successfully avoided talking to him just the same as talking to anyone. She nodded hello to him in science but kept her eyes on her desk so he wouldn't talk to her. The only person she'd had any kind of conversation with had been that girl, Avery, who she'd walked to first period with since the first day of school. She hoped he wasn't remembering how she'd ended up in tears the week before.

"So, like . . . we're here . . . ," he said, looking at Chewie and nodding his head. "Cute dog."

"Thanks," she said. "His name's Chewbacca." She let Chewie's collar go.

"Hey there, Chewbacca," Mo said, squatting down and scritching Chewie behind the ears.

"I'll be right out. I've got to go say bye to my mom."

He said, "Okay," then straightened up, standing there

for a second, like he was going to wait for her on the steps. Then he turned and went out to the car. She ran upstairs, two at a time, to her parents' bedroom. Chewie followed her and jumped up on the bed with Daisy's mom.

"They're here," Daisy said, sitting on the edge of the bed. Her mom sleepily opened her eyes. "Do I really have to go?"

"Lovie," her mom said. "You *like* Hebrew school. You've got friends there. Morah Jill's nice."

"Morah Jill cries all the time, because everything is so 'moving.'" She made air quotes. "She's annoying."

"She's a nice lady. And she means well." Her mom yawned and closed her eyes again. "Aunt Toby will scoop you guys up at the end. And she's picking up Thai for dinner."

. Daisy sighed.

"See you later," her mom said, reaching out and absently patting her on the leg.

The first thing Daisy noticed when she got into the car was that Moise Like Louise was sitting in the back seat with her. Which was weird and awkward, like they were five years old and he wasn't allowed to sit in the front seat yet.

Mo's dad passed a paper bag over the seat. "Here, give some to your friend," he said to Mo, smiling at Daisy. Then he turned up the radio, which was on the '80s on 8 station.

Daisy wanted to say to Mo's dad, *We're not friends*, but that would have been rude. His car smelled like peppermint and was much neater than her mom's car, which always had sweatshirts and tote bags and library books in the back seat.

"Jelly bean?" Mo said, offering the bag to her.

Ugh. Why did this kid have to like jelly beans? Daisy and Ruby both loved jelly beans. Ruby's favorites were the tropical ones. Daisy liked the sours.

She peeked in, looking for a good one. But they were all black.

"I like licorice," Mo said sheepishly, "and so does my grandma, who we live with, so she buys black jelly beans for us in bulk." He smiled and shrugged.

She plucked a jelly bean out and handed the bag back to Mo. She took a little bite with her front teeth. She wasn't sure if she liked black jelly beans.

He laughed at her. "I've never seen someone take a *bite* of a jelly bean." He shoved a handful in his mouth.

Her face got warm and she blushed. "I like nibbling," she said. "Besides, why do you even care?" She knew she was being rude. She could hear how angry she sounded. She glanced to the front of the car to see if Mo's dad had heard her, but he wasn't listening to them. His head bopped in time to the music on the radio. She wished Mo would stop looking at her. She wished he were sitting in the front seat. She wished she didn't have to carpool, or go to Hebrew school, or do anything, really.

She half turned her body toward the window and made a point to look out, the black jelly bean melting a little in her fingers. She took another tiny nibble. As they passed Mill Pond Road, where Ruby's house was, Daisy looked down at her lap. She blinked a couple of times, just in case any tears thought they might want to well up in her eyes.

"Sorry," he said softly. "I didn't mean anything by it. Nibbling is cool." She glanced at him and nodded. Then he turned and looked out his own window. She could hear him eating jelly beans a handful at a time. They didn't say anything else to each other for the rest of the ride. Mo's dad sang along to the radio in the front seat.

By the time they got to B'nai Shalom, Mo had eaten almost the whole bag of black jelly beans. She'd eaten her one jelly bean in three nibbles and hadn't asked for another. As they walked up the path to the synagogue door, Daisy said, "Sorry I was rude." She turned to look at him. There was black goo at the corners of his mouth. "It wasn't you, you know."

He said, "Um, I know."

How does he know? she thought.

"Don't worry about it," he said. "My therapist said when you're sad, sometimes it comes out as angry and gets on other people." He smiled, and his teeth were gray.

She frowned and nodded. *Who tells someone they hardly know that they have a therapist?* He was hard to take seriously with gray teeth.

Then he said, "Hey, I practiced saying that 'Mi Shebeirach' prayer at home this week."

"I like that one," she said, nodding again.

"I learned the tune on YouTube," he said. "But I've got a terrible voice, so . . ." He smiled, and in the place where his front teeth met, where it was a little crooked, a black glob of jelly bean was lodged.

He looked pretty ridiculous. She smiled a small smile back at him and pointed to her front teeth.

"What?" he said.

"You've got a big black glob between your teeth."

He smiled, then poked at it with his tongue.

"Did I get it?" he said, making his top lip disappear and making a silly face.

"Yeah," she said. She didn't want to, but she heard herself giggle. He was actually kind of nice. They were standing outside the door to the synagogue, but neither of them opened it, and the security guard was inside.

"Good friends always tell you when you have spinach in your teeth." Mo nodded at her, smiling. "Or jelly bean goo, I guess."

He'd called her a good friend, which made her feel weird inside. They'd only just met. They weren't even really friends yet. She smiled back at him awkwardly.

"So, do you think it works?" he said.

"Do I think what works?" she answered. Through the window she could see Morah Jill walking into their classroom.

"The prayer," he said. "Do you believe the 'Mi Shebeirach' prayer can really make someone get better?"

Her eyebrows drew together, and the smile faded from her face.

"I'm not a good person to ask," Daisy said.

How would she know if something like that worked?

"Nobody's a good person to ask," Mo replied, his own smile slowly fading. "Nobody really knows anything for sure."

They were going to be late. They should head into the synagogue.

"But I want to know what you believe," he said.

She looked down at her feet. "Why?" she asked. She nudged at the gravel on the path with the front of her sneaker. She looked through the window of the synagogue, where Morah Jill was standing at the door to the classroom now.

"Well," Mo answered, "sometimes you meet someone, and you just know." He shrugged.

"Know what?" she said.

"That they're the right friend for you," he said. The security guard came to the door and opened it. Mo walked in. He looked back at her over his shoulder. "My grandma calls it *bashert*."

"What's that mean?" she said, still standing there.

"Destiny!" he replied. He looked so goofy, grinning at her with his gray licorice-stained teeth. "Come on," he said over his shoulder, then nodded to the security guard who was holding the door open for Daisy.

But she just stood there for a minute, wondering why anyone would want to be friends with a sad girl like her. Wondering if *she* wanted to be friends with *him*. Wondering how he could know something like that—bashert—and why he'd say it to her. It made her feel like she had to do something that she didn't know how to do with his declaration of friendship.

When she got to Morah Jill's classroom, Mo had already sat down near the front of the room. He had his notebook out on his desk again. *Who takes notes at Hebrew school?* she thought. She took her seat near Rachel and Hannah and wondered if Morah Jill was going to make them find partners for something again.

Morah Jill said, "We're going to talk about tikkun olam today." Mo raised his hand. Morah Jill said, "Yes, Mo?" and you could tell she really wanted to call him Moise. Daisy stifled a laugh.

He glanced at her and smiled, then said, holding his notebook in front of his gray teeth, "Can you please spell that?"

"*T-I-K-K-U-N, O-L-A-M.*"

Mo put his notebook on the desk and began scribbling in it. Only Daisy knew his mouth was covered in gray goop. It was like a secret that they shared. And as much as the idea of them being destined for anything annoyed her, it was nice to have a secret with someone. She decided that Moise Like Louise might not be all that bad.

Morah Jill said, in a booming voice, "Now, let's talk about repairing the world!"

Avoidance Plan

Avery and Daisy were walking down the hall to Mr. Herman's class. Today Avery's shirt said FORGET PRINCESS. I WANT TO BE AN ASTROPHYSICIST. Avery said, "That spatially unaware kid is going to knock into us at 7:39. Let's make an avoidance plan."

Daisy looked at her. *Spatially unaware.* Avery was funny.

"How do you know it's going to be at 7:39?"

They were passing Madame Lecardonnel's French classroom. Avery nodded toward the bulletin board where a digital clock showed the time in France. "It was 13:39 in Paris the past four days that he knocked into us, so taking into account the New York–to–Paris time difference, and by means of deduction, I'm betting on 7:39 again." Avery grinned.

In response, a tiny smile tickled the side of Daisy's mouth. *By means of deduction.*

Avery said, "I say we make a plan to *thwart* being in the line of his propulsion."

The tiny smile bloomed into a full smile on Daisy's face. *The line of his propulsion.*

Avery grinned, and Daisy couldn't hold back a tiny giggle.

What other sixth grader casually uses the word "thwart" in everyday speech?

"All right," Daisy said. "What's our plan?"

Avoiding Carlos Ruiz, the kid who barreled down the hall knocking into everyone, became part of their morning routine. Every morning Avery waited for Daisy at their lockers, and they walked to Mr. Herman's class together. By the third week of school, Daisy had started expecting it. When they reached Madame Lecardonnel's room at 7:39, Avery would step all the way to the left, and Daisy would hug the wall on the right. Carlos would come running down the hall at full speed, and then the hall monitor would yell, *No running, Carlos!* Carlos always said, *I'm not running!* as he slowed to a jog, pretending to walk. As soon as he passed, the girls returned to strolling next to each other. Daisy was still mostly quiet, but Avery talked enough for the both of them.

Daisy learned that Avery had gone to private school until the previous year, when her parents got divorced. Then her mom decided she should switch to the public school. Roosevelt Cove Middle School was highly rated, her mom had said, so she was sure she'd be fine there. Avery said she didn't care where she went to school, because her best friend, Emily, had moved to Philadelphia, and anyway some mean kids had been teasing her at her old school. Changing schools was a relief, she'd said. Avery told Daisy she liked science, dogs, and mint chip ice cream. She told her that her dad lived in the city now, and her mom, who was a lawyer, worked *a lot.* She had a housekeeper named Melania, who didn't speak a lot of English and didn't pay much attention to her. Avery didn't like her. She told Daisy she had an older brother named Alex, who went to boarding school, but because he played hockey, they gave him a scholarship when her mom was going to pull him out because of the money.

Every morning as they walked down the hall to first period, Avery chatted and chatted and chatted. Daisy gladly listened and nodded a lot. It was pleasant. Avery asked her questions too, and most of the time Daisy didn't mind answering them.

"What's your favorite kind of cupcake?" Avery had asked. Daisy's was vanilla with chocolate icing, but Avery's was devil's food cake with vanilla icing.

"I definitely like both dogs and cats, but dogs are better," Avery said one morning. "I'm, like, maybe sixty percent dog-liker and forty percent cat-liker." Daisy was firmly anti-cat, and that led to a long conversation about what were reasonable expectations to have from a pet. Daisy told Avery about Chewbacca and how he was the best dog ever and how his eyebrows moved when he ran after squirrels in his sleep. She almost told Avery that she didn't know what she would have done these past months without Chewie. But she swallowed that sentence down because then she would have had to talk about Ruby. And that was something she did not want to do. Not with Avery. Not with anyone.

One morning Avery told Daisy that over the summer she'd gone out east to the tip of Long Island for a week, and they'd visited the lighthouse there. She talked and talked and talked about how much she loved Montauk. She asked Daisy if she'd ever been to the Montauk Lighthouse, or if she ever went out to the Hamptons.

Daisy shook her head, looked away, and didn't say anything. It would be weird to be walking down the school hall and telling Avery about all the time she'd spent in the Hamptons at Ruby's house, like it was just some casual memory. Then she'd have to explain who Ruby was and everything. Avery was considerate, though, and didn't push when she saw that Daisy didn't want to talk.

Another morning Avery asked, "Do you like math or science better?"

"I like reading," Daisy answered.

"Okay, but if you *had* to pick one, math or science?"

"If I had to pick one, I guess it would be science," Daisy said. "But only because I like figuring out what the science words mean by looking at the prefixes and suffixes and stuff."

Avery nodded.

"And I like to think things through," Daisy said. "Figure stuff out for myself, you know?"

Avery nodded again. "Valid. Valid reasons," she said. "I like science because I like knowing how things work. Like how cells divide—you know, mitosis and meiosis—or why chemical reactions happen, or . . ."

Daisy listened as Avery went on and on about why she loved science. And every time Avery said something like *Statistically speaking, the probability of Mr.*

Herman wearing a bow tie versus a regular tie is fairly high, it made Daisy giggle. Avery wasn't anything like Ruby, so it felt easier to like her, because it didn't feel like replacing Ruby. Daisy didn't think Avery was the kind of person who believed in magical things at all. Daisy definitely didn't think she could tell Avery about seeing the fairy.

So in the fourth week of school, when Avery didn't show up at their lockers one morning, Daisy noticed. She waited a few minutes but didn't want to be late, so she started down the hall to class. She avoided getting bumped into by Carlos Ruiz at 7:39 and took her seat behind Avery's empty desk in Mr. Herman's class. Mo was already in his seat, right next to hers, like every day since that first one. He grinned at her when she sat down. She half smiled back.

"Oh hey," he said. He pushed his glasses up on his nose. "Did you figure out a tikkun olam project yet? I was thinking about some of the things Morah Jill said the other night at Hebrew school, and I've got an idea, but I don't know if I'm getting it right, you know?"

She didn't want to talk about Hebrew school or tikkun olam right then, though. She couldn't stop wondering where Avery was. Her eyebrows drew together, and she said, "I don't know what I'm doing yet."

She took out her homework and looked toward the front of the classroom, hoping Mr. Herman would start class soon. She was getting used to carpooling once a week to Hebrew school with Mo. Sometimes it still felt uncomfortable and weird. She didn't mind that he wanted to be friends in regular school, but she didn't want to talk about tikkun olam there. The kids at regular school didn't know what that was. Sometimes it felt like Mo was a bit too much, with his "bashert" destiny stuff. It was like he needed something from her, and she didn't know what it was. She didn't have anything to give anyway. Losing Ruby had taken everything away from her. She could manage starting to become friends with Avery because it didn't feel like Avery needed anything from her. Avery just took her as she was.

"Where's Avery?" Mo said.

"I don't know," she replied.

She was probably just running late. Or maybe she had a cold or something.

The bell rang, and Mr. Herman closed the door.

Then Daisy's brain kicked into overdrive. She couldn't stop the cascade of thoughts that followed. She put her head down on her desk.

"Today we're going to talk about ecosystems," Mr. Herman's booming voice exclaimed, "about biological communities of interacting organisms and their physical environments!"

What if something really bad had happened to Avery? Like, what if she died?

Daisy closed her eyes. She knew that was a stupid thing to think.

That couldn't possibly happen to two kids I know. Could it?

She wanted to go home. She thought, *Avery would probably say something about the statistical improbability of having that happen to two friends in one year.*

"Are you okay, Ms. Rubens?" Mr. Herman asked.

"Sorry, I'm fine," Daisy said, picking her head up.

She swiped at her eyes. She could feel everyone looking at her. She could feel herself blushing. She wished she were anywhere except right where she was.

"Okay then!" Mr. Herman said, and gave her a nod. She nodded back. He went on. "Ecosystems are complex biological networks. They are interconnected systems. . . ." His voice rose up and down, up and down with excitement. Mr. Herman really loved science. But to Daisy it just sounded like he was saying, *Blah blah blah blah blah.*

She made it through the rest of class without putting

her head down again or tearing up. She'd just met Avery a few weeks ago. They barely knew each other. Why was she worrying about her? As she tried to quiet the thoughts running around in her head, Daisy also couldn't stop thinking about Ruby, and how she hadn't even had a chance to be worried about her. Ruby had been gone for three whole days before Daisy knew about it. Daisy had been kayaking and eating hot dogs cooked on the campfire and talking to frogs, and Ruby had already been gone. That was just wrong, and it wasn't fair. Thinking about eating s'mores when her best friend had died and she didn't even know it made her feel like throwing up.

She wanted to go home. And she really hoped Avery was okay.

The next day Avery was back at school, explaining everything to Daisy. "I just had a teeny-tiny sore throat, but my mom had already left for work, and Melania made me stay home." Avery rolled her eyes. "I didn't have a fever. I didn't have any symptoms of strep. It was so annoying. All I said was 'My throat hurts,' and she made me stay home."

Daisy shrugged. "You didn't miss much in Mr.

Herman's class." She looked at Avery's T-shirt, which had a picture of a ginger cat on it and it said, THREAT LEVEL HIGH.

Avery saw Daisy looking at her shirt. "It's a *Captain Marvel* reference," Avery said, looking a little embarrassed and uncomfortable.

"I know," Daisy said. "I love Goose."

Avery smiled and relaxed a little. "Flerken," they said at the same time. Avery laughed.

Daisy felt a pang of something, thinking back to all the times she and Ruby had watched Marvel movies together. It wasn't guilt. It was more complicated than that. Ruby had liked Marvel, but it was really Daisy's thing. Ruby might not have remembered that Goose was actually a Flerken and not a cat. But Ruby would have loved that Avery did. She would have liked Avery.

Daisy swallowed as they kept walking down the hall. She looked straight ahead so Avery wouldn't see that her eyes were brimming.

"So, what did we do in class?" Avery said.

"Oh, we were talking about ecosystems," Daisy said. She cleared her throat.

When they got to Madame Lecardonnel's doorway, they fell into their usual routine. Avery stepped all the way to the left, Daisy hugged the wall on the right,

Carlos ran past them, and then they stepped back next to each other.

"I was going to text you, but I don't have your number," Avery said.

"I don't have a number," Daisy said. "I was supposed to get a phone when school started, but my mom didn't get to it yet." They were at the door to Mr. Herman's class, but they had a few minutes until the bell rang, so they hung out for a minute in the hall. "My mom was going to help me pick it out, but she's too pregnant and tired and distracted."

Then she frowned. She and Ruby had been looking forward to getting their first phones together when they started middle school. *Another thing we didn't get to do. Ruby never got a cell phone. She never would.* Daisy swallowed, trying to make the lump in her throat go away.

"What's wrong?" Avery said.

"Nothing," Daisy said, clearing her throat again. "I just thought of something." For the millionth time, tears filled up behind her eyes. Avery's eyes got wider, and she looked like she was going to say something else. "It's nothing," Daisy said, turning away.

"All right," Avery said softly. When they went into class, Daisy could tell Avery hadn't believed her. She'd given her one of those fake smiles that means something like *I know you weren't telling the truth, but I won't push.* Daisy appreciated that Avery, who could talk and talk and talk, and who could be pretty persistent when she was looking for an answer, had let it go. Ruby had been like that too. Daisy hadn't thought that anything about Avery was like Ruby, but this was. She wasn't sure how to feel about that.

Drowning

O n Saturday, Daisy's mom shouted from the living room, "Dad's going to pick up Tex-Mex for dinner. What do you want?"

"Ugh," Daisy grumbled. She stopped working on her homework and shouted back from the kitchen. "I don't want Tex-Mex. Why do we have to have Tex-Mex *again*? Why do we have to order in *again*?" She wasn't trying to, but each time she said "again," it was coming out whinier and whinier. She could hear it, but that never made a difference. She still couldn't stop doing it.

A loud, dramatic sigh came from the living room. Daisy braced herself for the lecture she knew came after one of those Mom sighs. But instead of a lecture her mom said, "Daisy, I just can't. I'm not doing this."

"Oh brother, here we go again," Daisy muttered under her breath. Her mom was saying *I just can't* about everything lately.

Her mom must have heard her *oh brother*, though, because she said, "I don't need to defend my decision to order takeout to my kid," in a tight voice. Daisy couldn't tell if her mom was talking to her or not. They were sitting in separate rooms, within eyesight of each other, but not looking up. For a long minute there was silence, and then her mom said, "What—do you want—from Tex-Mex?"

Daisy rolled her eyes and said, "Geez, Mom, I don't care. A burrito or whatever," and she went back to doing her homework.

"I don't know what a *whatever* is." Her mom's voice was rising, getting shrill. Daisy heard her heave herself off the couch with a little grunt, and then she waddled to the kitchen door and said, "Please, just tell me what kind of burrito you want. Is that so difficult?"

Daisy slowly looked up from her homework. Her mom looked like she was going to cry. She had been snapping at her and Daisy's dad for weeks now. Her pregnant belly strained against the fabric of her yoga pants, distorting the picture on the front of her

T-shirt. The baby was due soon, and the big T-shirt was hugged so tightly on the underside of her mom's belly, you couldn't read the words printed at the bottom. Her popped-out belly button pressed outward through the forehead of a distorted, stretched-out picture of Supreme Court Justice Ruth Bader Ginsburg. Daisy looked away.

Going back to her schoolwork, she said, "Geez, I'm sorry." She knew she didn't sound sorry at all, though. She was so angry, but she didn't know why. And she knew she sounded bratty, but she couldn't help it. She thought about Mo telling her what his therapist had said, about sadness coming out as anger. "Just get me a chicken burrito. Enchilada style," she muttered.

She used to be happy to order in. She and Ruby loved getting tacos or pizza or sushi. But now Daisy just wanted regular dinners, like before, when her mom cooked something weird and delicious. Like that curried purslane soup that they'd never gotten to have. That seemed like so long ago.

Daisy's mom was supposed to be on what was called "modified bed rest" now because of something having to do with the baby. Apparently "modified bed rest" meant lying on the couch and working on her computer, like she always did, but it didn't include making dinner.

Each day as it got closer to the time for the baby to be born, her mom was hardly cooking at all, and Daisy really missed it. All they did was order in.

Mom waddled to the back door and shouted, "Will! Daisy wants a chicken burrito, enchilada style! Get me whatever. I don't care. And put the baskets on your bike! We need milk and eggs, too!"

Why could her mom tell Daisy's dad she wanted *whatever*, but if Daisy said it, that wasn't okay?

"They're called panniers, not baskets," Daisy said under her breath.

Her mom turned and said, "Please cut it out. Don't be snippy with me. I just can't take it. With *him* trying to save the world by insisting on riding his bicycle everywhere, with your Aunt Toby who's supposedly here but never actually *here* . . ." Daisy tried to tune her out, but her mom just kept going on and on. "I mean, how does she magically get clients here when she lives in Seattle? And *you* sassing me about every little thing . . . I just can't—" Then her mom stopped in the middle of her rant, got a funny look on her face, and put her hand on the side of her belly.

"Mom?" Daisy said, standing up. "Is it now?"

"Nope. It's nothing," her mom said. Daisy sat back down. "I'm fine, sweetie."

This had been going on all week, with her mom stopping midsentence, or in the middle of doing something, out of nowhere. The other day Aunt Toby had pulled the car over when they were all on their way home from the library. Daisy's mom was in the passenger seat, gazing out the window, with her hand on top of her stomach, still as a statue. Aunt Toby just waited and was as calm as ever. Daisy's heart had beaten so hard in her chest, she thought it would explode. Was this it? Was the baby coming? But whatever it was that her mom had felt, it had subsided, because when Aunt Toby said, "You good now, Lori-Lu?" Daisy's mom had said she was fine, and they'd driven home like nothing had happened.

With another week left to go until it was safe for the baby to be born, every time her mom did that, the whole world went on pause until she said she was okay. Daisy's mom kept trying to be reassuring, telling her it was all normal. The last time, she'd said, "It's just Braxton-Hicks contractions, which are my body's way of practicing to give birth. Isn't that cool?"

Daisy didn't think it was cool. It was scary. She didn't trust that things would work out for the best anymore. So many things felt scary. When the midwife put Mom on this modified bed rest thing, *just in case*, Daisy didn't ask *In case of what?* but her brain kept coming up with horrible possibilities. Anything that put that particular funny look on her mom's face frightened Daisy. She didn't care if it was a Braxton-whatever contraction.

And she didn't have anyone to talk to about it. She used to be able to talk to Ruby about anything. But Ruby wasn't here. She didn't really talk to Avery about feelings and things. Mo probably would have understood, but that would be weird. And Aunt Toby had hardly been around recently. It seemed like she was always visiting friends in Brooklyn and teaching yoga classes out east.

"I'm going back to the couch," Mom said.

Daisy let out the breath she'd been holding and said, "Fine," then went back to her homework.

Sometimes it felt like she and Mom were in a fight even when nothing had happened.

"Did you sign the permission slip yet?" Daisy called from the kitchen. "I have to hand it in by Monday." They were going to the Bronx Zoo with Mr. Herman's class.

Mom called back from the couch in the living room. "I already signed it. It's in your school folder upstairs on my desk." Daisy flipped through her textbook. A soft sigh came from the other room, followed by the sound of typing on the keyboard. Then Mom called from the couch, "Can you get me a glass of water, lovie? I'm just—my back hurts—and I'm so exhausted."

Tears welled up in Daisy's eyes. She felt bad for her mom, but she was tired of fetching glasses of water, tired of eating takeout, tired of being the one who had to be understanding and generous and patient. She wasn't ready to be that person, not when the pain of losing Ruby was still so overwhelming. She wanted her mom to be the one who was understanding and generous and patient to *her*. That was how it was supposed to be.

She went into the kitchen and got her the glass of water, though, then set it on the side table next to Mom, who smiled up at her. "Thank you," she said.

Mom looked really tired. Daisy knew none of this was really her mother's fault. Nobody had planned for her to be exhausted and pregnant right when Daisy needed her most. She just wanted to crawl onto the couch and cuddle up in her mother's lap. She knew that was dumb, because she was way too big and too old for that. And Mom didn't really *have* a lap anymore anyway, because of her belly. So she plopped down on the floor next to the couch and rested her head against Mom's thigh. Things would be changing again. *Why does everything always have to change?* And soon. They'd have a new baby. She'd have a baby sister or baby brother. They were all looking forward to that. They all were. She was.

But still.

Mom drank some of the water Daisy had brought and with one hand softly stroked Daisy's hair. They sat quietly, the bickering put aside for the moment. She cuddled into Mom's leg, then looked up. From this angle she could read the words on the bottom of the T-shirt. It said, I DISSENT! She sure related to that. More often than not these days, she dissented too.

Mom took another sip of the water, then put it down on the side table. Daisy reached up. With one hand she placed her palm on her mother's belly, gently pushing against it to feel the baby, solid underneath. "The bump has been moving around a lot today," Mom said. Daisy's other hand found her mother's fingers. They both gave a squeeze.

Mom stroked Daisy's hair some more and held her hand with the other hand. Daisy's tears were coming, and she didn't try to stop them this time. The baby moved under her palm, shifting under her mother's skin. She got goose bumps. A shot of fear about the birth pulsed through her. *What if something happens to Mom? You can die having a baby. What if something happens to the bump?* But when she looked up, Mom looked so calm—so strong and count on–able. She pushed the fear away. She couldn't go there. She wouldn't. *Nothing bad will happen.* It just couldn't.

As soon as she pushed the fear away, though, the familiar sorrow rolled in in its place. There it was, the inevitable swell of sadness about Ruby flowing over her, threatening to engulf her, to drown her. She took her hand off Mom's belly and swiped at her eye with her palm. Was this how it was going to be from now on? Waves of sadness following waves of fear, until more waves of sadness rolled in? She loved Ruby—had loved her—but she couldn't bear this. She didn't want to feel like she was drowning all the time.

Once, two summers before, she'd almost drowned for real when she and Ruby were at the beach. She and Ruby had been bodysurfing, riding waves in, then swimming back out to wait for another. They were in chest-deep water, had just turned around to catch the next wave, when they were both caught off guard. A huge wave broke on both of them, and Daisy had been knocked down, shoved under the water, tossed, and turned upside down.

Her head hit the bottom with a big clunk. She was disoriented and started to panic. She'd breathed in water, and for a second she couldn't tell which way was up. Then her instincts kicked in. She always felt strong and confident being in the water, and especially in the ocean. She opened her eyes and pushed herself up from the darkness, her face breaking through the surf, into the sunlight and air.

Ruby had been knocked over too, but she hadn't been pummeled under like Daisy had. She said, "Are you all right? I couldn't find you!"

Through her coughing Daisy had replied, "I almost couldn't find me either!"

Later, when they were wrapped up in their beach towels, warming themselves on the deck of Ruby's beach house, Ruby had said, "I was really scared before, Daze. I'm glad you saved yourself." Daisy remembered knowing she hadn't had a choice. Her body, her whole being, had pushed her toward the light, toward being alive. She knew she *had* literally saved herself.

Daisy put her hand back on Mom's belly. Mom caressed her hair again. Even though she wasn't actually drowning now, sometimes it felt like that. There was the deep, unrelenting sorrow about losing Ruby. And now her sorrow was morphing into fear about the birth, terror that something bad would happen to Mom or the bump. She needed to do *something*. She just couldn't keep on feeling these feelings. She had to figure out how to save herself. The bump gave a kick, and Mom laughed. "The bump's saying hi," she said, smiling down at Daisy.

"That was a big one," Daisy replied, gently rubbing Mom's belly where she'd felt the kick. Then she said, "There's a girl at school, Mom. . . ." She took a deep breath, and Mom looked down at her. "Her name's Avery and she's new." Mom waited. Daisy was pushing herself toward the light when she said, "Next week, after the Jewish holidays, can I invite her over?" Asking felt a little like she was shoving herself away from the darkness. Like she was saving herself.

Mom said, "Yes, lovie. After the holidays. That would be nice."

High Holiday Reverie

The Jewish holidays aren't as good with Mom pregnant, Daisy thought. Her mother's "bed rest" meant everything was different. Usually Mom spent a week cooking for Rosh Hashanah. Brisket in the oven and the smells of oniony potato kugel and cinnamony sweet potato tzimmes wafting through the house were the heart of Rosh Hashanah for their family. And every year she helped her mom with the matzo ball soup. Mom said, *Making good matzo balls is an art form.*

There was a very specific way her mother said it should be done. First they'd wet their hands in cool water, then gently, gently, gently pat the matzo-meal batter into walnut-sized spheres, delicately dropping them into the clear chicken broth, where they would magically turn into the lightest, fluffiest matzo balls ever. *My bubby taught me how to make matzo balls when I was a little girl,* Mom would say. And even though Daisy knew that and had heard the story every Rosh Hashanah since she could remember, she would let Mom talk. She'd hear about the Matzo Ball Wars—how Mom's family had been divided over whether the perfect matzo ball should be light and fluffy, or so dense it would sink to the bottom of the pot. She and Aunt Toby loved light, fluffy matzo balls, but their cousins loved the sinkers.

Every year Mom would tell Daisy that the secret ingredient for truly delicious chicken soup is a chunk of fresh ginger. She'd go on and on about how much she had loved watching her grandma make matzo balls because that was when she first noticed their hands had the same squarish shape. Daisy loved that part of the matzo ball story the most, because then her mom always paused and said, *And look, your hands are shaped that way too!* as if every year it was the first time she'd noticed. Daisy loved her mother's hands—her strong, square palms and long fingers—and it felt good knowing she had those same kind of hands.

But this year was different. Mom wasn't even

cooking. Dad had just gotten back from a business trip, and Aunt Toby was finishing up some kind of yoga training thing in the city. Mom had to stay off her feet, and cooking was just too much for her. Dad's cousins and their kids weren't coming to Roosevelt Cove for Rosh Hashanah dinner this year. Grandma was staying in Florida because she was too old to travel to New York by herself—something about her hip. So Daisy, Mom, Dad, and Aunt Toby were going to have dinner, just the four of them. Mom ordered the whole thing from the kosher deli. Chicken instead of brisket, because the deli made their brisket too salty, Mom said. Aunt Toby made an apple cake.

At synagogue the first morning of Rosh Hashanah Rabbi Aaron said the sound of the shofar was supposed to wake people up out of their spiritual sleepiness. He called out, "Tekiah!" and Cantor David blew a long blast on the shofar. It did its job. Daisy sat up a little bit straighter in her chair. Rabbi Aaron said, "Shevarim!" and Cantor David answered by blowing three staccato notes from the shofar. She thought about what he'd said, and how the sound of the shofar was to remind them to pay attention to the important things in life. He called out, "Teruah!" and Cantor David responded with three sets of three notes on the shofar.

Aunt Toby leaned over to her and whispered in her ear, "Hearing the call-and-response of the shofar being blown is my favorite part of the High Holidays."

Daisy nodded. "Mine too."

When the long blast of the tekiah gedolah sounded, Aunt Toby said, "Hearing that sound, coming out of an actual ram's horn, reminds me how amazing it is to be Jewish, and how we're part of something that goes back thousands of years."

Daisy smiled at her aunt, who grinned back. *I'm going to try to pay attention to the important things in life,* Daisy thought. Sometimes it was hard to notice what was important, though, right when it was happening. Especially when you just wanted things to go back to normal, back to the way they were.

Usually they went to the stream in Dower Nature Preserve to do tashlich. Walking in the woods between the morning and evening service to symbolically throw their sins into the running water of the stream also helped them not feel so fidgety for the afternoon service. But Daisy asked if this year they could go to the nearby Sound Beach instead, and Dad said sure. Daisy hadn't gone into the preserve since that day with Ruby, and she didn't want to go now. As Dad and Aunt Toby and Daisy drove to the beach, Dad said, "You know, we really shouldn't use bread for tashlich. It's not good for the birds."

"Well, since seagulls eat garbage out of trash cans," Aunt Toby said, "I don't suppose snacking on our expensive stale organic whole-grain bread is going to kill them." Sometimes when Aunt Toby laughed, it reminded Daisy of wind chimes tinkling in a breeze. "Anyway, tashlich is about atonement—or as I like to think of it, at-one-ment—so I don't need bread crumbs. I'll send my sins out into the ether."

Daisy just looked out the car window, holding the bag of stale bread. Chewbacca sat next to her, happy to be in the car, one paw resting on Daisy's leg, like he didn't want her to forget that he was there.

When they got to the beach, Aunt Toby plopped herself down on a blanket, crossed her legs into lotus position, placed her hands palms-up on her knees, and closed her eyes. She looked like a yoga statue. Daisy loved how her aunt was so comfortable interpreting Jewish customs to suit her own beliefs. Aunt Toby took to heart the Reconstructionist saying that Jewish law has a vote, not a veto. Dad and Daisy walked toward the water, holding hands, for a more traditional tashlich.

"How are you doing, Buddy-Girl?" he said.

"I'm fine," she replied. She wasn't in the mood for a deep and meaningful talk and hoped he wasn't going to start one. He crouched down and let the dog off the leash, and Chewie sprinted away. Instead of there being crashing waves like there are on the South Shore, the tides of the Long Island Sound lapped their way in and out more gently. It was breezy and sunny, and the light danced and bounced on the ripples of the water. They walked down to where the sand was damp, and Daisy's and Dad's feet made prints as they got closer to the water. She stuck her hand into the bag of stale bread.

"Should we recite the prayer?" Dad said.

"Okay," she replied.

"Usually Mommy brings a printout," Dad said. She looked up at him. Mom was home resting, as always now.

"You didn't bring it, did you?" she said.

Dad shook his head sheepishly.

"Well, we could hum the Avinu Malkeinu tune and say 'Avinu Malkeinu' at the right parts," she said. "I don't know all the words."

So that's what they did, saying "Avinu Malkeinu" interspersed with a lot of humming. Daisy had always liked the tune of it but had been annoyed when she found out that it meant "our Father, our King." She didn't think about God like that, like as a king or a queen, a man or a woman. She wasn't thinking about any of that now, though, mostly just humming.

She ripped off a piece of bread and threw it into the water to symbolize the casting away of sins.

For not always being nice to my mom.

She threw another.

For being jealous of the bump, who isn't even born yet.

And then another.

For not wanting to talk to Maria and Leo at the funeral.

For not appreciating Ruby enough when she was alive.

For not being kinder to Mo, who just wants a friend.

For not telling Avery about Ruby.

Dad said he hoped the seagulls weren't going to have a bad year, because as soon as their sin-soaked pieces of bread hit the water, the seagulls gobbled them up. When the bag of bread was all gone, Dad whistled, and Chewie came running back. Aunt Toby finished meditating, and they all drove home.

In synagogue the following week on Yom Kippur, Daisy's stomach growled. She was trying to fast until sundown this year. Last Yom Kippur she'd tried but had given up by the afternoon. She'd gotten too hungry and cranky and ate a bowl of soup when they went home during the break between morning and afternoon services. But this year she hadn't eaten anything. The morning service was almost over, and even though she was hungry, she knew she'd be able to make it. She yawned. The sun streamed through the windows to the right of the bimah, where the rabbi and cantor were leading services. It was warm in the sanctuary with so many people in it. There was something hypnotic about all the standing up and sitting down, singing the prayers in Hebrew, reading the words in English, listening to the rabbi speak and Cantor David's chanting.

When they'd first gotten to synagogue, she saw Rachel and her family already sitting toward the front of the sanctuary. Hannah wasn't there. She'd told Daisy she was going to her grandma's in Brooklyn. Daisy had waved to Rachel, and then she and Dad and Aunt Toby found seats farther back. Mom stayed home again. They were expecting the baby any day now, and Mom was more uncomfortable than ever. Her belly looked enormous.

Daisy saw Mo come in with his dad, a lady who must be his mom, and his grandparents. His mom definitely looked sick. She was wearing one of those scarves on her head that people with cancer wear, and she had dark circles under her eyes. She was skinny and pale, and her skin looked yellowish. His dad was holding her by the elbow, and Mo was on her other side, with his arm around her waist. Mo didn't see Daisy, and she didn't do anything to get his attention.

Rabbi Aaron was giving the morning sermon. He usually talked about politics and Israel during the Rosh Hashanah sermon, and most years Daisy zoned out. She didn't like that political things and synagogue got mushed together. But this year when he started talking about a Reconstructionist Jewish response to school shootings and how to lobby for gun control, she paid attention. Kids getting shot in school. Kids dying. When they did lockdown drills at school, it never felt real, like that could really happen in Roosevelt Cove. But there'd been another school shooting just the week before. It didn't matter that it wasn't even in New York. Her heart hurt, listening to Rabbi Aaron talk. Wanting to pay attention to his sermon made her feel more grown up, because she could relate to what he was talking about in a way she hadn't before. *It's so weird that having a friend die can make you feel both like a little kid and an adult at the same time.*

Rabbi Aaron said, "Our kids are growing up with firsthand knowledge of the precariousness of life; this generation of children is cognizant of how fleeting our time on this earth can be." Daisy swallowed the lump in her throat. To her right Dad took her hand and gave it a squeeze. On her other side Aunt Toby leaned in to her a little bit, and she gently pushed back, acknowledging Aunt Toby's gesture.

When everyone stood up, she stood up, and Dad dropped her hand. Her stomach growled again. They said another prayer, and then she sat as everyone sat down. Cantor David started strumming his guitar, a soothing, repetitive song, which he accompanied by a melodic, wordless tune that was somewhere between a hum and a prayer. The combination of the guitar and his singing was making her sleepy.

Rabbi Aaron started speaking again. He said, "Our Jewish tradition encourages us to bridge the gap, in our Yizkor service, between the living and the dead."

A beam of sunlight shone through the window and cast a shadow that looked like an elephant onto the floor. Daisy watched dust motes dancing in the sunbeam. Her eyelids were so heavy.

He continued, "In secular culture, outside in the world, we are encouraged to see the dead as totally gone."

Daisy's eyes had fallen closed, but she was trying to listen. She hated that word. "Dead." She strained to stay awake, to hear what Rabbi Aaron was saying. She took a long drawn-in breath, filling her lungs up, and then it slowly whispered away again, leaving her hollowed out. It felt like a very Yom Kippur thing.

"But thinking of death only in a scientific way leaves us spiritually stranded—in a place where the chance of connection with our loved ones is forever gone—as if we're standing on the precipice of an unpassable span."

Daisy imagined it exactly like that, as if she were standing on the edge of a cliff, looking over a deep, wide ravine, and Ruby stood on the other side, so far away. There wasn't any way to get across. Her friend would be forever unreachable.

Rabbi Aaron's soothing voice continued, "But like our other Jewish mourning rituals—shiva, kaddish, and yahrzeit—Yizkor provides us a certain kind of access to our family who are no longer with us."

Daisy's dad put his arm along the back of her chair again.

"Yizkor is when we consciously generate sacred time and space, and this allows us to open our hearts and our minds to the possibility of connecting with our loved ones no longer residing in the world of the living."

Finally Rabbi Aaron finished with "Saying *Yizkor* can provide a bridge to our loved ones." But Daisy had fallen asleep in the warm sanctuary. She'd just barely heard the last bit, about how to connect with lost loved ones. It didn't matter, though. Daisy would always feel connected to Ruby. There might be a huge chasm between the living and the dead, but a part of Ruby would always be here with her. She slept with her head gently resting on her dad's arm. As mourners in the congregation around her rose to say the prayer for the dead, Aunt Toby stood for her, her hand gently resting on Daisy's head. Aunt Toby said, "Oseh shalom bimromav, hu ya'aseh shalom aleinu, v'al kol-yisrael, v'imru amen," and something shifted in the air around them, like a gentle exhale.

Moment by Moment

The morning after Yom Kippur, Dad came in to get Daisy up. She should have known something was going on. It was cold for October, and her bed was warm and cozy. She kept her eyes shut, pulled the blanket up, and cuddled deeper into the pillow. She was going to try for five more minutes. Dad whispered, "Chewbacca, off!" Chewie sighed but didn't move. "Chewie!" Dad whisper-shouted.

Daisy kept her eyes closed. She didn't want to get up. Everything felt like too much. It was Friday, and she just wanted to sleep in. School had been closed for Yom Kippur, and it was stupid to have to go back just for one day before the weekend. After synagogue the day before,

Dad's cousins Mitch and Stacey had come over to break the fast with them. They'd brought bagels and lox and rugelach, and Dad and Aunt Toby had done all the running around in the kitchen that Mom usually did. Daisy did manage to fast all the way through to the end. When they'd gotten home from synagogue in the evening, she was starving but proud of herself.

Now Chewie sat up on the bed, circled around and around, and settled, making himself comfortable behind Daisy's knees. He moaned a dog sigh.

"Daisy," Dad softly said, gently shaking her shoulder. He sat next to her on the edge of the bed and said, "Time to get up, Buddy-Girl." He pushed her hair away from her face, and she half opened her eyes, which was less effort than pretending to still be asleep. Dad was still in his pajamas and was wearing an old-guy hat with a plaid band on it that she and Mom had given him for Father's Day. He looked funny wearing the hat with his pajamas, but he was always complaining his bald head was cold.

She closed her eyes again and pulled the blanket closer.

Mom usually crawled into bed with her in the mornings, cuddling her awake. Daisy never had to pretend to be sleeping to get an extra five minutes with Mom.

Lately, though, when Mom crawled in, they'd both fall back asleep. Daisy had been late to school twice already, which was not good. She cuddled in her blankets, but Dad persisted in his gentle shaking and prodding of her shoulder.

"Come on, Buddy-Girl," he said.

She mumbled half into her pillow, "Where's Mom?" followed by "Do I have to go to school?" and then "Can you make pancakes?"

"Mommy's still in bed," Dad said, petting Daisy's hair. "I'm not making pancakes. You can have a freezer waffle."

She was about to start begging when she heard a weird sound. At first it was hardly noticeable, blending into the other background noises. Like maybe it was from outside, the whine of a leaf blower or something. She opened her eyes a little and looked up at Dad. His mouth smiled down at her, but his eyes were doing that thing where they didn't match what he was making the rest of his face do. His mouth was smiling, but his eyes looked worried.

He petted Daisy's hair again, and she frowned. The sound was coming from *inside* the house. She couldn't tell what it was exactly. She listened closely, but it stopped. Chewbacca heard something, though. He stood up, did a dog stretch, and jumped off the bed. His toenails tick, tick, ticked on the floor. She heard him plop down in the hallway and sigh another dog sigh.

Then there it was again, this time louder. It was like growling or groaning, and it was coming from her parents' room.

She sat straight up in bed. "Dad?" A scared, empty hole punched itself into her stomach. "Is it happening? Is Mom okay? Is it now?"

Again, only Dad's mouth smiled. The hole in Daisy's belly started to get bigger.

"She's all right, Daisy. Don't worry. It's just . . . It's just the baby coming. It's normal. Everything is totally normal." He wasn't being convincing at all. The hole in Daisy's belly froze to ice.

"Daddy! Why didn't you tell me right away?" she said.

Dad nervously adjusted his hat. "I'm sorry," he said. "I didn't know how to say it. I don't want you to worry, because everything is really okay. She's okay." Then the sound started again. Daisy thought, *Why is she making weird noises?* Her mom had explained to her, step-by-step, in excruciating, agonizingly vivid detail, what was going to happen when the baby came. She had gone over it a million times with Daisy. She had told her exactly what was going to be happening to *her* body during the birth, what would be happening to the *baby's* body during the birth, and about the whole physiological process. Daisy thought it was totally disgusting, but Mom just hadn't stopped talking. She'd kept saying, *It's just biology, lovie, totally natural, and someday if you have a baby, it will happen to you, too.* Daisy had tried not to say *Yuck!* out loud.

But Mom hadn't ever said anything about noises. She'd asked Daisy if she wanted to be at the birth, in the room when the baby was born, *to welcome your new sibling.* Daisy had decided she didn't want to be there. Even though Mom thought everything about having a baby was awesome, Daisy thought it sounded pretty gross. She wanted to see the baby right away, but being in the room? *No thanks,* she'd said. *I'm good!*

But now maybe she *did* want to be in there, to make sure her mom was okay, to ask her why she hadn't said anything about groaning, moaning, animal-like noises. The sounds subsided again, and Dad just kept sitting next to her on the bed. Mom must be okay if he was still in here with her. She lay down again and pulled the blankets close around herself, staying very still next to Dad, and listening. Then they both heard Mom yell, "Will, for crying out loud, get in here now!" and then she yelled, "Jee-zuss!" plus a bunch of swear words. Dad kissed Daisy's head and told her she did not have to go to school, but she should get up and get dressed. He looked like he wanted to be doing pretty much anything but going in to Mom, who had started swearing *a lot*.

Daisy got herself dressed, pulled her hair into a ponytail, brushed her teeth, and then crept down the hall. It was quiet inside now. She waited outside the door to her parents' bedroom for a minute and then tentatively peeked in. "Are you all right?" she said softly. She didn't go all the way in, hovering near the door.

Mom was in bed, in her nightgown, lying on her side. She looked like she was sleeping, but she opened her eyes when she heard Daisy's voice.

"I'm fine. It's going to be all right, lovie," Mom said. "Promise." Then her eyebrows drew together, and she moaned and closed her eyes again, her arms wrapped around the bottom of her belly.

Dad was sitting next to Mom on the bed. "Go eat something for breakfast," he said to Daisy. "Aunt Toby will be here soon."

Aunt Toby had slept at a friend's house in Brooklyn. Daisy thought she might have a new girlfriend or something, which would be great, but right now she wanted her here by her side. Dad was going to be with Mom, and Aunt Toby had promised she'd stay with Daisy through the whole birth.

Dad looked at her. "And don't worry, Buddy-Girl."

But she couldn't help it. The same scared phrases kept hammering inside her head.

What if something happens to Mom?

What if something happens to the bump?

What if the worst thing that could happen happens?

She went downstairs and ate a frozen waffle. After a little while, Dad came down and sat at the table with her. She could hear Mom going into the bathroom upstairs and the water turning on for the shower. Dad poured himself some cereal and started eating. Which was weird, because he was a smoothie guy. He never ate cereal. They sat there together for a few minutes, with him crunching. They heard Mom making sounds again upstairs, and the doorbell rang. Chewie started barking, and Dad jumped up and sprinted toward the front door. "It's probably the midwife," he shouted over his shoulder. *Why is he shouting?*

Daisy got up and followed him to the foyer, but it wasn't the midwife; it was Aunt Toby.

"Blessings! Blessings! Sorry, I forgot my key!" Aunt Toby said. "Happy Birth Day, Will!" She said it with a big pause between the words "birth" and "day," making it mean a whole different thing. Aunt Toby shone a huge smile at Dad, but when she swept into the house, she went right to Daisy, swooping her into a big strong hug, enveloping her in her spicy, smoky smell.

"Why did it take so long for you to get here?" Daisy said.

"There was traffic on the Expressway" Aunt Toby replied, kissing the top of Daisy's head. She leaned back, looking into Daisy's eyes. "Honeypot! We're growing more family today!" she said. "Isn't it glorious?" Then she pulled Daisy back into a hug.

Sometimes it was as if Aunt Toby's voice had a song hidden in it, like everything that came out of her mouth was an expression of joy. Being inside her hug, Daisy relaxed a little. Just having her home calmed Daisy down.

"How's she doing, Willy?"

"Okay so far. I think she just went into the shower," Dad said, and they all looked toward the stairs when they heard Mom singing or moaning. Or something.

"Maybe my sissy wants company in the shower!" Aunt Toby said. She gave Daisy one last squeeze and started up the stairs.

Dad said, "Company in the shower? Um, well . . ." Daisy knew Aunt Toby would totally jump in that shower with Mom in a hot minute if Mom wanted her to.

As Aunt Toby reached the bathroom, she sang out, "Lori-Lu! You want me to come in that shower with you?"

Before she closed the bathroom door, Daisy heard Mom laugh, and she relaxed a tiny bit. She sat down on the bottom step of the staircase and put her chin in her hands, leaning on her knees, and looked expectantly at Dad. He shrugged.

The doorbell rang again, and Chewie started barking frantically once more. This time it *was* the midwife. Dad looked so relieved. Daisy still didn't want to be in the room when the baby came. Dad said that was fine and suggested Aunt Toby and Daisy go out for a while, run some errands, pass the time somewhere outside the house. Apparently it takes a long time for a baby to be born.

Dad told the midwife, "She's upstairs. I'm not sure, but I think her sister *might* be in the shower with her." He was shaking his head when he said it, with a quizzical expression on his face. Daisy scooted to the side so the lady could go upstairs. The midwife looked at Dad, shrugged, and said, "It wouldn't be the oddest thing I've ever seen. I'll go up and see where we are." Dad nodded his head, as if knowing it wasn't the oddest thing she'd ever seen somehow made everything more normal.

If Aunt Toby really *had* gotten in the shower with Mom, maybe Daisy wouldn't have to go run errands with her. Everything was happening *here*, and Daisy didn't want to leave. She wanted to stay and make sure she was here when the bump was born. Not in the room, but she wanted to make sure nothing bad happened, as if her being here, even in the next room, might somehow *do* something.

Dad sat down on the step next to Daisy. "Don't forget to take the tote bag with Mom's library books," he said. "They need to be returned."

"All right," she said. "But do I have to leave?"

"You don't have to, but I think it might be better for you to take a little break, Buddy-Girl."

When he looked at her, his eyes and the rest of his face finally matched. Now the whole thing looked lost. His eyebrows drew together.

"You okay, Dad?" she asked.

He was quiet for a moment, then said, "Yeah, I am." He leaned into her a little. "I know Mommy will be fine. She's so strong and in control."

Daisy thought that was true; Mom *was* very strong and did always seem to be in control of things. But would that be enough? Ruby had been one of the strongest people she knew, but she hadn't been able to control what had happened to her. Daisy rested her head on Dad's shoulder. Anything could happen at any time, and nobody was in control of anything. It was scary.

"You know, when you were born in the hospital, it was so clear what the rules were," Dad said. "But having this baby at home is different." He nodded. "I'm not sure what the rules are, or if there are any rules, or where I'm supposed to be."

Daisy understood that. She said, "Probably the best plan is to just do whatever Mommy wants, then, right?"

He laughed. "Yeah, that's probably a good plan. And how are you doing? Are *you* okay?"

Knowing that Dad was unsure about what he was supposed to do—and he was a grown-up and everything—weirdly made her *less* scared. She felt warm in her chest, thinking about that, like her heart filled up with love or something. Being scared or unsure *with* someone else, like Dad, made her a tiny bit braver, a little less frightened. That was one of the things she missed about Ruby. Being with Ruby had made her feel a little braver too.

"I think I'm okay," she said. "I mean, like, right *now* I am." She nodded.

"Sometimes we have to take life moment by moment," he said, his nod bobbing in time with hers.

She thought about it—moment by moment—because things could totally change in a moment.

"I should probably go up there to be with Mom," Dad said. But he didn't get up. Then he reached out and took Daisy's hand.

"Yeah, probably," she said.

"Right," he said, taking a deep breath.

"Right," she said, feeling slightly better.

They sat there for a while, just holding hands, taking it moment by moment.

Right at Home

They returned books to the library. They bought stamps at the post office and picked up milk, bread, and eggs from the grocery store. Aunt Toby took Daisy out to lunch. She had pizza, and Aunt Toby had salad. Then they dropped off the dry cleaning and went to the local farm store to buy some squash and onions. When they got home, Daisy ran through the front door, not waiting for Aunt Toby. She stopped in the foyer a moment, just listening. She could hear them walking around upstairs. She ran up but stopped when she got to the top step, her hand clutching the wooden rail tightly.

The three of them—Mom, Dad, and the midwife—

were at the far end of the hall, in a small huddle at the doorway of the bedroom. The midwife was holding Mom on one side, and Dad was holding her on the other, their hands under Mom's arms. The three grown-ups took a couple of steps into the hallway, not noticing Daisy standing at the top of the stairs. Mom was humming, her head thrown back, and her long, curly hair a mess, like she hadn't bothered to comb it after the crazy singing shower that morning. Although she had a purple terry-cloth bathrobe sort of thrown over her shoulders, she was basically standing in the hall naked.

It wasn't like Daisy hadn't seen Mom naked before. They weren't very private about that kind of stuff. Dad walked around in his boxers all the time, and it was normal for Daisy and Mom to change in front of each other, or for Daisy to make a naked dash from the bathroom to her bedroom. Bodies weren't a big deal in their house. But Daisy had never seen Mom full-out naked while she was a million months pregnant.

And usually when Daisy looked at her mom, she just saw . . . *Mom* cooking dinner for her and her dad. *Mom* asking her about her homework. *Mom* writing, or reading, or working, or not paying attention to Daisy at all. Or *Mom and Dad* leaving her with a babysitter to go out to dinner or a movie. When she looked at Mom, or

Dad for that matter, she pretty much only saw them in relation to herself. She'd never really thought about who they were as people other than her parents.

But looking down the hallway at Mom standing there, held up by the midwife and Dad, for a brief flicker of a moment, Daisy saw her mom as a woman, Lori, doing something that very much had nothing at all to do with her. It made Daisy feel untethered. She gripped the railing tighter. Her vision went a little dark around the edges.

Dad and the midwife were totally focused on Mom. And Mom was looking through everything and everyone. She was there but not there. Still, none of them had noticed Daisy standing at the top of the stairs. They took two steps down the hallway. And Daisy couldn't look away.

They stopped, and Mom made a deep growling sound, and the three of them squatted down together, right there in the hall. Daisy saw her mom's belly get tight, and it looked a little smaller, and the outline of what must have been the baby was visible through her skin. It was like a science-fiction movie special effect. It was like a computer-generated belly, doing something implausible and incredible. Dad was whispering something in Mom's ear, and she could hear the midwife saying, "You can do this, Lori. You're doing great. Just breathe."

A shiver ran through Daisy. Why were they all so calm? Was Mom going to push the baby out right there? Just because she had decided to have the baby at home, was it going to get born right on the floor? Shouldn't they go into the bedroom or something? This couldn't be happening. This couldn't be true. This couldn't be what they'd planned. Daisy thought, *Oh my god, who gives birth to a baby in the hallway?*

Then Aunt Toby came to the top of the stairs behind her and enfolded Daisy in a hug. "I had to let Chewie out," she said. Then she whispered, "You okay, honeypot?" Daisy was wrapped up in Aunt Toby's spicy, flowery smell. But no, she wasn't okay at all.

In that moment when her mom was there but not there, and Dad hadn't even turned his head to acknowledge her, it hit her. When this baby was born, actually here in the world, not just an idea of a brother or a sister, she might feel like *this* for the rest of her life—so very alone. If Ruby were here, and Daisy had told her how she was feeling right now, Ruby would have said something like, *You've got me, Daze,* and she would have felt a little better. Now she didn't have her best friend anymore either.

Then Aunt Toby hugged her closer. "Look at her, Daisy. She's so beautiful and strong, my sister," she said in a choked-up voice. But Daisy turned and looked up at her aunt instead. Aunt Toby was looking at Mom and Dad and the midwife in their huddle, and she had a look of wonder on her face. And it was unabashedly full of love.

Low animal noises were coming from somewhere deep inside her mother now, but Daisy kept her eyes on her aunt. Just like Daisy, she had tears in her eyes. Daisy pushed herself a little deeper into Aunt Toby's hug.

"I'm scared," Daisy whispered to her.

"I know it's a little scary," Aunt Toby said, "but it's going to be okay. Your mom is like an Amazon warrior. She's spectacular. She's Wonder Woman and Katniss and Captain Marvel, all wrapped up into one breathtaking woman." Aunt Toby rocked Daisy in the hug, and the tears started to run down Daisy's cheeks.

"I love you, honeypot. Don't worry," Aunt Toby said, as if she could read Daisy's mind. "Let's go downstairs and make cookies until this baby's finished being born. I don't think they need us here. We'll come back up when there's someone new in the world to cuddle, okay?"

They were about to go downstairs when Mom looked up and noticed them at the end of the hall. She gasped and said in one big sort of whispery exhale to Dad, "Will, make sure Daisy comes up and meets this baby as soon as it's out of me." She was looking right at Daisy, right into her eyes, totally there, and she smiled. Daisy was about to smile back, but another pain must have come over Mom, because she closed her eyes, furrowed her brow, and scrunched up her face, and she was gone again.

One of the best things about having a mom with a twin sister is that Mom and Aunt Toby were like those psychically connected kind of twins that you read about, even though they weren't all the way identical. So when Aunt Toby squeezed Daisy's shoulder, it felt like the squeeze came from Mom, and Daisy felt like she was right there in the circle with them.

The first time Daisy held her sister, Dahlia, they were in Mom and Dad's bed. Mom was sleeping, and Dad was making lunch, and Daisy was cuddled up napping next to Mom. She woke up when Aunt Toby sat next to her, holding the small package that was the baby, all wrapped up in a blanket like a burrito. Aunt Toby whispered, "You haven't held her yet, honeypot." She hadn't, and she wasn't sure she was ready to. She seemed so little, though the midwife had said she was a nice-sized seven pounds, eight ounces. Daisy was afraid she would somehow break her or do something wrong. She knew there was something you weren't supposed to do with babies' heads, too, because they were soft and squishable.

"Scoot up," Aunt Toby said. Daisy sat up next to Mom, who hadn't woken up. Aunt Toby whispered, "Put the nursing pillow on your lap." Daisy took the weird C-shaped thing and stuck it around her waist. Then Aunt Toby gently placed the baby burrito into Daisy's arms, resting on the pillow. The bundle of baby was so tiny and warm. In her mind Daisy kept saying, *Careful, careful, careful,* the entire time she held her. Then the burrito started to cry, a furious, high-pitched noise that sounded like a yowling cat. Aunt Toby took her back and rocked her until she quieted, and Mom kept sleeping. Dahlia was three hours old.

The second time Daisy held Dahlia, she was sitting on the couch in the family room. Dad was upstairs napping, Mom had fallen asleep in the rocking chair, and this time when Aunt Toby handed the baby burrito to Daisy, Dahlia was already awake and a little squirmy. Daisy carefully put her hand under Dahlia's neck like Aunt Toby had shown her, and in her mind she said, *Don't drop her, don't drop her, don't drop her.* When Dahlia started to cry, Daisy gave her back to Aunt Toby, who brought her to Mom to nurse. Dahlia was five and a half hours old.

The third time Daisy held Dahlia, Daisy was the one sitting in the rocking chair. Aunt Toby had handed her to Daisy and was helping Mom in the bathroom. Dad was in the kitchen making dinner. It was the first time Daisy was alone in the room with the baby burrito. Dahlia wasn't sleeping and she wasn't crying. She was looking straight up into Daisy's face, or maybe she was looking at Daisy's ear; it was hard to tell. Dahlia puckered her lips in a way that made Daisy think of a baby bird. Then in the course of ten seconds it looked like her face went through all the possible expressions a human face could make. She smiled, she grimaced, her forehead furrowed and un-furrowed, she looked surprised, then scared, and then perfectly calm. And then with a tiny little squeak she closed her eyes.

Very slowly and carefully Daisy lifted Dahlia up toward her face and sniffed her right where her face met the knit baby hat on her head. She didn't know why she did it, but Dahlia smelled so good. It wasn't like anything she'd ever smelled before. It was like the earthy smell of fallen leaves on the floor of the woods in autumn, with warm milk added, and baby powder sprinkled on top, and then some other unnamable smell mixed in, and all put together on the head of the baby burrito. She wished she knew the word to describe that whole baby smell.

Then Mom and Aunt Toby came back into the room, and Aunt Toby walked Mom over to the couch and got her comfortably settled with pillows and a blanket. Mom looked so tired. "I should try to nurse her again," she said. That third time that Daisy held the burrito, Dahlia was eight hours and twenty minutes old. And that was when Daisy fell in love with her sister.

Aunt Toby took Dahlia and gave her to Mom, then went in the kitchen to help Dad with dinner. Daisy watched her mom and the baby, and it clicked in her head that it had gone okay. She could stop worrying. Watching Mom nursing Dahlia, she was a little jealous, too.

Mom looked up at her and softly laughed. "This kid hasn't quite gotten the nursing thing yet," she said. "You knew how to nurse from the very first time." She caressed Dahlia's cheek. "This one, not so much. But she'll learn."

It was silly, to be proud of something she'd done when she was a baby, especially something like breast-feeding, which she hadn't even known was something you had to learn. But Daisy was; she was proud of her former baby self's ability to nurse.

"Come look," Mom said. "She looks just like you, lovie." Mom sighed. "So beautiful and tiny." Daisy went and looked down at her nursing sister.

Then Daisy felt something big. The love she had for her mom and dad, and for Aunt Toby, had grown. It included Dahlia. Aunt Toby once told her that there isn't a finite amount of love, that the more you give love, the more love you have to give. Having this baby had created more love in their family.

But even behind all that extra love, Daisy still felt the pain that had become a part of her ever since Ruby died. She wanted so badly to call Ruby and ask her to come over. She couldn't believe Ruby would never get to meet her baby sister and Dahlia would never know a world that included Ruby. Incredible sadness and happiness apparently can exist in a person at the same time, though. Because this was very good. This was the first time in a long time that she didn't feel like her sadness was overflowing, like it might pour out of her at any second. She was too filled with love for her sister. For a moment she saw a glimmer of what it might be like to feel okay again.

Another Way In

Wait, what? Your mom didn't go to the hospital to have the baby?"

Daisy and Avery were eating lunch at a picnic table in the courtyard at school. Daisy kept her eyes on her sandwich. People had been weird when they'd found out Mom was having the baby at home. Dad's cousin Mitch had said it was irresponsible. He'd had a lot to say about it while eating bagels after Yom Kippur. His wife, Stacey, kept telling him to be quiet. Dad had stuck up for Mom's decision and answered all Cousin Mitch's comments with facts and statistics.

"No, she had a home birth," Daisy said. She took a big bite of her sandwich. Turkey with mayo. Good, Dad remembered she didn't like mustard when he'd made her lunch that morning.

She looked up, still chewing. Avery's eyes were wide.

"She just, like, had her—gave birth—in the house?" Avery asked.

"Well, with a midwife," Daisy added. "Somebody who knows how to deliver babies."

"Oh," Avery said, nodding.

Daisy said, bragging a little, "I was there when she was born." Avery's eyes widened even more. Daisy went on. "Well, sort of."

"Wow!" Avery said. "But was that safe for her to do?" She looked concerned, Daisy could see, but also Avery's scientific nature was peeking out, wanting the facts. She was wearing a purple T-shirt that said SCIENCE > OPINION, which was very Avery. It was one of the things Daisy liked about her. She thought things through, like Daisy did, looking at the pros and cons of every situation. She was measured and practical, but still funny and fun. She seemed, to Daisy, like somebody you could count on. Someone you could trust.

"Of course it's safe," Daisy replied. "Women have been having babies at home for centuries. Or, like, forever. Besides, my mom wouldn't do something not safe." Now that it was over, and everything had gone okay, it was easy to say that. She and Aunt Toby had been down-stairs making cookies in the kitchen when Dahlia came out, so she wasn't *actually* there when Dahlia was born.

"My dad told me there are tons of scientific studies that show it's as safe as a hospital, and sometimes even safer."

"Really?" Avery said. "That's amazing. Was it gross?"

For a second Daisy wanted to lie. She wanted to tell Avery that it was so gross, and make up some details about it, like something super weird and cool. But she didn't.

"Well, I wasn't in the room when the baby, like, came out," she said sheepishly, wrinkling her nose up. "But I *heard* it all."

Avery had stopped eating, her sandwich held between her fingers, hovering near her mouth. She was so riveted, she'd forgotten to take her next bite.

Daisy said, "I mean, I kind of saw part of it. Sort of."

"What part?" Avery asked.

"The labor part, when my mom was walking around and stuff," Daisy said. "I thought she was going to have the baby right there in the hallway."

"Whoa," Avery said. "And did she?!"

"No, but at one point it looked like she had an alien trying to get out of her stomach."

"Whoa!" Avery said again. "So, is she cute?"

"My mom?" Daisy said.

"No! Your sister!" Avery said, laughing.

Daisy laughed too. "It's so weird to hear somebody say, 'your sister,'" Daisy said. "She's still all red and wrinkled. I don't think I'd really call her cute yet."

The corners of Avery's eyes scrunched up when she smiled. "I bet she's cute," she said. "Baby anythings are cute."

"Yeah, that's true," Daisy said.

"Except baby naked mole rats," Avery said.

Daisy laughed.

"No, really! Have you seen what they look like?" Avery continued. "They're so gross. . . . They look even more . . . naked!"

She and Daisy giggled.

"Yeah, my sister is definitely cuter than a naked mole rat," Daisy said.

"What's her name?" Avery said.

"We called her the bump when she was in my mom's belly, so I kind of still think of her as the bump. But her name's Dahlia," Daisy said. Then she took a deep breath and said, "So, like, if you want . . . you could maybe . . . Maybe you could come over sometime? And you could see her?" She'd meant her sentence to be an invitation, but it came out strange.

Avery said, "Sure. That would be cool!" Then she took a bite out of her sandwich and smiled.

Daisy cleared her throat. She looked over Avery's shoulder, not wanting to meet her eyes. She didn't know why she felt so awkward about asking, but she did. "Do you want to come over after school *today*?"

"Sure," Avery said. "But will that be okay with your mom?"

Daisy hadn't thought about that. Mom had said she could invite Avery over after the Jewish holidays, but that was before Dahlia was born. Dahlia was only three days old. Maybe she needed to ask first. If she had gotten a phone, like she was supposed to, she could just text her now.

"I can ask," Daisy said. "I'll go to the office to call home."

"You can use my phone," Avery said. "But we have to go where the teachers can't see us."

"I'm getting a phone soon," Daisy said.

"Dahlia's a pretty name," Avery said.

"Thanks," Daisy said. "It's a kind of flower."

"That's funny," Avery said. "You both have flower names."

"My dad's sort of into gardening," Daisy said. "Well, mostly he's into foraging."

"What do you mean?" Avery said.

"Like, picking edible stuff on the side of the road or eating stuff that most people think are weeds."

"Cool," Avery said.

"I guess," Daisy said. "But he basically loves all kinds of plants, so me and my sister got flower names."

"Valid reason," Avery said. "I'm glad my dad didn't name me for something he's into." She went on. "I would have been named Stock or Commodity or Golf Cart or something."

Daisy laughed. They finished eating their sandwiches, threw away their trash, and went out to the yard behind the school. "Kids go back over there, behind those trees, when they want to use their phones," Avery said. "There's cell service, and the teachers pretend they can't see you."

They passed Carlos and a bunch of other boys playing soccer in the field. A girl named Rayna was sitting with her back up against a tree, reading. Her friend Michelle sat next to her, also reading. As Avery and Daisy walked by, Michelle said, "Hey," and the girls answered in unison, "Hey!" Then Michelle said, "I like your shirt!"

"Thanks!" Avery said. Daisy saw Amanda and her friends sitting on the lawn, laughing and talking. Daisy and Ruby had always called them "the horsey girls" because at recess when they were little, they used to pretend they were horses. They were nice enough. Now that they were in middle school, they'd graduated to competitive riding of actual horses.

Ruby and Daisy hadn't really been good friends with too many other kids. They'd always been friendly enough to everyone, and everyone was friendly back to them. It was just that she and Ruby didn't need anybody but each other. It felt good to be walking in the schoolyard with somebody now. It was weird that it wasn't Ruby, and Daisy felt kind of guilty about it. It had only been four months that Ruby was gone. Daisy had been so lonely without her. But she liked Avery. She knew Ruby would have liked her too. Sometimes she'd forget for a minute and think, *I've got to tell Ruby what Avery said!* Every time she had that thought, the emptiness in her chest came back, and the knowledge that Ruby was gone—gone forever—would hit her again. She sighed.

"Daisy," Avery tentatively said.

Daisy's attention came back to Avery and their walking across the schoolyard. They were on the grass, near the trees now.

"Yeah?" Daisy answered.

"How come you do that?"

Daisy frowned, her eyebrows drawing together.

"Do what? What do you mean?" she said. She slowed down, her sneakers scuffing in the grass. Avery wasn't looking at her.

Avery said in one big breath, "Well, sometimes when we're talking, it's like you're thinking about something else, and you have a super-sad look on your face, and then I have the thought, 'She looks so sad,' and then you sigh. Why do you do that?" She blurted it all out, then looked up at Daisy. "Why do you get so ruminative?"

"Ruminative?" Daisy said.

"It means super thinky," Avery said.

Should she tell her? How should she say it? What would Avery do?

Daisy didn't say anything, though. They'd gotten to the trees, where the lunch monitors couldn't see them using Avery's phone. They stopped. Avery looked at Daisy.

"Oh god, I'm sorry," Avery said. "My mom said I have no filter sometimes." Daisy hadn't answered her. "I shouldn't have asked," The pressure behind Daisy's eyes that was the beginning of tears started to build. She put her fingers in the corners of her eyelids, pressing in, willing the tears not to come.

"Forget it," Avery said softly. "I'm so sorry."

Daisy was trying to figure out what to say, but nothing was coming out.

Avery looked embarrassed. "It's okay if you don't want me to come over today. I know that was rude. I don't mean to pry."

Daisy finally said, "You weren't rude. It's okay." Her voice cracked. She still didn't answer Avery's question, though. She was starting to feel bad about not talking to Avery about Ruby, telling her who Ruby was, and what had happened. But she didn't know how to do it, or what to say. She cleared her throat and said, "I want you to come over. I'll call my mom." They stepped behind a tree, and Avery handed her the phone.

And there behind the tree was Mo. On his phone. Crying.

"I've got to go," Mo said into the phone, and then he shoved the phone into his backpack. He pulled his baseball cap out of his back pocket and stuck it on his head, backward. He tipped his chin up at the girls in a silent hello, then turned away, swiping at the tears on his face as he walked back toward the school building.

"Oh my gosh, what do you think that was about?" Avery whispered.

Daisy almost blurted out, *His mom's got cancer*, but she stopped herself. She thought about that first day at

Hebrew school when she'd met Mo and how brave it was of him to tell her about his mom. How he'd looked when he told her why he was going and what he was hoping to do. Raw, open, vulnerable. She thought about how he'd never brought up, afterward, what she'd told him. About Ruby dying. He'd never said anything about the fact that she'd cried the first time she met him. He'd known that she didn't want to talk about any of it. And yes, sometimes it felt like he was kind of needy, trying to be friends when she wasn't sure she wanted to. And he was so bold and self-confident about it, telling her their friendship was bashert, destiny, whatever. But he still respected her privacy. He hadn't brought it up again to her.

"That kid is in Mr. Herman's class with us," Avery said. "You know him, right?"

Daisy said, "Yeah, Mo Hammonds. We go to Hebrew school together."

"He was really crying," Avery said. "I hope he's okay. I wonder what happened."

"Yeah," Daisy said. "I wonder."

It turned out that Daisy went to Avery's house after school, instead of Avery coming over. When Daisy called home, Mom said she wasn't ready to have people over yet. Which was okay with Daisy. She wanted to see where Avery lived and meet the mean housekeeper, Melania. But mostly she just wanted to feel like Avery was a friend, not merely someone she talked to at school. It didn't matter whose house they went to.

Avery lived pretty close to the school, so they walked to her house. "My mom or Melania drives me to school in the morning, but until it gets really cold out, my mom said I have to walk home." As they strode up the long, winding drive, they came to a big house, what Aunt Toby called a McMansion. As they entered the large foyer, a house alarm signaled with a subtle ding that the front door had been opened. But nobody came to greet them. Avery threw her backpack onto a plush velvet bench near the double front door. "You can just put your backpack there," she said. Daisy dropped her backpack and gazed up at the double-height ceiling with a gigantic crystal chandelier looming over them. They went through the foyer and into the kitchen, and Avery looked around and said, "I don't know where Melania is." She sighed. "I texted her you were coming over. Whatever." Daisy could see a pool and a tennis court out the back slider.

Avery's house was the kind of house that had been put together very intentionally, where everything matched and nothing was out of place. There was a beautiful floral centerpiece on the kitchen table, and on the wall were at least a dozen framed pictures of Avery and a boy who must be her older brother, from when they were babies until what Daisy guessed was probably last year. It looked like a professional photographer had taken the pictures. Daisy thought they were fancy enough to be in a magazine. There was a television mounted on the kitchen wall that had a frame around it like a painting.

As Daisy looked around, she thought about Ruby's house, which was also one of the bigger houses in Roosevelt Cove, just in a different neighborhood. The Affinis' house had always felt lived in, and not as fancy as this one. Leo was always in the kitchen cooking something and making a mess. Just the night before, he'd dropped off a celebratory lasagna for Daisy's family because of the baby. Gazing around Avery's kitchen, Daisy couldn't imagine anyone ever cooking in it. It felt like a movie-set kitchen or a museum.

"Let's go up to my room," Avery said.

Avery's bedroom looked like a picture from a magazine too. The floral throw pillows on the bed matched the fabric of the curtains, which coordinated with the striped upholstery of the chair at the desk and an easy chair in the corner. It all complemented the pattern on the wallpaper, in different shades of blue and yellow. Daisy thought it was beautiful, but it wasn't what she'd expected, and it wasn't very Avery-ish.

"Wow," Daisy said. "Your bedroom's really pretty."

Avery shrugged. "My parents had a decorator do it all. My mom hates doing stuff like that."

Daisy sat in the easy chair, and Avery perched on the ottoman next to her. It looked fluffy and soft.

Avery's shoulders hunched forward. "My mom said we might have to sell the house because of money, because of the divorce."

Daisy leaned back in the big cozy chair. "That would stink," she said. She pulled her knees up and wrapped her arms around her legs.

"I don't really care about the house itself," Avery said. Her hands stroked the soft cloth on the ottoman, her fingers making patterns in the fabric as they moved back and forth. "But I don't want to change schools again."

"I hope you don't have to move," Daisy said.

"And there are scientific studies that show moving again will impact my grades," Avery said. "Statistically speaking."

Daisy looked up at her.

"I like it at Roosevelt Cove Middle. Moving would be the worst thing ever," Avery said. "I mean, besides my parents splitting up."

Daisy didn't say anything. *There are even worse things than that,* she thought.

"So, do you want to do homework," Avery asked, "or just hang out?"

"Maybe just hang out," Daisy said.

"Good," Avery said. "Let's get a snack and go outside. I want to show you something."

They went back to the kitchen, and this time the housekeeper, Melania, was there. Avery had said she was mean, so Daisy had assumed she'd be ugly, too. In the movies mean people are always ugly. But Melania was pretty, like a model. She hardly even looked at them, though, when they came into the room, just kept wiping the counter.

"We're going outside," Avery said. Melania nodded. Avery opened a cabinet, and it was full of snacks—bags of chips, granola bars, cookies. "Pick whatever you want," Avery said to Daisy. They each took a bag of popcorn, and Avery grabbed two bottles of water from the fridge. They went out the back slider, and Daisy looked over her shoulder at Melania, who hadn't said a word the whole time and wasn't even looking in their direction.

"Is she always quiet like that?" Daisy asked as they walked across the deck.

"Yep," Avery said. "And now that my brother's back at school, and my mom's working all the time, I've *really* got nobody to talk to." They went down the stairs at the end of the deck and walked across the lawn.

"You've got me to talk to," Daisy said. Avery looked at her, and they both smiled.

"Come on!" Avery said, and she started jogging toward the tennis court. Daisy followed. When they got to the fence on the far side of the court, Daisy saw what Avery wanted to show her.

There was a gate in the fence. On the gate was a small metal plaque that said NO ENTRANCE, and underneath that, DOWER NATURE PRESERVE LAND TRUST. Even though they didn't live in the same neighborhood, Avery's house bordered Dower Nature Preserve too. Daisy's house was on Cedar Road, on the eastern edge of the preserve, near the bluff. Mo's house wasn't too far away. He lived on Birch Court, closer to the entrance of the preserve and the parking lot, but basically directly across the preserve from Daisy's house. But Avery's house was on Willow Lane, all the way at the far end of the preserve, down near the pond and the gazebo, probably about a mile from Daisy's house.

"Whoa!" Daisy said. "I live right on the other side of the preserve. We could literally *walk* to each other's house."

"Really?" Avery smiled.

"Yeah, and Mo Hammonds, the kid from the schoolyard today? His house backs up on the preserve too."

Avery stuck her fingers through the chain-link fence and looked through.

"Are you friends with him?" Avery asked.

"Sort of," Daisy said. "We're the only kids from Roosevelt Cove who go to our Hebrew school, so we carpool. He's pretty nice."

Avery nodded. "Hey, let's go in," she said. "Me and my friend Emily used to sneak in together, before she moved," Avery said. "But she never really liked it. She only went because I wanted to."

Daisy's momentary bubble of happiness, realizing she could walk to Avery's house from her own, quickly popped, leaving the hollow feeling behind her ribs. She hadn't gone into the preserve since before the summer. The last time she'd been there was with Ruby. She stood next to Avery, looking through the fence.

"You're not supposed to go in this way," Avery said. "But who cares!" She opened the gate. "There used to be a lock, but I don't know what happened to it." Daisy's heart was pounding in her chest. "We're kind of near the gazebo," Avery said. "Let's go eat our popcorn there."

Daisy didn't say anything.

"Come on!" Avery called. Daisy wasn't sure she could do this. She didn't know if she was ready to go back into Dower Nature Preserve yet. She took a deep breath. Avery turned around. "You okay?"

Daisy frowned but didn't say anything, following Avery in.

"Just so you know," Avery said quietly, walking ahead of her, "you just got ruminative again." Daisy consciously un-frowned her face, but Avery didn't turn around, so she didn't see. "Don't worry. I won't ask you anything," Avery said over her shoulder. "But if you want to ever tell me, you can."

Could I? Daisy thought. *Could I tell her? Could I say those words again to someone?* She didn't want to say it out loud again. It was bad enough she'd told Mo that first day she'd met him at Hebrew school. But he'd just told her about his mom being sick, so somehow it seemed right that she'd told him. But to just come out and say that to Avery? *My best friend died last summer. Not a day goes by where something doesn't remind me of her.* She wasn't ready. But she followed Avery into the preserve, and they ate popcorn in the gazebo. She could do that.

Carpooling

The next day it was Dad's turn to drive to Hebrew school. When Daisy got in the back seat of their car, Dad asked why she wasn't sitting in the front.

"God, Dad, it's just how we do carpool," Daisy had answered, as if Dad should have known.

"All righty, then," he said.

When Mo got in the car, Dad said, "So, I'm Will Rubens, Daisy's dad." He looked at Mo through the rearview mirror. "You can call me Will."

"Oh hi. I'm Mo," Mo said. "You can call me, um, Mo." Dad nodded to him in the rearview mirror. Mo gave him a thumbs-up.

"Daisy tells me you're in science class together."

Oh god, why did Dad have to tell Mo that she'd been talking about him?

"Yes, Mr. Rubens, Mr. . . . I mean, sorry . . . Will." Mo laughed nervously.

"Don't you want to listen to the radio, Dad?" Daisy said.

"The radio?" Dad said. "Oh sure. I can listen to the radio." Then he turned it on, winked at Daisy, and made the obvious move of not looking at them in the mirror. It was a jazz station, and every now and then Dad got super into it, drumming on the dashboard and saying, "Yeah!"

When they passed Mill Pond Road, where Ruby's house was, Daisy looked down at her lap and bit her lip. They were both quiet for a couple of minutes. She'd been waiting to ask Mo about what she and Avery saw at school. Finally she said, "Are you okay?" in a low voice.

"Oh," Mo said softly. "Yeah, that was embarrassing, but I'm all good." He nodded and pressed his lips together. "So," he said, immediately changing the subject, "Morah Jill said we have to tell her what our projects are going to be by the first week in December."

"Are you sure?" she said. "You looked really upset."

But Mo just kept talking as if he hadn't heard her.

"I'm going to make an owl box for Dower Nature Preserve," Mo said proudly. "Or maybe a bat house."

"You're what?" Daisy said.

"Mr. Rosen, the guy who runs all of Dower Nature Preserve, is a friend of my grandpa's," Mo said. "And when I told him I wanted to do a community service project there—you know, for tikkun olam—he said I could make an owl box or a bat house to put in the preserve." He grinned at her. "Cool, right?" He looked pleased with himself.

"That's a tikkun olam project?" Daisy said.

"Of course it is," he said, looking at her like that was a silly question. "It's about balance, and ecology, and supporting animals in our community. That's repairing the world too." He was holding a paper bag, which he held out to her. "I brought jelly beans," he said. "Want to nibble?"

She couldn't tell if he was making fun of her or being sincere.

"Take some," he said, pushing the bag toward her. She peeked in, expecting them to be all black, but they were multicolored. "Fruit-bowl flavored," Mo said with a smile. "The white ones are supposed to be coconut, but if you ask me, they taste like soap."

Was he just going to pretend it hadn't happened, that he hadn't been crying at school, that she and Avery hadn't seen him?

She took a handful of jelly beans, avoiding the white ones, and nibbled as they rode to Hebrew school. Mo talked and talked and talked about his project, and how his dad was going to help him with the woodworking part, what kind of owls might nest in them, and how many bats were usually in a bat house.

When they got to synagogue, they jumped out of the car. "Thanks, Mr.—oh right—Will!" Mo said.

"Bye, Dad," Daisy said, not even looking at him.

They walked up the path together. Daisy slowed down as they neared the building, and Mo matched her pace. Then she blurted out, "But, Mo, why were you crying at school yesterday? What happened?"

"Ohhhhh . . . ," he said. "I was hoping you were going to forget about that."

Forget? That I'd found him crying at school?

"I'm sorry. I couldn't forget about it," she said, swallowing. "You looked . . ." She didn't finish her sentence. When she'd seen him in the schoolyard, he'd looked like she'd felt for months.

"I know," he said. "That's dumb." They stopped walking.

Rachel and Hannah came up the path from the parking lot. "You guys coming in?" Hannah said to them. The security guard held the door to the synagogue open for the girls.

"We'll be in in a minute," Daisy said. Rachel looked away, like she couldn't look at Mo and Daisy together. She grabbed Hannah's elbow as they went in. Ever since the first day of Hebrew school Rachel had been crushing on Mo. But Daisy and Mo were just friends. Why did Rachel have to be so weird about it? Mo didn't say anything. He took a deep breath.

"I mean," Daisy said, "is everything okay? Like, with your mom?" He swallowed and looked down. Another kid passed them, walking into the synagogue. Mo stuck his hands into his pockets. Unconsciously mirroring him, Daisy stuck her hands into her pockets too.

She recognized the look on his face. She imagined it was the same look she'd had on her own face the day before when Avery had told her she sighed all the time and looked sad. But she waited to see if he'd say anything else. It was like one minute his face had been open and bright and hopeful when he was telling her about building owl boxes, and the next minute a storm came in, and he shut down, his face turning cloudy and downcast. And she had made that happen. She shouldn't have asked. But he didn't go into the synagogue. He stayed standing there with her.

"Um." He looked up at Daisy, and she was afraid he was going to cry again when he said in a low, soft voice,

"My mom had to go back to the hospital." Daisy took a deep breath and held it. "She's doing chemo," he said, "and she got an infection or something and had to go back to the hospital."

Daisy exhaled. "Wow, I'm sorry," she whispered.

"Yeah," he said. "Thanks."

Through the window they could see Morah Jill at the classroom door, looking toward them.

"I guess we should go in," Daisy said.

Mo straightened his shoulders, like someone had told him to stand up and march. "Yep!" he said. "Let's do this."

Toward the end of class that night, before the challah and grape juice, Morah Jill asked them to find partners. As usual, Rachel and Hannah paired up, but Daisy saw Rachel look at her, then at Mo, who hadn't gotten up yet. He was still writing in his notebook. Rachel had told Daisy again that she thought Mo was cute and that Daisy was so lucky they went to regular school together. Daisy had told her it was no big deal. Daisy looked at Rachel and nodded toward Mo, mouthing, *Go!* But Rachel grabbed Hannah's hands, started giggling, and shook her head violently.

So Daisy went over to Mo and said, "Want to be my partner?"

"Sure," he said. Daisy couldn't remember who she used to pair up with before Mo came. She didn't remember them doing so many find-a-partner things in Hebrew school before. Morah Jill passed around a handout for them all to work on. The class was paired off, two by two, desks pushed together.

"I haven't told anyone at school that my mom's sick," Mo said, fiddling with the handout. "This school or regular school either." He was looking down at the desk, his fingers pushing the paper back and forth.

"Okay," Daisy said. Her eyes were on the paper too. She didn't want to look at him in case he started crying again. She thought she might cry if he did.

"Except you," he continued. "I only told you." And there it was again. That feeling like he wanted something from her, needed something from her, but she didn't know what it was. Why had he picked her? Was it because she was sad too?

"Okay," Daisy said again.

Morah Jill talked about the activity—a word search—and how they should discuss the terms as they found them, but neither Daisy nor Mo was paying attention to that.

"So, do you want to meet me in the preserve sometime?" Mo said. "I can show you where I might put the owl box."

"Sure," Daisy said.

"Or bat house," he said.

Daisy glanced toward Rachel.

"I mean, they'd go in different places because owls and bats like different things," Mo said.

What would Hannah and Rachel think if they knew Mo had just asked her to go to the preserve?

"Owl boxes usually go up in a tree," Mo said.

It didn't feel like he was asking her for any reason other than that they both lived near the preserve. She hoped not, anyway, whatever Hannah and Rachel thought. Even though she rode to Hebrew school with him, she wasn't sure if they were going to be real friends.

"But you can put a bat house on the side of a building, if you want," he added.

Daisy finally decided she didn't care what Rachel and Hannah thought. It was too much work to try to figure that kind of stuff out. So she and Mo worked on the handout together, finding the words in the word search. *Community. Identity. Truth.*

Mo told her about where he used to live, in western Massachusetts, and how different it was living in Long Island. *This kid is so easy to hang out with,* Daisy thought. He told her about the time his mom planted carrot seeds and how one morning they saw a black bear, right in the backyard, digging in their vegetable garden, eating a carrot.

"We definitely don't have bears here," Daisy said. "But there are foxes and sometimes deer."

"I saw a porcupine once in the Berkshires," Mo said. "It was waddling right across the road."

"That's so cool," Daisy said.

"We drove past it, and I was like, 'Hey! That's a porcupine!' And my mom backed up so we could get a closer look."

When Mo imitated the hoots of the barred owls that he used to hear in the trees near his old house, Daisy looked up and saw Rachel and Hannah staring at them. She didn't actually roll her eyes, but she felt like it.

"We found a possum sleeping in the bottom of . . ." She stopped talking for a second. "Um, in the bottom of my friend's garbage can once," Daisy said. She felt a little panicked. It was weird to talk to Mo about something that had happened with Ruby. It felt weird to say, "my friend" and not just "Ruby," and that he didn't know she meant the best friend who wasn't here anymore. She frowned and swallowed the lump she felt in her throat.

Mo stuck his tongue out. "Ew," he said. "Possums are . . ." He did a full-body shudder.

"I know," she said. She relaxed a little. "They're so gross."

"So gross," he said.

She took a deep breath. She felt her jaw loosen up. She hadn't realized she'd been clenching it. Sometimes it felt good to just feel a little normal, like talking about regular things, even if she felt kind of guilty when she did. Like she was somehow letting Ruby down.

They did more of the word search together. *Culture. Belief. Justice.*

After class they sat next to each other on a bench in the synagogue lobby, waiting to be picked up on the car-pool line. She forgot to look and see if Rachel and Hannah were staring at them.

"I know you were talking about your friend before," Mo said, bumping his shoulder into hers. "The one who . . . you know . . . ," he said. "With the possum."

"Yeah," Daisy said. She sighed.

"Don't worry," he said. "I know you get sad when you talk about her." In a softer voice he said, "It's okay to be sad. No judgments here." Sometimes Mo sounded like such a grown-up, like someone way older than another eleven- or twelve-year-old kid. It was kind of nice.

"Thanks," Daisy said. "And don't worry. I won't tell anyone about your mom being sick."

"Thanks," Mo said, believing her.

And Let Us Say

Garlic mashed potatoes, sweet potatoes with marshmallows, chestnut stuffing for Aunt Toby because she doesn't like the mushroom one, Grandma's cranberry sauce, and Auntie Christi's brussels sprouts, and of course turkey," Mom called from the couch, where she was nursing Dahlia. "Don't forget to write 'turkey,' or I literally might forget to buy one!" Daisy heard Dahlia burp. "How many pies do you think we need?" Mom shouted.

Daisy was sitting at the kitchen table writing it all down. "Umm . . . how many people are we going to be? Who's coming?" she replied.

Mom was *back*. Next week was Thanksgiving, and

it would be as good as always. Nothing like that store-bought Rosh Hashanah dinner they'd suffered through in September. And now that Mom was back, when they went around the table at Thanksgiving sharing what they were thankful for, Daisy could say that she was thankful for her baby sister without any reservations. Dahlia was almost six weeks old, and besides the fact that all she did was breastfeed, poop, and sleep, Daisy liked having a baby sister.

"Well, it's us and Aunt Toby and the Connecticut Rubens."

"Why isn't Grandma coming?" Daisy asked.

"She can't do it, sweetie," Mom answered. "She said, and I quote, 'I love you madly and want to see the princesses. . . .'"

"Princesses," Daisy repeated, rolling her eyes.

"But she can't fly by herself," Mom said. "It's too much for her, with her hip. Then she asked if we'd consider going to Florida for Thanksgiving." Daisy heard Mom laugh. "She'd want to make a reservation somewhere, and I'm not doing *that* on my favorite holiday." Mom continued, "Maybe we can go to Florida for February break."

"Welp," Daisy said. "Then we only need four pies, if we're eight people. That leaves lots of leftovers."

Mom said, "Pumpkin, apple, pecan, and . . ."

Daisy said, "Chocolate pudding!" Then she wrote them all down.

It was quiet in the other room.

"Okay?" Daisy said more loudly. "Chocolate pudding?"

Mom answered in a softer voice. "Shhh . . . she's almost sleeping. . . ."

Aunt Toby came downstairs and into the kitchen. "I'm heading into Brooklyn," she said to Daisy. "But come with me. I want to pick some flowers to bring to my friend Caryn."

"It's November," Daisy said. "There aren't any flowers."

"There are asters down near the stone wall," Aunt Toby said. "And the sage isn't done, and that's pretty in a bouquet."

Daisy went into the family room, where Mom was still on the couch. She was holding Dahlia, who was mostly sleeping, half nursing, her eyes closed but her little mouth occasionally still giving a suck. Mom was all the way sleeping, though, her head gently resting on the couch cushion. Maybe Mom wasn't *all* the way back. Daisy put the list on the coffee table in front of her and scrawled *Out back with Aunt Toby* on the bottom.

Aunt Toby grabbed the clippers Dad kept with the

gardening gloves and bug spray near the back slider. Daisy put on a hoodie, and with a glance over at Mom and Dahlia she and Aunt Toby quietly slipped out to the yard.

They gathered what fall flowers were left—a bouquet of golden black-eyed Susans, fading purple asters, and one lone stalk of sedum with its cluster of reddish pink blooms—and then they hopped up to sit on the stone wall, gazing out over the Long Island Sound. A cloud passed in front of the sun, and for a second there was a chill. Daisy zipped her hoodie up. The cloud continued on, though, and then the sun shone on them again.

"So, who's Caryn?" Daisy asked. "Do you like her? Is she your girlfriend?"

"Am I that obvious, honeypot?" Aunt Toby laughed. "I don't know if I'd call her my girlfriend just yet, but yes, I do like her."

Daisy nodded. "Is she nice?"

"Very nice."

"Is she pretty?"

"Well, I think so," Aunt Toby said, grinning.

"Good," Daisy said. "Maybe you'll get married this time."

Aunt Toby laughed again, shaking her head.

"Slow down, honeypot," she said. Then they sat in

companionable silence, looking out at the water.

After a little while Daisy nodded toward the fallen tree. "That's the tree Ruby and I climbed over last spring, to get into the preserve."

The fence was still squished. She wondered if Mr. Rosen, the man Mo had mentioned was the caretaker at the preserve, even knew it had happened. Her mom and dad certainly hadn't been focused on something at the far end of their property. It was hard to believe it was only five months ago. It felt both like such a long time and like it happened only yesterday. Aunt Toby looked in the direction of Daisy's nod.

"It's where we thought we saw the fairy," Daisy said softly. She'd never told anyone that they'd sneaked in. She'd told Aunt Toby they'd thought they'd seen a fairy, but she hadn't told her about going into the preserve by themselves or climbing over the tree.

Aunt Toby gazed at the fallen tree, the squished fence. She pulled her legs up under herself so she was sitting cross-legged on top of the wall.

"Ah!" Aunt Toby said, nodding her head. "It's an oak." She looked at Daisy knowingly. "They're pretty magical." She shrugged. "Not surprising."

What other grown-up would say that? Daisy thought. *Aunt Toby is the kind of adult Ruby would have grown up to be.*

Thinking about that made her feel a little dizzy.

"Have you climbed back in, to see if it's still there?"

"If what's still there?" Daisy asked.

"The fairy," Aunt Toby said. "Don't you want to see it again?"

Did she? She wasn't sure anymore that what she and Ruby had seen really was a fairy. Did she want to see it again? Would it make it better or worse if she saw it again?

"I don't know," Daisy said. She cleared her throat. "I haven't climbed back in." Aunt Toby nodded. "I've only been back in the preserve once, with Avery." Aunt Toby didn't say anything. "It's kind of hard to climb over the tree and stuff," Daisy said.

They were both quiet. They sat, looking out at the Long Island Sound, at the shadows and patterns the clouds made on the water, as they moved in front of the sun.

Aunt Toby said, "Let's say a prayer." She looked at Daisy. "Want to?"

"A prayer to the fairies?" Daisy asked, thinking Aunt Toby meant some kind of hippie yoga thing.

"I don't ever know who a prayer is *to*," Aunt Toby said. "But I know that I like to reach out and see what I can connect with in the Universe."

Daisy pulled her feet up and sat cross-legged atop the wall like Aunt Toby. "Okay," she said. "I can try that." If anyone else had suggested saying a prayer to "the Universe," Daisy would have rolled her eyes. But when Aunt Toby said stuff like that, somehow it was different.

Aunt Toby put the flowers down. She adjusted her legs, placed her hands on her knees, closed her eyes, and took a deep breath in, which made her back draw up straighter. Daisy kept her eyes open, watching her aunt, but sat up straighter too. If there was one thing she could count on, it was that she never knew what to expect from Aunt Toby.

Aunt Toby tilted her face back, letting the sun shine down on it, and with eyes still closed she began to sing, "Mi shebeirach avoteinu, m'kor hab'racha l'imoteunu . . ." Daisy's eyes filled with tears. For sure, that wasn't what she'd expected. Aunt Toby was singing the prayer for healing. "Mi Shebeirach." Aunt Toby continued, "May the source of strength, Who blessed the ones before us . . ."

Aunt Toby's voice reached out over the Sound.

"Help us find the courage to make our lives a blessing . . ."

Aunt Toby sang, "And let us say . . . ," and Daisy joined in, singing, "Amen."

Aunt Toby took another deep inhale and a long, drawn-out exhale. Daisy swiped at the tears running down her cheeks with the backs of her hands.

The prayer floated out into the crisp air, was lifted up onto the breeze, whirled around them, and spread out over the trees on both sides of the fence, over their yard and across Dower Nature Preserve. The prayer danced among the tree branches, settled down into autumn's fallen leaves in the underbrush on the ground, and dusted the wall on which they sat, shimmering.

Daisy sat silent and motionless. With her eyes still closed, Aunt Toby said to Daisy, "Let's sing the second part, honeypot. Take a deep yoga breath in, and let's do it together." Daisy didn't reply. Aunt Toby said, "I know you know the words."

Daisy drew a deep breath into her lungs. When she inhaled, it felt clean—sparkly—like the cool air itself was full of energy, or spirit, or magic. Aunt Toby began singing again, and Daisy let her eyes softly flutter closed and joined her.

"Mi shebeirach imoteinu, m'kor habrachah l'avo-teinu . . ." Aunt Toby's singing was kind of off-key, and Daisy's voice cracked when she sang. The breeze danced across her closed eyelids. "Bless those in need of healing with r'fuah sh'leimah," they sang. The breeze ruffled Daisy's curls, lightly kissing her forehead. "The renewal of body," they sang. "The renewal of spirit . . . and let us say, 'Amen,'" they finished.

When they were done singing, something shifted, and a stronger gust of wind blew in off the Long Island Sound, rustling through the trees around them and into the preserve. Daisy listened, eyes still closed, and the *shush shush shush* of it surrounded her like a hug.

She felt like she'd been scrubbed clean inside. Had the prayer done that?

Aunt Toby put her hand on Daisy's knee and said, "It's okay to feel sad and still see the magic in the world, honeypot."

Daisy opened her eyes and looked out over the water. She didn't know if she'd be able to see magic in the world again. She didn't know if she'd ever see the fairy or whatever it was either. But she knew one thing she could do. She could climb over that tree and at least look for it. Even if this time she was alone.

Magic, No Rules

Aunt Toby kissed her on the head, took the bouquet of flowers they'd picked, and went back to the house. Daisy looked across the top of the stone wall, her gaze stopping where the branches of the tree rested on it, and past that to the crushed fence beyond. The leaves had all dropped, and the branches were now bare. The tree had settled. Even though it was windy, it looked firmly set in place now.

She still wasn't sure if she was allowed to go in there by herself. She'd never told her parents that she and Ruby had gone in there without a grown-up. But she doubted she'd get in trouble about it now. A lot of the rules were different now that she was in middle school.

Her parents acted different with her ever since Ruby died too. And since Dahlia had been born. They were more—she tried to think of the word—was it "gentle"? Not that they'd ever been harsh or anything. But sometimes she really needed gentleness.

Daisy stood up on top of the wall and looked out over the water again. It was so beautiful and sparkly. She heard a high-pitched chirping, looked up, and saw the osprey. The large bird looked suspended in midair as it rode a thermal above her. She hadn't seen the bird since the day she and Ruby saw the fairy. Which wasn't surprising. She hadn't been able to bring herself to come down here since then. If she had, she was pretty sure she would have seen it. Its nest was probably nearby. And yet, she couldn't help feeling like it was a good-luck sign, like what she was going to do was just the right thing.

She inhaled another deep breath of the crisp air and decided—the time was now. She walked across the top of the wall and barely felt afraid. She wiggled her body between the empty branches of the fallen tree, reached up, grabbed a big branch, and started climbing toward the trunk. The knuckle of her middle finger scraped against the bark. She stuck her finger in her mouth for a second, then looked at it. It wasn't bleeding. The wind blew her curly hair into her face. She didn't have a ponytail holder, so she just shook it out of her eyes and kept climbing. She pulled herself up onto the trunk, first on her belly, and then sitting up. There was nobody saying, *Are you okay?* There was nobody telling her she could do it.

But she *was* okay. And she was *doing* it. She stood up, holding on to one of the bare branches until she got her balance. Then she just let go and started to walk. It wasn't as hard as she remembered. It wasn't even that far. Just a few steps, really. She got to the fence and stopped. The sad had come back.

Saying the prayer had made a difference for a minute. That was the thing that had gotten her up and moving and climbing the tree. Because here she was! She stepped into the preserve, her fingers tightly gripping the fence one last time before letting go, as she inched her way across the trunk. When she got to the part where she should jump, she just did it. She landed in the soft bed of fallen leaves—brown and gold and scarlet—and even though it had been easy, her heart was thumping hard in her chest.

She looked at the top side of the fallen tree's root system, where it looked like a piece of the ground had tipped up and was still holding the tree. A lot of the soil had crumbled away from the roots now, and she couldn't tell where the window had been, where they'd looked through from the other side when they saw the fairy. She walked around to the underside and looked again. There were more holes now where the dirt was missing, any one of which might have been a magic window.

The breeze picked up, and a few leaves that had been clinging to the bare branches of the tree above fluttered down to join their colleagues on the forest floor. A beam of sunshine shone through the spaces between the lace of the roots, and dust motes sparkled. But that was it. They were just sparkly dust motes. She didn't see anything extraordinary fluttering on the other side.

Turning, Daisy meandered through the trees, leaves crunching underfoot, until she got to a path and a wooden park bench. It was broken. The slats had rotted away in spots, and one of the arms had a big crack in it. Daisy sat down on the one small spot that wasn't about to fall apart, remembering a time before she and Ruby had sneaked into the woods, before the tree had fallen and invited them into the preserve.

Ruby had always said there was going to be something magical in the woods. She just knew it. Was that why they'd seen the fairy?

"Magic is everywhere in nature," Ruby had said. "I'm sure we'll find something, if we can just sneak in."

But Daisy hadn't just wanted to *find* something. She had wanted to *know* magic was real.

"*Evidence* of magic and *proof* of magic are two very different things," Daisy had said as she'd considered it. "Evidence would mean a possible *sign* of something magical. Proof would be *confirmation* that it really exists."

Ruby had looked at Daisy like she was nuts. "Proof? Evidence?" Then Ruby had laughed a huge laugh, her head thrown back, her arms outstretched. Daisy remembered it exactly. It was such a Ruby move. "But it's *magic*, Daisy!" she'd said with a big smile on her face.

As they'd walked past the play set in Daisy's yard that day, Ruby had given the swing a big push, then spun away as it swung back toward her. For a second Daisy had thought Ruby was dancing with the swing, until she'd skipped away onto the grass.

So, as always, Daisy had skipped to catch up to Ruby. They'd walked side by side for a moment, and then, as if by silent agreement, they'd broken into a run. That's how it always was with Ruby. They didn't even need to talk; they just knew what the other was thinking.

"You're probably right," Daisy had said, catching her breath when they stopped running. "I bet the rules about finding evidence of magical things are different than when you try to prove nonmagical things." She gave a little nod to herself and hitched at her backpack straps as she thought about it.

"Oh definitely," Ruby had said, pulling a pretend-serious face. "There must always be *very* specific rules. . . ."

"Come on," Daisy had said, "you know what I mean." Ruby's teasing was like that—kindhearted, never hurtful.

Ruby had leaned into Daisy then. "Magic!" she'd sang out. "No rules!" She'd wiggled her fingers at Daisy, and they'd both laughed.

Thinking about it now, sitting on the broken bench, Daisy missed Ruby so much. The air smelled like autumn, like decaying leaves and overripe apples. "Magic! No rules!" she whispered to herself, wiggling her fingers. And then she saw somebody walking up the path toward her. Her face got hot, and she started to blush. She really, really, really hoped they hadn't seen her wiggling her fingers and talking to herself.

It was a lady and a little girl, and the little girl was crying, tears making streaks down her plump cheeks. The woman looked distressed, her forehead wrinkled and tense. "Excuse me," she said to Daisy. The little girl swiped at her cheek with one hand, holding tight to the lady's hand with her other. "Can you tell us how to get back to the entrance, where the parking lot is?" The little girl squished herself against the lady's leg and inhaled a deep, shuddery breath, trying to stop crying. "There aren't signs anywhere."

"Just go back the way you came," Daisy said, pointing. "Then when the path splits, go left, and the parking lot is just past the bend."

The lady picked up the little girl and hugged her. "See, Chloe, we weren't really lost. We just missed the fork." She looked over at Daisy. "Thanks," she said, the worry gone from her face, replaced with a mischievous gleam in her eyes. "I read Chloe too many fairy tales about getting lost in the woods, so when we got spun around, she started to get really scared." The lady hiked Chloe up on her hip. "Didn't you, Chloe?"

The little girl nodded.

"There's nothing worse than feeling lost," the lady said, pulling the little girl into another hug and giving her a kiss on the cheek. Daisy couldn't tell if she was talking to the little girl or to her, so she just nodded. The lady put the little girl down and took her hand, and they walked back the way they'd come. The lady playfully kicked at some fallen leaves on the path and shouted back, "Thanks!" Then the little girl laughed, gave a quick look back over her shoulder at Daisy, and kicked at the leaves just like the lady had.

There are a lot of ways to feel lost, Daisy thought as she picked her feet up onto the bench, arms around her knees. She leaned back, gently testing to make sure the back of the bench wasn't rotted through. She wished she could find her way out of the lost feeling she carried around all the time just by asking someone which way to go, and then going that way. It wasn't that easy, though. Aunt Toby tried to lead her sometimes. Avery did too. But walking your way out of a maze of grief is different from finding your way out of the woods. When you get lost on a path in the woods, all you need to do is ask someone or follow a park sign.

Daisy gazed down the path where the lady and the little girl had gone. Dower Nature Preserve didn't have any signs on the paths to guide people. An idea started fluttering around in her head. And that's when Daisy figured out what she wanted her tikkun olam project to be.

Carpe Diem

After that first time climbing over the tree bridge by herself, Daisy had gotten good at it. It was pretty easy now. She was a few inches taller than she'd been five months ago, when she and Ruby had sneaked into the preserve. The first few times after that, when she'd done it alone, she'd been tentative, but she'd heard Ruby's voice in her head saying, *Outlook Good!* After a while, though, she didn't need the memory of Ruby's encouragement to get up and over the fence. She just did it without thinking.

She made her way over to the pond, where there was a wooden deck that jutted out over the water. It was chilly out. She reached the pond, and there was a breeze.

With a gloved hand she pulled the zipper of her jacket all the way up to cover the small bit of her neck that was unprotected. Mo was sitting on the edge of the deck, with his legs dangling over the water and his chin on his arms, which were folded on the bottom rail. He slowly kicked his feet back and forth. As always, he was wearing his Vans.

Daisy sat next to him. He reached into his pocket and pulled out two apples. Every time they met at the pond now, he brought fruit.

"What kind?" she asked.

"Honeycrisp," he said.

"My favorite," she answered.

"I like these too," he said. "But there are these ones called Mutsu that we used to pick at an orchard near my old house." He took a bite of his apple and chewed. "They were so good," he said. "Kind of sweet but also tart. My dad can't find them at the supermarket here."

They sat quietly together, eating their apples, Mo slowly kicking his feet back and forth.

Daisy bit off a piece of her apple and dropped it in the pond. Three enormous fish swam up to eat it, breaking the surface of the water as they fought to get to it first.

"Carp," Mo said.

"I know," Daisy said. "I came here once with

my dad when I was little, and he told me how his great-grandmother used to buy a live carp and keep it in the bathtub until it was time to make gefilte fish for Passover."

Mo laughed.

Daisy shook her head. "You can laugh, but I can't eat gefilte fish because of that," Daisy said, smiling.

"I think a lot of people don't eat gefilte fish," he said.

"Well, definitely nobody not Jewish," she said.

"Yep," he said. "Same with chopped liver."

"I love chopped liver," Daisy said. She took another bite of her apple.

"Me too."

"So, what did you decide about your tikkun olam project?" she said.

"I don't know," Mo said. "Mr. Rosen said I can make either a bat house or an owl box, and I don't know which one to do."

"Okay, so think it out logically," she said.

"Well, they're both woodworking projects," Mo said. "And my dad can help me with either one of them."

"All right."

"And bats are pretty cool. But owls are kind of awesome."

"So are there pros and cons to each of them?"

"Yeah," he said. "But the pros and cons balance out. It's not helping me decide."

He took another bite of his apple, and neither of them said anything. Daisy always appreciated being able to sit quietly with other people. She liked talking, but she also didn't mind not talking. Not everyone was comfortable with silence. Aunt Toby was the best at sitting quietly together. Probably a yoga thing. But Ruby had been good at it too. Maybe because they'd known each other since they were little. Avery was surprisingly good at companionable quiet, given she could be such a chatterbox. And being with Mo was just easy, so even though she was thinking about it now, she barely ever thought about it usually when they were quiet together. It was just comfortable.

Daisy took another bite of her apple, which was almost down to the core.

"I know," Mo said. "We can toss our apple cores into the pond, and if mine goes farther, I'll make an owl box, and if yours goes farther, I'll make a bat house."

"You want to decide by having a littering contest?"

"It's not littering. Apples are organic and break down," Mo said. "We're adding to the ecosystem." He smiled at her.

"Okay," Daisy said, taking one last nibble of the apple. "Not really based on logic, but fun!"

They stood up and looked out over the pond. It was sunny, and the light sparkled on the surface of the water. The leaves on the trees were still red and gold and brown, with the evergreens providing contrast.

"I'm not a very good throw," Daisy said.

"Me neither," Mo said. "If it were a soccer ball, it would be a whole different thing."

He took one last bite of his apple.

"Ready?" he said.

She nodded.

"One, two, three!" he said. They both threw their apple cores into the pond. Daisy's arced high and fell into the water with a plunking sound, and the carp went crazy. Mo's hadn't gone as high but went just a tiny bit farther, plopping into the water, attracting a couple more of the big fish.

"Owl box!" Daisy said.

"Whoa!" Mo said, pointing. "Look how big that carp is!"

"Lots and lots of gefilte in there!" Daisy said, laughing.

Mo smiled.

"What about yours?" he said. "What did you decide to do?"

"I hope it's okay with you," she said. "My project is for the preserve too."

"Of course it's okay," Mo said. "I like that the preserve is something we're both connected to."

So Daisy told him about meeting the lady and the little girl who were spun around. And how the lady had said there weren't any signs in the preserve, which gave her the idea for the project. And that it would be *really* in her own community, since the preserve was basically her backyard. Almost.

They were walking on a trail that went from the pond over to a group of wooden Adirondack chairs in a clearing, in the direction of the main entrance to the preserve, down near Mo's house.

"I emailed Mr. Rosen," Daisy said. "He said the board of trustees liked the idea. They had been wanting to do something like that for a while."

"Cool," Mo said.

They sat next to each other on a double bench that was like two Adirondack chairs stuck together.

"And," Daisy said, "they want me to be as creative as I can be."

"What's that mean?" Mo said. "Like, if you want a sign to say, 'Quickest Way to the Bathroom,' it would be okay?"

"Mr. Rosen said as long as I wasn't rude about anything, I could have the signs say whatever I want."

"Mr. Rosen's the best," Mo said, shaking his head in appreciation.

"Yeah, the board of trustees said putting in regular signs—like 'This Way to Exit' and stuff—wouldn't be as interesting as putting in creative ones."

"What kind of signs are you thinking about?"

"Like, maybe one pointing to the pond that says, 'This Way to Gefilte Fish,'" Daisy said, holding back a smile.

"Really?" Mo said.

"Nah," Daisy answered. "Not enough Jewish people around here. They wouldn't get it. But stuff *like* that."

"So, all you have to do is think up creative signs for your whole tikkun olam project?" Mo said. "I don't think Morah Jill is going to approve that."

"No," she said. "I'm also going to raise money to donate to Dower Nature Preserve."

"I want to raise money for the preserve too," Mo said. "We should work together."

"Do you think we'd be allowed?" Daisy asked.

"Signs point to yes!" Mo said.

"What?" Daisy said, furrowing her eyebrows.

"Magic 8 Ball," Mo said. "It's one of the answers in the Magic 8 Ball."

"Yeah, I know," Daisy said. "What made you say that, though?"

"I don't know," Mo said, shrugging. "Don't you have a Magic 8 Ball?"

"No," she said. "My . . . My friend did, though."

"Oh, sorry," Mo said. "I didn't mean to . . ."

"No, it's okay," Daisy said. "You didn't know."

They got up and walked together in silence until they reached the split in the path where you could turn to go toward Mo's house, or back to the tree bridge and Daisy's house, or toward the gazebo and Avery's house.

"If you put a sign here," Mo said, "what would it say?"

"I don't know," Daisy said, thinking.

"Maybe something like Narnia, Neverland, and Middle Earth?" Mo said. "But only if I get Middle Earth."

Daisy laughed. "I don't know . . . ," she said again.

"Which one do you think Avery would like?" Mo said.

"I think Avery would like inventing things in Tony Stark's lab or designing tech with Shuri in Wakanda."

"Man, you're all Marvel, all the time," Mo said.

She smiled and shrugged. "It is a good place for a sign," she said. "But I'll have to think about what it might say."

Mo smiled back, made finger guns at her, and said, "Concentrate and ask again!"

"Okay, MO-gic 8 Ball!" Daisy replied, shaking her head, giving him a wave, and starting down the path toward her house.

Mo waved back and began the walk to his own house. "See you tomorrow at school!"

"Byeeee!" Daisy said, heading off.

It was weird that Mo could quote the Magic 8 Ball like Ruby used to. What were the chances of that? She didn't want to think about it too much, though, or she might start believing in Mo's bashert, and that made her feel uncomfortable. It gave her a squidgy feeling in her stomach. She walked down the path with her hands in her pockets, as it was getting chillier. It felt good to hang out with somebody who was goofy in that same way Ruby was.

She knew Ruby would have liked Mo, which made her happy, because knowing that felt like it was okay to be friends with him. But it also made her sad, because obviously Ruby would never meet him. Would she even have become friends with Mo if Ruby were still here? She sighed and kept walking toward home. There was no way to know. If she had a Magic 8 Ball to ask, it would probably say *Reply Hazy, Try Again,* even if she wished it were a *Yes—Definitely.*

Mappa

*D*ahlia was crying in her car seat as Daisy and Aunt Toby pulled into the preserve parking lot. It was weird now, to drive to the other side of town to get to the entrance when she knew she could just climb the fence to get in. But obviously she couldn't climb over the tree bridge with Aunt Toby and Dahlia. Daisy sat next to the crying baby in the back seat, whispering, "Shh shh shh, we're almost there," trying to be soothing but wishing Dahlia would just stop. And Dahlia wasn't just being a little fussy; she was really screaming.

She wasn't old enough that her crying sounded like crying, though. It was frantic and desperate and high pitched, more like a screeching cat than a human baby.

Daisy bounced Dahlia's foot and smoothed a finger across her cheek, which was red and hot from all her wailing. Aunt Toby had wanted to take Dahlia and Daisy for a walk in the woods before it got too cold to walk with a baby. But Dahlia wasn't great in the car seat. It was annoying. She'd only ever settle if someone was holding her.

Aunt Toby slid the baby sling over her head. It looked like a scarf, dark purple and bright yellow, with stars and moons and planets scattered across the fabric. She adjusted the part that went over her shoulder and unfolded the part that draped across her body. Daisy expertly unbuckled the car seat so Aunt Toby could scoop the squishy baby up. Between the two of them they maneuvered sad, screaming Dahlia into the pleats of the fabric. She fit into the folds comfortably and immediately snuggled up against Aunt Toby's body. She nuzzled her face back and forth against Aunt Toby's breast. "Nothing for you there, babycakes. Your mama just nursed you," Aunt Toby said. They started walking across the parking lot. Dahlia quickly settled down.

Daisy loved going to the wildlife sanctuary at the preserve. There aren't so many wild animals in Long Island; an occasional possum or fox would need help before being returned to the wild. Mostly what got rescued were birds. Owls and hawks and sometimes an eagle. Occasionally a seagull or other waterbird. A lot of the rescued birds couldn't be released back to the wild, for one reason or another, so they lived in outdoor aviaries, which were large screened-in sheds.

They crossed the parking lot, and Daisy said, "See, there could be a sign right here in the parking lot, pointing to the rescue center and saying something like which way to the gazebo, which way to the pond."

"Agreed," Aunt Toby said. "And signs for which way to all the magical places!" She laughed her windchime laugh, the breeze carrying it tinkling through the crisp autumn air.

Daisy couldn't tell if Aunt Toby was kidding or not. She thought, *If it was only as easy as following a sign to find magic.*

Then Aunt Toby said, "Although I think the magical signs are already there, and you just have to know how to look for them." Daisy felt the hollowness in her chest. Maybe Aunt Toby was right, even though she was kidding. Maybe Daisy just didn't know how to look for magic in the right way anymore, and that's why she never saw the fairy again.

"Mo and I are putting a donation box near the entrance, and another one near the animal rescue, so we can do the donation part of our tikkun olam projects too," Daisy said. They walked over to the aviaries, first passing one that housed hawks. Aunt Toby wanted to see a specific bird that she'd read about in the *Roosevelt Cove Herald*—a peregrine falcon that had been injured and rehabilitated and was being released back to the wild the following week. Gravel and leaves crunched under their feet as they walked the winding path between the cages.

They passed a barn owl hiding up in the rafters of its aviary. It made Daisy think about Mo's tikkun olam project. He'd told her he was researching how to make owl boxes and was hoping to attract barred owls. Aunt Toby grabbed Daisy's hand and swung it back and forth. "I remember when you were as little as Dilly Dally here," she said, gently patting the sling with her other hand.

"Weird," Daisy said. "I wish I could remember being a baby."

They passed a big black crow that let out a *caw!* as they went by.

"Caw to you, too, mister!" Daisy said.

"What's your earliest memory?" Aunt Toby said.

"I don't know." Daisy thought for a minute. "There was this time I got lost at a museum. I don't know how old I was. I was pretty little. Maybe around four?"

"What do you remember?"

Daisy's mom had taken her into the city for a special mommy-daughter day at the museum. She remembered sculptures and drawings and some cool carpets that an artist had designed, which had been laid out on the floor like paintings. She'd thought that was funny. And there were lots of maps. What she remembered in particular was a gigantic, colorful embroidered map of the whole world. Her mom was trying to get as near as she could, to look closer at the individual countries. But Daisy was ready to get to the part of their visit that included eating ice cream, so she'd gone and sat on a bench in the corner of the gallery, to wait until Mom was done looking.

She had a full view of the biggest map, and it was huge! It took up a whole wall. Her mom had told her it was called *Mappa*. Daisy remembered saying that *Mappa* wasn't a very creative name for a map, and Mom had laughed. She remembered sitting on the bench and thinking it was pretty, though. Each country was filled in by the color and pattern of its flag. Red, white, and blue stars and stripes for the United States. Red and white with a maple leaf for Canada. Green, white, and red for Mexico. Africa was big and made up of so many different flags, with lots of reds, yellows, and greens. And there were words all around the border. Daisy had started picking out the letters that she knew. *D* for Daisy. *R* for

Rubens. *A*, the first letter of the alphabet. But when she stopped looking at *Mappa* and looked around, her mom was gone.

She remembered her heart beating like it was going to burst out of her chest, the thump of it pulsing in her ears. She remembered how it had started to get black around the edges of her vision when she couldn't see her mom anywhere.

Then out of nowhere Mom had plopped down next to her on the bench. "I went to ask why Israel isn't on that map," she'd said. Daisy looked up at her and burst into tears.

"What's wrong, lovie?" Mom had asked as she'd enfolded Daisy in a big, tight hug.

"I was looking at the *Mappa* of the world, but then I got lost," Daisy had said through hiccups and sobs

"You weren't lost," Mom had said. "I could see you the whole time." She'd hugged her tighter. "I was right over there, asking the lady about the map," she'd said, pointing to a museum guide standing in the back corner.

"But I couldn't find you," Daisy had said as tears slid down her face.

"That must have been scary," Mom had said. Daisy remembered that they'd sat there for a few more minutes, looking at the big, beautiful embroidered map of the world together. And then they'd gone out for ice cream.

"Mom said that even though I thought I'd lost her, she'd never lost me," Daisy said to Aunt Toby.

"Yes," Aunt Toby said. "And you still have people who will never lose you, even when you feel lost."

Daisy leaned her head into Aunt Toby as they looked at the peregrine falcon together. Aunt Toby put her arm around Daisy's shoulder. The bird was cool, but it didn't look so different to them than the other hawks. It hopped up to a higher perch, away from them, out of view.

"Fine, be that way," Daisy said to it.

"Let's keep walking," Aunt Toby said.

They left the wildlife sanctuary and headed down a path through the trees. They kicked their way through the crunchy leaves, like they were the only ones in the whole preserve. When the sun peeked from behind a cloud and there was a sparkle overhead, Daisy looked hard at the branches, searching for a fairy, for something out of the ordinary, for anything slightly magical. But she didn't see anything.

They walked around the pond and stopped on the deck over the water to look down at the giant carp. Then they took the path into the woods. Aunt Toby sneezed. Dahlia made a squeak in the baby sling, then settled back to sleep. Daisy took two apples out of her hoodie pocket and handed one to Aunt Toby.

"Another sign should go here," Daisy said as they took the left path.

"Yep," Aunt Toby replied. They ate the apples and walked, not talking much. Aunt Toby took big, messy, random bites of her apple, and the juice dripped down her chin, leaving a tiny piece of apple skin flecked at the side of her mouth. Daisy took methodical bites, starting in one place and nibbling her way evenly around. When they were finished, though, the cores looked the same. They tossed them into the trees on the side of the path, and Daisy crossed her fingers that a squirrel or chipmunk would find them.

They took the right path when it split again, and Daisy said, "And another sign here, showing that the other way leads to the pond."

"Definitely," Aunt Toby said.

Daisy said, "What's *your* earliest memory? Do you remember being little?"

Aunt Toby said, "I don't know. I don't remember a specific thing. What I remember most from being little is your mom taking care of me. She was always there for me. I was super shy, and she was so much better at school than me, and she always had a lot of friends."

"It's funny to think that you were shy when you were little. Neither of you are shy now. And even though you're twins, you guys are so different from each other."

"Well, we share a lot of the same values, and we have some similar interests, but yeah, I think we're pretty different," Aunt Toby said.

"Mom acts like she's so much older than you," Daisy said.

"She is! She's two minutes older than me," Aunt Toby said, smiling.

"I know she's two minutes older, but that's not really *older* older."

"I'm immature," Aunt Toby said, and laughed. Dahlia burped in the sling, cried for a few seconds, and then went back to sleep.

"I'm eleven and a half years older than Dahlia," Daisy said. "I hope I can be there for her like you are for Mom. I'm going to be, like, grown up by the time she's my age."

"She'll be lucky to have you as a sister, no matter the age difference," Aunt Toby said. "It would have been nice if you could have been closer in age, but sometimes things don't work out the way we want them to."

"That's for sure," Daisy said.

Aunt Toby stopped walking, said, "Shhh . . . ,"

and pointed. Daisy's heart sped up, and she held her breath. *Was it a fairy?* But Aunt Toby was pointing to a brown rabbit about fifty yards in front of them. As soon as it spotted them, though, it darted into the leaves on the side of the path and hopped away.

Daisy let out her breath in a big sigh. "Sometimes I think about those times Mom was pregnant before, and how old one of those babies would be now if she hadn't had a miscarriage. And I wonder if they would have been a brother or a sister."

"Yeah, it's strange," said Aunt Toby. "But think . . . if any of those pregnancies had lasted, then you wouldn't have this little bundle," she said, stroking Dahlia's back through the fabric. One of Dahlia's little hands was clutching the hem of the sling, and Daisy noticed it was squarish, just like hers and Mom's and Mom's bubby's.

Daisy said, "Yeah, I'm glad we have *this* baby, *this* Dahlia. Here and now."

Aunt Toby said, "I'm so glad I came back to New York to be with you guys, to be here when Dahlia was born." Daisy nodded. She was really glad Aunt Toby was here too. "I've missed being here with you and your family these past few years," Aunt Toby said. "I don't think I realized how much, but . . ."

It felt like Aunt Toby was getting ready to say something, maybe that she was finally going back to Seattle.

"I've been thinking," Aunt Toby said, putting her hand on Daisy's shoulder as they walked. "I can't live in your guest room forever." Daisy got ready for it. It was going to stink having Aunt Toby on the other side of the country again. But Aunt Toby was looking at Dahlia and smiling, stroking her back through the sling as they walked. Then she squeezed Daisy's shoulder and looked over at her. "And I'm not going back to Seattle."

"Wait, what?" Daisy said. Her heart was racing. How could this be?

Daisy stopped walking.

"The Greenes have an apartment in Brooklyn that I'm going to rent," she said. "I'm moving in January."

"The rich couple from Southampton?" Daisy said. She was beaming.

Aunt Toby laughed. "Yes," she said. "Bill and Garry, the lovely people from Southampton, who also happen to be wealthy. And lucky for me, they have a beautiful apartment in Park Slope."

Brooklyn wasn't that far at all. Not as far as Seattle was.

"But what about your job? What about the spa?" Daisy said. This was the best news ever.

Aunt Toby said her business partner was going to buy her out of her share of the spa, and she knew enough people on the east coast to keep herself busy teaching private yoga. Brooklyn wouldn't be the same as Aunt Toby living in the guest bedroom next to hers. But the plan had always been to make that a room for Dahlia, once she wasn't sleeping in Mom and Dad's room.

Dahlia squeaked in the sling, and Aunt Toby shushed her. Daisy and Aunt Toby both started walking again. Daisy felt such a sense of relief. She hadn't realized how much she'd been dreading Aunt Toby leaving.

"How about putting a sign here?" Aunt Toby said, pointing to the next fork in the path. One direction, the way they'd just come, led back to the entrance, to the rescued birds, over near Mo's house. Another path led to the gazebo and the part of the preserve down near Avery's house. A third path led to the spot where she'd first seen magic with Ruby—to the tree bridge where they saw the fairy—and the way back to her backyard. If she were to put a sign here, what should it point to? What would it even say?

Plotting Signs

Avery had come to Daisy's house a few times now. She'd met Dahlia and Chewbacca. She'd tried Aunt Toby's turmeric lemon bars, and Mom had made them tea with mint from the garden. But this was different. Daisy wasn't sure she was ready to do *this* with Avery.

She looked up at the tree. All the leaves were completely gone now, and there was more than a little chill in the air. Daisy stood back, watching as Avery reached up and grabbed a branch. The tree was settled firmly on the top of the stone wall now and didn't even budge as Avery effortlessly pulled herself up to the first branch.

She climbed onto the next branch easily too, and then she was atop the trunk. She looked down at Daisy.

"Hand me the stakes."

Daisy handed up the cloth bag of stakes that they'd tied orange plastic flagging tape to. Mr. Rosen had told her to put a stake wherever she wanted a sign to go. She also had to decide what each of the signs was going to say.

"Come on!" Avery said. "Let's do this."

Daisy's heart was thumping in her chest. It was one thing to cross the tree bridge by herself. That wasn't a big deal at all anymore. But nobody else had ever gone over the tree bridge. She'd never gone into the preserve this way with anyone but Ruby. Avery had never climbed over the tree bridge, but it didn't seem to be a big deal to her at all. And Avery had no idea what the tree meant to Daisy. She didn't know that sneaking into the preserve with Ruby was the last best thing that Daisy had done with her. Avery still didn't even know that the girl that everyone in town knew had died at the beginning of the summer—Ruby Affini, who lived in Roosevelt Cove—had been Daisy's best friend. Avery didn't know because Daisy hadn't told her any of those things.

"Daisy!" Avery yelled, already over by the fence. "What are you doing?"

Daisy looked up at the tree bridge. Her throat tightened. "I'm coming," she said, her voice cracking a little. She sighed and pulled herself up to the top of the trunk and made her way over to the fence.

"You're being kind of ruminative," Avery said. "What are you so thinky about?"

"I'm not thinking anything," Daisy said.

Avery crossed into the preserve. "We're always thinking," she said. "Even when we try not to, we're thinking about not thinking. Which is still thinking."

Daisy didn't say anything.

"And you were definitely being ruminative," Avery said.

Daisy crossed into the preserve behind Avery but still didn't respond.

Avery jumped down, turned, and looked up at Daisy, who stood on top of the trunk. "Like now. You're thinking again."

And Daisy was. She was thinking that Ruby had been tiny, dark haired, olive skinned, and pixielike, like she'd come straight off the pages of a fairy tale. On the other hand, Avery was tall and blond and down-to-earth. So very real. Ruby was all about magic, and Avery was the most practical, scientific girl she knew. She was thinking that Ruby always knew what Daisy was feeling. She could tell just by looking at her. Avery was becoming a good friend, but she always had to ask.

"I was just—" She didn't know what to say. "Nothing. I was remembering coming here another time," she said. She jumped down, landing next to Avery. "Let's keep going."

Turning to look back at the underside of the roots, Avery said, "Wow. This is amazing!" She pointed. "Look, Daisy. It looks like lace!"

Daisy swallowed, trying to loosen the tightness in her throat. She turned to look with Avery, wishing with all her heart that *this* wouldn't be the moment she saw the fairy again. Because that would be awful. It would feel like she was betraying Ruby. She'd looked and looked every time she'd come here by herself. But of course there wasn't ever anything. If something magical did show up now, what would she do? It was so confusing, because when she and Avery looked and there wasn't anything there, as always, she still felt disappointed. She couldn't figure out how she could both want something to be there and not want something to be there at the same time.

"It's beautiful," Avery said. More of the soil had fallen away from the roots, and the dust motes sparkled and danced behind the lacy openings. "It looks magical."

Daisy didn't say anything. She wouldn't have

expected Avery to use that word. After a minute Daisy said, "Let's go put the stakes where we want the signs to go. Come on." She turned and started walking through the trees toward the path.

"Okay," Avery said, catching up to Daisy. "Hold the stakes. I'll get the list." Avery was the one who thought to make a list of all the possible places Daisy wanted the signs to go. Daisy had permission for no more than fifteen signs. They were going to scout them out together, to pick the best places to put them. Avery had designed a scale of one to five, to rate each spot. Daisy grabbed the sack with the stakes, and Avery started digging through her messenger bag as they walked. She pulled out two peeled carrots, stuck one in her mouth, handed one to Daisy, and kept rummaging. Daisy looked at the carrot.

"Found it!" Avery said, the carrot in her mouth. She pulled a crumpled paper out of the bag and took a bite of the carrot. "My mom told Melania I have to eat more vegetables." She rolled her eyes. They came to the path and stopped. "I'm trying to figure out where we are relative to my house." Avery looked left. "Is that the way toward the rescued birds?"

"Yeah," Daisy said. "But let's go the other way."

"So that way is toward my house, then?" Avery said.

"Sort of," Daisy said. "You kind of have to go that

way, and then there's a split where the trail toward your end of the preserve circles around and meets it."

"Okay, so where's the first spot you thought would be good, then?" Avery said, looking down at the list.

"There's a bench," Daisy said. "That's where I got the idea to put the signs up in the first place. Let's look there." She took a bite of her own carrot, and they walked together. Avery was chattering on and on about her spot-rating system, and the list, and whether Daisy wanted the signs to say practical things or poetic things or factual things, and what colors the signs would be painted so they were optimal for seeing in the dusk in various seasons.

Daisy stuck her free hand in her pocket, holding the bag of stakes with the other. Avery slipped her hand in her messenger bag again and pulled out a black wool beanie with a white chess piece embroidered on the front that said QUEEN under it. She pushed her hair away from her face and pulled the hat on. When they reached the bench, the girls squished together and sat on the part that was still intact, looking at the list Avery had written.

"I thought this would be a good spot," Daisy said. "We could have one arrow pointing toward the trail to the gazebo and one pointing the other way, to the front entrance and the birds."

"What would be printed on them?" Avery said, wiggling the loose arm of the bench back and forth.

"I haven't figured that part out yet," Daisy answered.

Avery rummaged in her messenger bag again, and this time she brought out two bags of popcorn.

"Mo's dad helped him make the donation boxes," Daisy said. "We put one near the birds and one near the entrance."

"Cool," Avery said. "Did anyone give money yet?"

"Yep, but not so much. I go to collect it and give it to Mr. Rosen once a week," Daisy said.

"So, for the rating system, you want to give this a five, right?"

"Okay," Daisy said. She wasn't sold on Avery's rating system. She wanted to just walk around the preserve and stick the stakes in where it felt like they made sense. She took a piece of popcorn out of the bag, nibbled off all the parts that were sticking out, then popped the rest in her mouth. Avery took one piece of popcorn out of the bag, tossed it in the air, and caught it in her mouth. She looked over at Daisy. Daisy nibbled another piece of popcorn, and Avery missed the second time she tried tossing a piece into her mouth. They heard footsteps crunching on the path, which glittered with a slight sparkle of frost. Two grown-ups were walking toward them. Daisy felt like she'd been punched in the stomach.

It was Maria and Leo Affini. Ruby's parents.

Avery Asks

Ruby's mom looked from Daisy to Avery and back to Daisy again. Then she reached out and took Leo's hand. They stopped walking. Daisy felt embarrassed, like she'd been caught doing something wrong. She stood up and took a step toward them. She felt so awkward. Was she supposed to introduce Avery? Would Maria and Leo think having a new friend meant she didn't miss Ruby anymore? That she wasn't sad anymore? That she didn't think about Ruby all the time anymore? That she'd somehow replaced Ruby with this tall blond girl in a goofy hat? She felt ashamed and self-conscious.

"Maria," she whispered. Ruby's mom came toward

her and wrapped her in a Maria Mom hug. Daisy sagged a little, leaning her cheek against Maria's shoulder.

"Oh, Daisy, sweetie," Maria said. Leo's hand awkwardly patted her back.

She was crying then—no, she was sobbing—erasing the past few months when her grief had settled down a little under her skin and hadn't constantly been boiling up and overflowing all the time.

"Are you all right, sweetie?" Maria said. She put Daisy at arm's length and looked at her. "It's okay, it's okay," she said. Daisy hiccupped as she tried to stop crying. "And who's . . . Who's your friend?" Maria asked.

"That's Avery," Daisy said, not looking at Avery. "I know her from school."

"Hi, Avery," Maria said. Maria's forehead wrinkled up. Avery looked at Daisy and then back at Maria.

"Hi," Avery said, frowning a little and sticking her hand out to shake Maria's hand.

Why does Avery want to shake Maria's hand? That is so weird.

Maria took Avery's hand and shook it. And then Leo did too. Daisy swallowed. She wished with all her heart that they hadn't come to the preserve today. Why, of all days to run into Ruby's parents, did it have to be today, with Avery?

"You were on the bench," Maria said.

"The bench?" Daisy said, turning around to look at the broken thing.

Maria said, "My father was a birder. He used to come here all the time. When he passed, we donated a bench in his memory. This was it."

"It's broken," Avery said.

Why did Avery have to point that out? Anybody can see it's broken.

Leo said, "Yes, we haven't been in here in a long time. We were coming to inspect it before—" He looked at Maria, who gave the tiniest shake of her head. Maria took Leo's hand again, and Daisy saw her squeeze it.

"We're having it replaced," Maria said. "The bench." She cleared her throat. "We were planning on calling your mom soon," Maria continued. "We wanted to come over to tell all of you our news in person."

Maria and Leo have news? What kind of news? Is it about Luca?

Maria pursed her lips. Avery came to stand beside Daisy. Leo put his hands in his pockets. It was getting cold out. Daisy swiped at her nose, which had started to run. The silence lasted a bit too long to just be a pause, stretching awkwardly out until Daisy couldn't stand it anymore and said, "What news?"

"Well," Maria said. She cleared her throat again and took Daisy's hands. "We've sold the house, sweetie," she said in a soft voice. "We're moving to California, to be near my family."

Daisy felt a little dizzy. She hadn't seen Maria since Ruby had died. She'd only seen Leo because he dropped a lasagna off when Dahlia was born. She never saw Luca, because he went to a Catholic school that was all boys. She knew her mom talked to Maria on the phone sometimes, but that was it. Even though she'd dreaded the thought of running into Maria or Leo or Luca, because it felt so painful, she never thought the Affinis wouldn't still be there, in Roosevelt Cove, in case she did want to see them. If they moved all the way to California, she wouldn't only be losing them, which felt horrible, but it would also feel like losing Ruby again. And another family would move into their house.

Somebody else would move into Ruby's *room*, where Daisy and Ruby had made pillow forts when they were little and had read books together. Where they'd cried when they were six because they'd found a dead baby rabbit in the yard. Just last year they'd laughed till tears ran down their faces when Daisy got stuck under the bed trying to reach the Magic 8 Ball when it rolled underneath. They'd been breaking Maria's no-food-in-the-bedrooms rule in that room since they were eight, always with pretzels. Some other person would live and sleep in that room, and it would be like Ruby had been totally erased.

Even though Daisy had never run into Maria or Leo or Luca at the library or the supermarket or the park or anywhere in the six months since Ruby had died, she might have. If they moved, though, then even the possibility of running into them would be gone. Like Ruby already was.

"But what about the beach house?" Daisy said in a small voice. She and Maria were still holding hands.

"Oh, I can't go back there," Maria quickly said, giving Daisy's hand a squeeze. Leo shook his head and pursed his lips. "All the joy of the Hamptons house was swept away last summer."

Daisy could understand that. But still.

She felt Avery standing next to her. It was like the energy of Avery was vibrating in anticipation. Like she was a big question, waiting to be asked.

"Oh," Daisy said. "When . . . When will you be leaving?"

Maria took a deep breath and held it for a moment, then said, "We'll be out of the house before Christmas. I just can't—"

Leo said, "We don't want to be here for Christmas. It would be too hard."

Before Christmas. That meant they were leaving in a few weeks.

"I've been meaning to call your mom," Maria said. "But maybe we can come by before then."

Daisy felt the pressure of tears building up behind her eyes. "Okay," she said.

Maria pulled her in for another hug. It was strong and solid, but it wasn't reassuring. Instead, it felt very final.

As the girls walked down the path, away from the bench, Avery said, "Who was that?" Daisy ignored the question, avoiding it like she did anytime Avery, or anyone, asked something that felt too painful to talk about.

"I don't want to do this anymore," Daisy said. "It's too cold, and we can put the stakes in another day."

"But why were you crying, Daisy?" Avery asked softly.

Daisy didn't say anything, and Avery sighed. The only sound was the *crunch crunch crunch* of the freezing leaves under their feet as they walked.

"You don't want to look at the other spots?" Avery said. "What about the chart I made?"

Daisy kept walking. "I don't want to rate the spots. I don't need the chart to pick." She knew she was being mean. She turned off the path into the woods, walking back toward the lacy root system of the fallen tree. She wiped her running nose with the palm of her hand, then wiped her palm on her jeans. Avery followed, the crumpled chart clutched in one hand. Her eyebrows were drawn together in a frown, her gray eyes were dark, and her lips held together in a straight line.

When they got to the fence, Daisy started climbing. She'd gone into the preserve by herself so many times now, it was easy to get back to her backyard without getting scraped up at the top of the fence. When she was three-quarters of the way up, she reached her foot out, grabbed a branch, and did a half jump to swing herself to the top of the trunk. Then she started to walk over the tree bridge, back to her yard. Avery stood at the bottom, watching Daisy go.

"I don't understand what happened," Avery called up to her.

"I just want to go home," Daisy said, not even looking at Avery.

"Who were those people?" Avery said. "Why are they moving? Why were you crying?"

Daisy was on top of the trunk and walking through

the fence to her backyard now. She didn't answer Avery, who was still standing down on the preserve side, looking up at her.

"Daisy!" Avery called to her but got no reply. Then Avery shoved the crumpled chart into her messenger bag and adjusted the bag to her back. She narrowed her eyes and shook her head. Then she turned around and made her way home back through the preserve.

Blowup

D o I have to go to school?" Daisy whined. "I've got a headache." She pushed the cereal bowl away and put her head down on her arms. Dahlia screeched in her bouncy seat, which was next to the kitchen table, banging with her tiny fists until Daisy looked down at her. Dahlia smiled a wet, toothless smile up at Daisy and screeched again. Daisy closed her eyes and put her head back down.

Across from her, Mom said, "Take an Advil," not even looking up as she sipped her coffee and scrolled through the news on her iPad.

"I can rub peppermint oil on your temples," Aunt

Toby offered, talking around a mouthful of granola and flipping through *Yoga Journal*.

"When's Dad getting home from Texas?" Daisy asked, not picking her head up or opening her eyes. Her eyebrows drew together, and she took her fist and pushed on her forehead.

"Friday. It will be the first night of Hanukkah," Mom answered. She finally looked up. "Do you want to invite your friend Avery over for latkes and donuts?"

Aunt Toby added, "We're going to fry up some sufganiyot!" She always pronounced the Hebrew word for "donuts" with an exclamation point.

"Try to fry," Mom said. "No guarantees they'll be edible." They both cracked up like that was the funniest thing in the world. Dahlia screeched a high-pitched guffaw in response. Daisy kept her head down on her arms. They were all so annoying.

"What are you giggling about, Dilly Dally?" Aunt Toby said in a talking-to-babies voice, getting up from the table.

Mom said, "Tobes, pour me more coffee, would you?"

Daisy's head throbbed a dull, aching throb around her skull, like a baseball cap of a headache. "Avery won't want to come over for Hanukkah. She's not even Jewish," Daisy said.

"You don't have to be Jewish to go to a friend's house and celebrate, Daisy," Mom said. "Since when do you think that?"

Mom didn't say anything about all the times Ruby had come for Hanukkah or Passover or even to the Purim carnival at synagogue, or all the Christmases and Easters Daisy had spent at Ruby's house. But Daisy knew that's what she meant. She picked up her head and ate a spoonful of cereal, chewing and chewing and chewing. She swallowed.

"I don't want Avery to come over," Daisy said. "We're not such good friends anyway."

Mom didn't say anything for a minute. The only sound was the *squeak squeak* of Dahlia in her bouncy seat.

Finally Mom said, "Daisy?" There was a pause, and Daisy didn't say anything. "Did something happen yesterday, sweetie?"

Daisy sighed. "I don't want to talk about it." Aunt Toby handed Mom her coffee and went to stand behind Daisy. Daisy smelled peppermint. "Close your eyes, honeypot," Aunt Toby said softly as she started to massage the peppermint oil into the sides of Daisy's head.

Daisy swallowed down the lump in her throat.

"You should really take an Advil, lovie. You'll feel better," Mom said. "You're not staying home just for a headache. You've got a math test on Wednesday; you can't miss the work."

Aunt Toby gently massaged her head, and the band of ache subsided a little. Dahlia let out an ear-piercing scream, and Mom laughed.

"Come here, my big girl," Daisy heard Mom say. And then the sound of her scooping the baby out of the bouncy seat. "I'm going to nurse her," Mom said to Aunt Toby. "Can you get Daisy to school?"

"Sure. I'll drop her off," Aunt Toby said. "I'm headed out anyway. Go deal with Dilly Dally."

Mom kissed the top of Daisy's head, and a wet baby hand reached out and touched her cheek. But she just kept her eyes closed and let Aunt Toby keep rubbing her head.

Daisy took her time getting ready for school, so when Aunt Toby dropped her off, it was close to the first bell. She didn't want to have to walk from her locker to Mr. Herman's first period with Avery. She didn't want to be a part of the smooth choreography of their avoiding-getting-run-over-by-Carlos routine. She didn't want to feel Avery holding back from asking her the same questions that Daisy hadn't answered yesterday, because she knew Daisy didn't want to talk about it. Or see the hurt look in Avery's eyes when she ignored her. Aunt Toby dropped Daisy off with just enough time for her to run straight to Mr. Herman's class. She slipped in the door as the bell started ringing.

As Mr. Herman went to pull the door closed, Mo squeezed past him at the very last minute, as usual. "Sorry! Sorry!" he said.

Mr. Herman rolled his eyes. "Take your seat, Mr. Hammonds."

She and Mo walked to their desks across the row from each other. She avoided catching Avery's eye as she sat in her usual spot right behind her.

As everybody chatted and got settled and Mr. Herman started writing a list of scientific terms on the whiteboard, she saw Avery sit up extra straight in front of her. She could feel Avery noticing that she'd avoided looking at her. She knew Avery wanted to turn around and talk to her. How could Daisy have allowed herself to become friends with Avery so quickly? How could she have let herself move on, move forward? It wasn't right. Her head started to throb again. She rubbed at her temples, and the smell of peppermint came off her skin like a whiff of candy cane or the feeling of walking in cold, clean snow.

She made it through the morning, and after fourth-period social studies she just stayed in Mr. Nelsen's class and ate her lunch there. He showed movies in his classroom during fifth period for anyone who didn't like eating in the cafeteria. She quietly ate her turkey sandwich in the dim room, rewatching *Avengers: Infinity War* as the Guardians of the Galaxy got their butts kicked by Thanos, the Avengers did all the wrong things, and Marvel heroes turned to dust on the screen in front of her.

At the end of the period she went to her locker to put her lunch bag away and get her books for the afternoon. Avery was at her own locker, putting her things in. "Why didn't you come to the cafeteria?" Avery said, looking at her. "I don't understand what's going on, Daisy. Did I do something wrong?" she continued, barely taking a breath. "I'm sorry I asked you about those people in the woods yesterday. I didn't know you'd get mad at me."

Daisy didn't say anything. She put her lunch bag into her locker and took out her English book. Lava was rising from her feet up through her body, up her legs, into her stomach, where it roiled and boiled, then into her chest, which was going to explode, until it came out of her mouth in a burst of anger.

"Those were my best friend's parents!" Daisy yelled. "My best friend, Ruby," she screamed at Avery. "My best friend who's gone," she said. Avery's mouth hung open. Daisy wanted to slap her.

At first nobody noticed Daisy yelling at Avery. Carlos was running down the hall from his locker to get to sixth period, of course. His backpack bumped into Daisy's shoulder, and for a moment she felt like shoving him into the wall. Stupid Carlos was in middle school and still couldn't learn how to walk down a hallway.

"I didn't—" Avery started to say.

"You didn't know?" Daisy yelled at her, the tears welling up in her eyes. "Haven't you heard everybody's stupid pitying whispers all year?"

"But—" Avery tried to cut in.

"But nothing!" Daisy shouted. "You can't be my friend. I don't want any friends, Avery!" Daisy swallowed. "Don't you understand?"

"I thought—" Avery said.

"You don't!" Daisy said. "You don't think. You just talk and talk and talk. You are so stupid, you don't understand."

Now Avery looked like Daisy had actually slapped her.

Daisy heard somebody say, "Hey, hey, hey! You don't want to do that."

Avery clutched her backpack to her chest, her arms wrapped tightly around it. Her face was all pink now, and her light gray eyes had turned slate colored, but Daisy could barely even see her through her rage. She felt a hand on her shoulder, and she shook it off, turning to see Mo standing there, wide eyed behind his glasses.

He said softly to her, "Don't do this, Daisy. You're not really mad at her." His eyebrows drew together. She looked at him—at his one crooked front tooth and his big black glasses and his Vans sneakers—and it was finally too much.

"You don't know me," she said, turning her anger toward Mo. "You think you're special or I'm special or some stupid thing from your grandmother or whatever." Her voice was getting louder, and kids were starting to stare. "I don't know what you think," she said. More kids were in the hall now, and a small cluster of them were watching her yelling at Mo. Avery stood behind him, as if he were shielding her.

"I'm sorry your mother has *cancer*," she shouted at him. "But going to Hebrew school doesn't cure cancer!" Mo looked like she'd punched him. She turned to Avery and shouted, "And I'm sorry your rich parents are *divorced*, but . . ." Avery flinched. "Divorce isn't such a big deal. My best friend in the world died, and I'm not ever going to see her again, and she's never going to get to grow up. *Dying* is the most terrible thing in the world that could happen, and it's forever."

Daisy never knew what forever would feel like until Ruby was gone. And she hated it.

"I hate forever! And I hate you for being here instead of Ruby!" she said, looking at Avery. "And I hate you, too!" she said, turning to Mo.

When she was done screaming, Daisy looked around. Some kids had stopped and were staring at her. Avery's face was blotchy and red now. Mo had turned almost gray. And he looked smaller somehow. Like the words Daisy had thrown at him had shrunk him.

She blinked. Had she just told everyone his mother had cancer? The other kids had moved on as the warning bell rang, and Daisy stood there near her locker. Had she just mocked Avery for being rich or sad about her parents' divorce? She was breathing so heavily, she thought she might pass out, still staring at Avery and Mo. She heard Avery say to Mo, "Let's go," as she clutched him by the elbow, and they walked away from her together down the hall.

Aunt Toby picked Daisy up from school early. The nurse told Aunt Toby Daisy's temperature was 103. When they got home, Daisy crawled into her bed and cried herself to sleep, with Chewbacca at her feet, watching over her.

Lavender and Chamomile

*D*aisy was resting on the couch. Her head felt like it was splitting open. Each and every muscle in her body hurt individually and uniquely. It was work just to lift her head and look out the window. Her throat was the Sahara Desert. Her tonsils were bouncy balls lodged in the back of her throat, not letting her even swallow her own spit. When she coughed, her bones rattled, setting off a cascade of achy, scratchy suffering.

Chewbacca jumped off the couch and started snuffling at the front door. Someone came in, but Daisy was too miserable to care or open her eyes. She tried to get more comfortable. She was cold and wanted to cuddle into the afghan, but she was hot and needed to throw it off. She didn't know what day it was or even how many days she'd been sick. They all ran into one another, like a movie montage of a girl sleeping on a couch, with warm beverages brought to her and empty cups taken away, tossing this way and that, her fever going up and down and up again.

She felt a cold kiss on her hot cheek and the soft stubble of her dad's face. "Hey there, Buddy-Girl," he said softly.

"Daddy," Daisy said. "You're home." She coughed a big wet cough, and the rattling in her chest felt like glass breaking.

"Wowza, Buddy-Girl," he said. "You sound pretty terrible."

"I am terrible," she said, and fell back asleep.

Aunt Toby rubbed Daisy's feet with lavender, chamomile, and lemon essential oils. "You up to lighting the Hanukkah candles, honeypot?" Aunt Toby asked.

Daisy coughed, frowned, and tried to swallow before croaking, "I guess."

Aunt Toby's strong hands continued massaging, and Daisy sighed and closed her eyes. When Aunt Toby started massaging her hands, the scent floated up to her nose and like magic ignored the fact that her sinuses were stuffed as they did their job of casting a calming spell over her. She fell back asleep.

She had been sick for almost two whole weeks. It went from a nasty strain of flu to an even nastier case of bronchitis.

Mom took Dahlia to Florida to meet Grandma and get away from all the germs. Daisy knew Dad had come back from his business trip sometime when she was still fighting the fever, but she wasn't exactly sure how many days he'd been home. Aunt Toby took care of her, bringing her endless cups of tea and bowls of chicken soup as Daisy slept on the couch. Chewbacca never left her. He was more attentive than Nana, the dog in *Peter Pan*. Aunt Toby rubbed her feet and head and hands with all the soothing oils and kept her company, knitting or reading in the easy chair. Even during the worst of it, Daisy knew her aunt was there, and that made it the tiniest bit better. By the last night of Hanukkah, she finally felt well enough to get up.

Aunt Toby put the candles in the menorah. Dad had made latkes and cinnamon applesauce. Mom videocalled from Grandma's apartment in Florida as they lit the menorah for Dahlia's first Hanukkah now that they were all finally together, even if it was virtual. Daisy was too exhausted to sing or light the other candles with the shammash candle. She watched the flickering lights of the Hanukkah candles dance, and she wound up the silver musical dreidel, which played a plinky, tinkly version of "Ma'oz Tzur."

Dad handed her a small box. "Happy Hanukkah, Buddy-Girl," he said. She tiredly ripped the blue-and-silver paper open. It was an iPhone. They'd finally gotten her a phone.

"Thanks, Dad," Daisy said weakly. She had nobody to call now. "I'm tired," she said. "I'm going to lie down."

Dad took the phone and plugged it in to charge. Daisy cuddled into the afghan, and Chewbacca took his spot curled behind her knees. She put on *The Great British Bake Off*. She'd seen this season so many times, it didn't matter if she fell asleep again in the middle of it.

At last she'd gotten a phone. She sadly thought again that Ruby never got a chance to have one, and that she would never get to call or text Ruby on hers. That was awful. If her mom and Maria hadn't made their dumb rule about not getting them phones until middle school, she and Ruby would have had that fun together. Nobody ever thought she wouldn't make it to middle school.

So who cared about getting a stupid phone now? Who would she call or text? She'd made such a mess of things; she wouldn't be surprised if Avery never spoke to her again. She'd been so mean to Avery. And she'd done the worst thing she could do to Mo. He'd come to her so trustingly, sure that they were destined—bashert—meant to be good friends. He'd only ever been kind to her, at Hebrew school and regular school. He'd asked one thing of her—to keep his mom's illness a secret—and she'd screamed it at the top of her lungs where everyone could hear.

I'm the worst, she thought.

When Dad came in to ask if she wanted some latkes, she was sleeping again, Chewie curled up behind her knees.

How to Survive

*D*aisy missed school for the whole week before winter vacation and was sick for almost the whole school break. She missed two weeks of Hebrew school. Just in time for school to start back up, she finally felt a little better. Well, at least better from the flu, not about the things she'd said to Avery and Mo.

Avery must have gotten to school early on their first day back because Daisy didn't see her near their lockers in the morning. When she got to Mr. Herman's class, he had switched all their seats after vacation. Daisy was still sitting up front, near the door. But Avery's seat was toward the back of the classroom, near the window. She was already there, writing in her notebook. She didn't look up, and Daisy couldn't catch her eye.

When the bell rang, as always, Mo came rushing into class, saying, "Sorry!"

Mr. Herman didn't seem irritated this time, though. He stopped Mo before he went to his seat. Among all the chatter of the class getting settled, Daisy heard Mr. Herman quietly say, "You doing all right, Mr. Hammonds?"

Mo gave a quick nod, looked down, and softly said, "She's not back home yet." Daisy closed her eyes, pushing her palms against her eyelids, making sure no tears had a chance to even start to form. When she opened them, Mo was at his new seat, which was near Avery on the window side of the classroom.

She tried to pay attention during class, but all she could think about was how horrible she had been to Avery and Mo before vacation. When the bell rang, she gathered up her books to put in her backpack. Mo and Avery walked out of the classroom side by side, heads together, talking. As they passed her desk, Mo looked over his shoulder at her, but she looked away, afraid to make eye contact. She was so ashamed. She was such a horrible person.

She made it through the rest of the morning without talking to anyone, eating lunch in Mr. Nelsen's classroom again. She nibbled on cookies and watched the beginning of *Ant-Man and the Wasp*. After lunch she went to French, art, PE, and math. In French, Amanda, who'd always been nice to her, tried to strike up a conversation before class started.

"I got a puppy for Christmas," Amanda said, holding out her phone to show Daisy a picture.

Daisy tried to look interested. "Cool," she said. "My dog's old, but he's still cute." She took out her new phone and showed Amanda some pictures of Chewbacca.

"Rangez vos téléphones," Madame Lecardonnel said. Daisy slipped her phone into her backpack and managed not to talk to anyone else the rest of the day.

She didn't see Avery near their lockers before heading outside. As she was waiting to get on the school bus, she saw Mo and Avery in the car-pool line together. They got into a Range Rover, with stone-faced Melania at the wheel. They were talking to each other, and Mo laughed. They didn't see Daisy watching them as the car pulled away from the school. Daisy sighed, got on her bus, and took the seat behind the bus driver, which nobody ever wanted. She stuck in her earbuds and listened to *The Girl Who Drank the Moon* for the third time, all the way home, thankful that her phone could at least give her an escape from everything that was going on around her.

Daisy was dreading Hebrew school and carpooling with Mo. What would she say to him? How could she ever apologize for what she'd done? He'd trusted her, and instead of being a friend, or even just a regular decent person, she'd violated his trust. Why would he even forgive her?

She heard Mr. Hammonds honk.

"Go learn cool Jewish things!" Dad said as she walked out the door. "I'll pick you up at the end." She rolled her eyes. *Cool Jewish things. Oh brother.* When she got to the car, Mo was sitting in the front seat, next to his dad. She got in the back, and they drove off. Mr. Hammonds was friendly, as always, but Mo didn't even turn around. When they pulled up in front of the synagogue, Daisy jumped out of the car.

"Thank you," she said to Mr. Hammonds, and then walked quickly up the path to the synagogue and straight into class. Mo took a seat near Jacob, Zach, and Dylan Roth, and Daisy heard the boys all talking about a skateboarding video or movie or something. She sat near Rachel and Hannah and was very glad they didn't have to break into pairs for anything.

Morah Jill said, "I hope everyone had a joyous

Hanukkah and a restful winter break!" Nobody said anything. "Before we hear updates about your tikkun olam projects, let's talk about Tu BiShvat, the birthday of the trees." Daisy looked over at Mo, who was raising his hand and talking at the same time.

"Excuse me, Morah Jill, can you spell the name of that holiday, please?" As Morah Jill spelled it out and explained what Tu BiShvat was, Mo wrote it all down in his notebook. After Hebrew school, when her dad came to pick them up, Daisy quickly glanced at Mo before getting in the front seat of the car. Mo didn't say anything the whole ride home except "thanks" to her dad when he got out.

"Everything okay, Buddy-Girl?" Dad asked as they pulled into the driveway at their house.

"Yep," was all Daisy responded.

And that's how it went the rest of January and through February, when she turned twelve. For her birthday her parents took her to a Broadway show, and then they got extra-fancy sushi in the city. By March she was used to eating lunch at school in Mr. Nelsen's room and watching movies. She sometimes made small talk with Amanda in Mr. Herman's class or in French. Sometimes she'd talk to one of the other horsey girls during social studies. She made sure to quickly pair off with Rachel or Hannah when they did paired sharing at Hebrew school.

Daisy had math tutoring on Wednesdays, and Aunt Toby came out to Long Island from Brooklyn on Mondays to teach a yoga class, so Daisy started doing yoga. Sometimes Daisy went to the JCC with her mom after school. They swam laps together while Dahlia stayed in the baby-care room. Her dad occasionally took her into Manhattan on the weekend, to the Museum of Natural History or the Central Park Zoo, just the two of them. And every couple of weeks the whole family went to visit Aunt Toby in Brooklyn. Daisy felt very grown up when she walked down a city street carrying Dahlia in the baby backpack.

Aunt Toby and her friend Caryn officially became girlfriends. Daisy liked hanging out with them. Caryn was a teacher, so she knew how to be with kids the same way Aunt Toby did, treating her like a regular human without talking down to her. If it was nice out, they'd go to Prospect Park or the Brooklyn Botanic Garden. Sometimes they went to Coney Island and walked on the boardwalk.

It's not so bad, not having any friends, Daisy would think, as long as she kept busy enough to get through each day.

And each day, as long as it wasn't too cold, raining, or snowing, she managed to go into Dower Nature Preserve for a little bit. She'd sit on the Affinis' new bench, with the small plaque that had Ruby's grandpa's name on the front of it. Sometimes she brought a book and read. Sometimes she just sat and thought. Sometimes—she couldn't help it—she cried.

Back in January she had seen Mo's owl box up in one of the trees not too far from the gazebo. And by early March she was pretty sure an owl was nesting in it. She didn't see a bird, but she could see some feathers near the hole in the box where the owl was supposed to go in. Daisy thought they could get more people to donate to the preserve if there was a way to make the donation electronically. Everyone carried their phones, but not everyone carried cash. So she put a small laminated sign on the post under the donation box, with info so people could Venmo if they wanted. They'd collected over six hundred dollars so far, with most of it coming from electronic donations. So even though Mo had made the pretty wooden donation boxes for the collecting-money part of their tikkun olam projects, she felt like she had done her part with her good idea. Mr. Rosen said when the ground wasn't so frozen, they could install her signs. She still didn't know what she wanted them to say, though.

Occasionally Daisy's mom nudged at her, trying to find out what had happened with Avery. Her dad nudged at her too, trying to find out what had changed with Mo, since carpool was a quiet, awkward affair now. Of course, since Aunt Toby never nudged, she was the one Daisy was willing to speak to about what had happened.

On the first day of spring Aunt Toby and Caryn were visiting for the weekend. "It's the vernal equinox, honey-pot," Aunt Toby said. "Let's go into the woods to welcome Persephone back to the land of the living." Daisy looked at Caryn. Caryn smiled and raised her eyebrows.

Daisy rolled her eyes. "Fine," she said. "Let's go."

Caryn said, "You guys go have special auntie time together. I'll stay here."

Aunt Toby was going to drive them around to the entrance like always, but Daisy said they could use the tree bridge, since they didn't have Dahlia with them. She showed Aunt Toby how to climb over the tree from her yard into the preserve. When they got to the other side, Daisy jumped down onto the soft forest floor, still covered with leaves. She looked up at Aunt Toby.

"You coming?" she asked.

"I am!" Aunt Toby said. "But first I'll do tree pose on a tree!"

Balancing on one foot, the other tucked near her

thigh making a triangle with her knee, and her hands in prayer position above her head, Aunt Toby stood for a moment atop the trunk of the fallen oak. Daisy gazed up at her. She looked like she was part of the forest. She watched as Aunt Toby took a deep breath, held it a second, and exhaled. Then the moment was over, the magical bubble burst. Aunt Toby jumped down next to her, grabbed her hand, and they walked.

The crunch of leaves under their feet was soothing. It had been a mild winter, hardly snowing at all. Daisy had spent a lot of time walking these paths by herself, sitting on the bench, visiting the rescue birds, going to the gazebo and the deck near the pond, and trying to figure out what her signs should say. She both feared and hoped she'd see Avery or Mo, or both of them, but she never did.

Now it was finally spring. The frost was just about off the ground, and there were buds on the trees, plants pushing their way out of the soil toward the sun. An intrepid crocus poked its face out of the ground at the side of the path, the bright purple of the flower an exclamation point of color among the brown and gray leaves. As they came up near the brook, they were greeted by the smell of skunk cabbages before they saw the bright green leaves forcefully insisting on springtime.

They skirted around a big spot of mud on the path to get to the bench. Daisy sat down, and Aunt Toby bent to look at the plaque on it, which read, IN LOVING MEMORY OF ANGELO VITALI, AVID BIRDER AND NATURALIST, LOVING FATHER AND GRANDFATHER.

"So guess what?" Daisy said. "I found out this bench was in memory of Ruby's grandpa."

"Angelo Vitali was Ruby's grandpa?"

"Yep," Daisy said. "He was Maria's father."

"Really?" Aunt Toby said. "That's cool."

"I guess. I found out right before the Affinis moved," Daisy said.

Aunt Toby didn't say anything.

"Ruby never told me about the bench; I don't even think she knew it was here." Daisy leaned her head back against the top slat and gazed at the branches above their heads, the bright blue of the sky in stark contrast to the dark leafless branches. Daisy saw purplish buds peeking out here and there. She continued, "When we were little, and Mom and Dad, or Ruby's parents, brought us into the preserve, we never came over this way. It's pretty far from the front entrance." She swallowed. "Ruby and I only ever came in here alone together that one time." Aunt Toby's hand found hers on the bench, and their fingers intertwined. "We never got a second chance." Aunt Toby gave Daisy's hand a small squeeze.

"About that," Aunt Toby said.

"What?" Daisy asked, looking at Aunt Toby.

"You don't always get a second chance," Aunt Toby said. "We should take them when we can."

How could she have a second chance if Ruby was gone?

"I don't understand," Daisy said.

"Well," Aunt Toby said, "you had sweet friendships growing with Avery and that boy, Mo." Aunt Toby looked at her, and Daisy looked away. "I don't know what broke there, or why, but I bet if you tried, you could mend it," she said. "I bet they'd give you a second chance." Daisy didn't say anything, and Aunt Toby let her be. "I think our lives are much richer when we have friends to share them with," she went on.

"I'm good," Daisy replied. "I can survive without friends."

"I'm sure you can," Aunt Toby said. They sat together on the bench with their heads tipped back, looking up through the branches at the sky. Then Aunt Toby said, "But, honeypot, I think maybe we're meant to thrive, not just survive."

Asking Forgiveness

As much as Daisy missed Ruby, a part of her heart was resigning itself to the permanence of that loss. It didn't mean it hurt less, or that she missed Ruby any less, but a semblance of acceptance was settling in. She worried that she might start to forget her. She wanted to remember all of Ruby, the awesome parts of her, how she was always there for Daisy, supporting her and never making her feel bad for being kind of a follower. She wanted to remember how funny Ruby was and how friendly she was and how she was always up for an adventure. She wanted to remember how she could tell Ruby anything, and Ruby never thought it was stupid. She wanted to remember all the fun times they'd had.

But she didn't want to forget that Ruby wasn't perfect. How sometimes Ruby wouldn't take no for an answer but kept pushing and insisting until she got her own way. Daisy usually ended up going along and doing something that turned out okay, but sometimes she had been left feeling like she hadn't had a choice in the matter. She didn't want to forget that sometimes Ruby would talk over her too, leaving her feeling unheard. To be honest, sometimes Ruby was a little bit too much. But those things were part of the whole Ruby. And Daisy really wanted to remember the real girl, not just an idea of her.

Missing her friendship with Avery, and even Mo, was different. Her emotions were so complicated. She hadn't been friends with either of them for very long before she'd ruined everything. And even though they had been new friends, their loss hurt. They'd both appeared in her life at just the moment that she'd needed them the most. She'd appreciated how easy her friendship with Avery had been. Even though Avery could talk up a storm, she was an eager listener, always asking Daisy her opinion. Sure, Avery was quirky in some ways, but she hadn't ever been *too much*. Daisy felt bad even thinking about that, about comparing her to Ruby in any way.

Ironically, Mo *was* too much, but in such a different way than Ruby had been. Daisy thought Ruby's too much had come from being kind of oblivious, like she was so wrapped up in her own thoughts and ideas and flights of fancy that sometimes Daisy's thoughts and feelings got lost. But Mo's too much felt like too much of an expectation on her to be his friend. He'd chosen her, and he'd forgotten that for them to be friends, she had to choose too. And it wasn't like she didn't want to choose friendship, because she did, but it really bothered her that he just assumed. Perhaps it was because they'd both been so sad when they first met. Him and his stupid bashert.

Now it looked like Avery and Mo had become good friends. She saw them together at school a lot. Maybe they were even boyfriend and girlfriend. She didn't know. More kids were doing that now, going out with each other. Boy crazy and girl crazy. She didn't want Mo to be her boyfriend or Avery to be her girlfriend. She still felt like she was nothing crazy, like Ruby had called it. But she was jealous of Avery and Mo's friendship nevertheless.

Daisy didn't know if she really could get a second chance with either Avery or Mo, like Aunt Toby thought she could. But she did want to thrive, not just survive. So, she knew she'd have to figure something out. She'd have to figure out how to make things right with them. She couldn't bear the idea of losing anyone else.

Daisy thought Avery might forgive her if she apologized just the right way. If she could explain that she'd been sick, that she'd spent the whole winter vacation in bed with a high fever, that she really valued their friendship. If she told Avery just how sorry she was, Avery might understand. She could apologize about being so mean and horrible. She would tell Avery how she hadn't meant any of the things that she'd said, because she really hadn't. Avery would get it.

She would tell Avery everything. About Ruby and how hard it had been since Ruby died. About how learning that the Affinis were moving had pushed her over the edge. She'd even tell Avery about the fairy. It was a very personal, private thing to share—something she'd only shared with Ruby and Aunt Toby. Avery might not believe in fairies, but by Daisy telling her, she'd see how important she'd become to Daisy. Avery was a kind person. She'd told Daisy she was there to listen whenever Daisy was ready to talk.

Avery had to forgive her.

It was such a relief once Daisy had decided. She'd

figure out how to apologize to Mo after. But first, she'd walk through the preserve to Avery's house, apologize, and tell her how much she missed being friends. That would be a start to fixing things.

It was the last day of spring vacation, the Monday after Easter, when she walked through the preserve with her thumbs hooked in her backpack straps. Although it wasn't a done deal yet, she had a high level of confidence—as Avery would probably say—that her mission would be successful. She'd baked mini devil's-food cupcakes with vanilla frosting, because those were Avery's favorite. She'd placed six of them in a box, with pale blue tissue paper between them so they didn't jiggle around, and toothpicks with plastic wrap on the top, so the frosting didn't smush. They were her peace offering. She hoped Avery still liked vanilla on devil's food cake best. She'd carefully put the box in her backpack, making sure the whole thing stayed right side up. The smell of chocolate wafted over her shoulder from her backpack as she walked the path toward the gazebo.

There were butterflies in her stomach when she got to the gate in the fence to Avery's yard. What if Avery wouldn't talk to her? What if she wasn't really as understanding as Daisy remembered, and she didn't accept Daisy's apology? Daisy thought about what Aunt Toby had said about second chances. If she didn't at least try to apologize, she'd never know if she could have a second chance with Avery. She took a deep breath, opened the gate, and made her way across Avery's yard.

As she walked up the steps to the patio, her heart pounded in her chest. This was harder than she'd thought it was going to be. The sun shone on the glass of the slider, and all she could see was her reflection. She looked very small. If Avery didn't answer the door, would Melania even remember who she was? She leaned in, out of the glare, to peek inside and see if anyone was even in the kitchen. She pulled her face away and took a step back. *What?*

She leaned in again and pushed her nose up against the glass, looking around as best she could. The kitchen was empty. Not just empty like there was nobody in there. It was empty like all the furniture was gone; the big shiny kitchen table with the beautiful floral centerpiece was gone. The walls were empty. No more pictures of Avery as a baby and a toddler and in elementary school. No more pictures of Avery's brother. No fancy television on the kitchen wall. No chandelier hanging from the ceiling of the foyer.

Daisy tried to push down the awful feeling that was rising up from her belly. Avery had told her they might have to sell the house and move because of her parents' divorce. And now she was gone. It had really happened. There would be no second chance. Daisy had screwed it up so badly, and now she'd never be able to make it right again. She didn't even have Avery's phone number so she could text her and find out where she'd moved and if she was okay. She sat down on the patio, her back to the slider, and wrapped her arms around her knees. The tears came, and with them racking sobs. Another friend lost, and this time it was her own fault.

Her phone vibrated. She caught her breath and slipped her hand into her hoodie pocket. The only people who ever called or texted were her parents and Aunt Toby. This was a shout of a text from Aunt Toby, who'd finally gotten a smartphone. The text said, I'M DRIVING YOU TO HEBREW SCHOOL BECAUSE YOUR CAR-POOL FRIEND WON'T BE GOING. I CALL SUSHI TUESDAY!

Won't be going? Like today, or anymore? Oh god, probably anymore! Daisy burst into tears again. Why wouldn't Mo be going to Hebrew school? It had been so important to him. He'd told her that. Even though Daisy hadn't thought going to Hebrew school or having a bar mitzvah was a way to change anything, Mo had insisted it could help make his mother get better. The only reason Daisy could think that would make it not matter anymore was if his mom had finally succumbed to the disease. If she had passed away, Mo probably wouldn't want to keep going to Hebrew school or become a bar mitzvah next year or anything. Daisy remembered that one of the last things she'd said to Mo had been that Hebrew school couldn't cure cancer. She cried into her knees. She was the worst person ever.

Daisy barely remembered how she got from Avery's backyard into the preserve or how she came to be sitting on the Angelo Vitali bench. But there she was. She was so utterly alone and completely empty, like she'd never be able to hold a good feeling again—not love or laughter or joy. The Universe didn't want her to be happy, whether that was God or chance or luck or whatever—it didn't matter. It wasn't bad enough that her best friend in the world had died. But when she'd finally allowed a little bit of hope in, and made a new friend in Avery, and let in Mo, who needed a friend he could count on, she'd totally screwed it up. There were no second chances for her.

She rubbed at her tear-swollen eyes and leaned her head down on her knees. She sighed. If she couldn't apologize to her friends, she could at least send a prayer out for them. She bowed her head, closed her eyes, and began to sing.

"Mi shebeirach avoteinu, m'kor hab'racha l'imo-teunu . . ." Her voice cracked a little as she sang, and the tears leaked out the corners of her eyes. She continued, her voice getting stronger. "May the source of strength, Who blessed the ones before us . . ." Her prayer was borne on the wind, up into the trees. "Help us find the courage to make our lives a blessing . . ." Her voice was strong and clear when she sang. "And let us say, 'Amen.'"

As the prayer was carried by the breeze, something shifted in the air around her. A quiet settled on the trees as Daisy sang, "Mi shebeirach imoteinu, m'kor hab-rachah l'avoteinu. Bless those in need of healing with r'fuah sh'leimah—the renewal of body, the renewal of spirit—and let us say, 'Amen.'"

Her prayer reached the top of the trees, and the wind carried it north over the preserve all the way to Avery's house and west to where Mo lived. It was warm and sweet like the springtime, smelling of honeysuckle and sunshine.

Daisy breathed deeply and sat for a moment, her eyes still closed. Then she heard the squish of footsteps treading through the muddy patch on the path as some-one walked toward her. Of all the people in the world it could have been, when she opened her eyes, she was so glad to see that it was Mo.

Bashert

Mo sat down on the bench next to her. He pushed his glasses up on his nose. "Hey," he said, not looking at her.

"Hey," she said back.

She didn't know where to start. Should she say she was sorry about his mom? Or should she apologize first? Should she tell him how much she missed talking to him in the car and at Hebrew school, or would that be too weird? For the past three months, since she'd exploded and told everyone his mom was sick, they'd seen each other at school every day and once a week carpooling and not talked to each other. Now here they were, alone on a bench. And even with all the feelings she'd had and things she'd thought about saying, she was tongue-tied.

Mo said, "I heard you singing."

Oh god, he heard me singing.

"That's the 'Mi Shebeirach' prayer. I sing it every morning for my mom when I wake up."

"I'm really sorry about your mom," Daisy said quickly.

"Your voice is much better than mine," Mo said. "It sounded pretty when you sang it."

Daisy said, "I'm really, really, super sorry that I let everyone know your mom was sick." Her eyes teared up.

"I know you are," Mo said, shaking his head. He sighed. "I told Avery it wasn't your fault. My therapist said if Avery and I wanted to be your friends, we needed to let you be as sad about your friend Ruby as you wanted—even if that meant getting mad at us and stuff."

Daisy swallowed.

He continued, "I told Avery that all that stuff you said that day wasn't about us. It was just you getting mad at the way things are."

He leaned over a little, so their shoulders were touching.

"Gotta be honest, though. I was pretty hurt that you'd done that. But then my therapist reminded me why I wanted to be friends with you in the first place," Mo said.

"You told your therapist you wanted to be friends with me?" Daisy said.

"Yeah," he said. "I told you, Daisy. To me it's bashert."

She sighed. "I wish you wouldn't say that," she said. "Bashert. I don't even know if I believe in that."

"Well, I do," Mo said. "Definitely."

She looked at him. His head was tilted back, and he was looking at the treetops, just like she'd done the other day. He was thinking, and behind his glasses his eyebrows were drawn together in concentration.

"Daisy," he said, sitting up and turning toward her. "When we moved here, I didn't know anyone. We moved so my grandma could help take care of my mom and because the hospital in New York City is one of the best in the country for breast cancer."

Daisy was holding her breath, waiting for Mo to start crying or something, because his mom hadn't made it. But he just kept talking.

"Moving here changed everything for me. I got to go to Hebrew school and learn about being Jewish. And I really like that. I like some of those kids, and I like learning that stuff."

How can he be so positive and upbeat? she thought. *How*

can he look at the bright side of everything when he's just lost his mom? But she didn't say anything. She just let him talk, because it seemed like he needed to. Like he was getting to something.

"But also," he said, "when we first moved here, I spent a lot of time by myself in the preserve, and something happened that I never told anyone about." Daisy sat up straighter.

"What do you mean?" she said.

"It was last June, the first time I'd ever come into the preserve by myself, and I was walking on the paths and just looking around."

She felt goose bumps on her arms, and she crossed them in front of her chest.

"I heard people talking," he said. Now he was looking at her. "It was you and another girl. She was really tiny. She must have been your friend Ruby. She looked like a movie version of a wood sprite or something."

Mo was there the day she and Ruby came into the preserve?

Mo said, "I'd been sitting on this bench, before it got fixed, and I made a wish." Something shifted in the air then, like something was being made right in the world.

Daisy's eyes widened.

"I didn't know when I made it that my wish was

really going to come true, or I would have wished that my mom would get better," Mo said, looking down.

"So what did you wish for?" she asked.

"I wished for a friend," he whispered. "For someone who would understand what I was going through. Someone who'd like me even though I was sad and depressed."

Her eyes filled up with tears yet again. *How much more can one girl cry?* she thought to herself.

"So, you see, our friendship was definitely destined. It was definitely bashert. I saw you with your friend that day. You guys were looking at something—I don't know what—but you were both pretty excited."

He'd been there when they'd seen the fairy.

"And then there you were again, at Hebrew school. And when you looked at me, I could tell you saw me, behind my sadness."

"I'm so sorry, Mo."

"I told you," he said. "I forgave you a long time ago. I was just waiting for you to be ready to be friends again."

"No," she said. "I mean about your mom."

"My mom?" he said.

She couldn't take it. She knew how awful it was to lose someone. It had been so horrible when she'd lost Ruby. It still was. She couldn't imagine losing her mom.

She couldn't imagine what Mo must be feeling. How could he talk to her so easily? How could he be so calm about it?

"My mom is in remission," he said.

Daisy looked at Mo in confusion.

He said, "That means her cancer is gone. . . . Well, for now, at least."

"I know what remission is," she replied. "I just thought . . ." She didn't want to say it.

"What?"

"But how come you're not going to Hebrew school anymore?"

"I'm going to Hebrew school," Mo said. "What do you mean?"

"My aunt texted me that you aren't going to Hebrew school."

"I'm just not going *this week*," Mo said. "We're going to Florida, to Disney World, to celebrate my mom getting a clean bill of health." He grinned, his slightly crooked front tooth catching her attention, as always.

Daisy was wrung out. She'd felt so awful for so long that she'd hurt Mo by betraying his trust. She'd been devastated when she'd thought he'd lost his mother. Now finding out that not only was his mom not gone, but she was okay, and also that Mo had forgiven her a long time ago, she was overwhelmed with emotion. She hadn't thought she could cry any more. But she did. She cried and leaned into his shoulder, and through her sobs she told him how happy she was that his mom was okay. He didn't tell her not to cry or anything. He just let her do it, and she stopped when she was done. He told her Mr. Rosen had seen an owl going in and out of the box, with all kinds of small dead things to feed the owlets.

Then he looked at his phone and said he had to go. His parents would probably get mad at him because, as usual, he was going to be late getting back to the house, and he had to pack. Daisy sat for a minute and watched him walk away. Then she wished she'd thought to give him one of the cupcakes in her backpack.

Dear Avery

Dear Avery,

I'm sorry you had to move. You said that would be the second-worst thing to happen after your parents getting divorced. I think the third-worst thing to happen to you was becoming friends with me. I'm really sorry about the terrible things I said to you at school that day. I could blame it on being sick, because I left school with a super-high fever. But that's not really the whole truth. The truth is that I wasn't brave enough to talk to

you about my friend Ruby, and what
happened to her, and I blamed you
for that. Mo said I wasn't ready, so
for him, that's why it's okay. He and
I made up, by the way. I don't think
he's right, though. Because the way
I treated you wasn't okay at all. You
were always super nice to me. You were
also very patient. But I was a terrible
person to you. I hoped I'd get a second
chance, and I could apologize to you,
and we could be friends again. Because
I really liked being friends with you
a lot. It's funny, even though you are
super different than my friend Ruby
was, I'm pretty sure you would have
liked each other. I wish I'd had the
chance to tell you about her. I'm sorry
I didn't get a second chance to be
your friend, but I hope you make nice
friends in your new school. I'm really
sorry, and I hope you forgive me.

Your friend,
Daisy Rubens

Daisy put down her pen. When Mo came back to school after his trip to Florida, she'd see if he knew where Avery had moved. She slid the letter into an envelope and sealed it. Chewie barked at the back slider, and she let him in. Dahlia was in her bouncy seat in the kitchen, banging her toy with one hand and sucking her thumb on the other. Daisy bent down and kissed the top of her head.

"See you later, baby face." Dahlia popped her thumb out of her mouth and said, "Da!" at Daisy, reaching for her with a drool-covered fist.

"Gross," Daisy said, ducking away. "I love you, but you're disgusting."

"I loved you when you were a disgusting little baby," Mom said, coming into the kitchen and handing Daisy her backpack.

"Daisy was never disgusting," Dad said, coming in behind Mom.

"Dad, can you drive me to school? I want to get to first period early. Mr. Herman is giving out five extra points to the whole class if we're all in our seats before the bell. Since Mo's in Florida, and he's the only one who's always late, we actually have a chance at this."

*　*　*

When Daisy got to her locker, it wouldn't open. Five-thirteen-six. She twirled the combination around and did it again. Five-thirteen-six. But again it wouldn't open. Of all the days, she couldn't be late.

Then she heard a voice behind her say, "What are you doing?"

She spun around. It was Avery, and she was wearing a T-shirt that said I WEAR THIS SHIRT PERIODICALLY over the periodic table.

"That's my locker," Avery said.

Daisy looked over her shoulder. It was. She'd been trying to open the wrong locker.

"I thought you moved," Daisy said.

"Why'd you think that?" Avery asked.

"Because I went to your house over spring break, and it looked like you'd moved out."

"Why did you go to my house?"

Daisy blushed. This was it. Her second chance. She swallowed and tried to say something, but the words wouldn't come out.

"I wrote you a letter," she finally said. "I was going to try to find out your new address and mail it." She reached into her backpack and handed Avery the letter.

"Did you know snail mail has decreased by forty

percent in the past fifteen years?" Avery said, looking at the envelope.

Daisy shook her head and smiled. "Nope. Didn't know that."

"My mom decided to remodel the kitchen while me and my brother were on vacation with my dad over spring break," Avery said. "She's renovating and making Melania's bedroom into a home office."

"Wow," Daisy said. "Where's Melania going to sleep?"

Avery smiled at Daisy. "She fired her," Avery said.

"Yes!" Daisy said.

"My mom got a new job where she mostly works from home, so she said she doesn't need Melania. Plus, it's for more money, so we don't have to move. I think my mom was pretty happy to fire her."

Carlos was jogging down the hall, oblivious as usual. Avery stepped to the left; Daisy stepped to the right. The hall monitor wearily said, "No running, Carlos!"

Carlos replied, "I'm not running!"

Daisy's phone vibrated in her pocket. She sneaked a glance at the text, making sure the hall monitor didn't see and confiscate her phone. It was from Aunt Toby. It said, HAPPY MONDAY, HONEYPOT. SEE YOU AT YOGA LATER. LOVE YOU MADLY. Aunt Toby didn't understand that all caps was shouting.

"I have a phone now," Daisy said as they walked toward Mr. Herman's class.

"I know," Avery said. "I see you showing pictures to Amanda all the time."

"She got a labradoodle puppy," Daisy said. "So I show her pictures of Chewbacca, and she shows me her puppy." Avery smiled.

They got to Mr. Herman's class right on time, and he gave the whole class five points toward their final exam. They were going to watch *Blue Planet*—an episode all about the coral reef. Daisy took her seat. She gazed over at Avery, who had taken her seat near the window. Mr. Herman turned the lights off and put the movie on, and Daisy sighed and started watching.

After a few minutes Avery went up to Mr. Herman's desk and asked him if she could go to the bathroom. When she came back, she slipped Daisy a piece of paper on her way back to her seat. Daisy looked down at her lap, where the paper was. It was the envelope from her letter. She turned it over. It was empty.

On the back, in her tiny, neat handwriting, Avery had written her phone number and the words, *I did make nice friends in my new school. I believe in second chances.*

Amity

Hanging out with Mo or Avery or both together became usual again. "I like that sign," Mo said with a smile on his face as they walked past through the preserve.

The sign had an arrow pointing to a huge tree, and underneath it said DAWN REDWOOD [METASEQUOIA], but on the other side of the sign it said GNOME HOME TREE under the arrow because Daisy could imagine a little gnome with a beard popping its head out of one of the crevices in the bottom of the ropy trunk. Then it said GNOME: SMALL, DWARFLIKE FAIRIES WHO DWELL IN THE EARTH, GUARD ITS TREASURES, AND USUALLY WEAR POINTY RED CAPS.

"I like all of them," Daisy said. "I tried hard to make them useful but still fun."

"Petrichor," Mo said, taking a deep breath in through his nose.

"Huh?" Daisy said.

"Petrichor's the word for that yummy smell of the ground after it rains."

"Yeah, I know," Daisy said, breathing through her nose too. "I thought you were talking about the signs."

"Oh no," Mo said. He offered her a jelly bean from the bag he was holding. She looked in, and they were all black, so she just took one.

"Did you figure out how many babies there are?"

"Baby owls are called owlets," Mo said, "I think three. It's hard to know until they come out of the box."

The path was soft from the previous night's rain, but not too muddy. The owl box that Mo and his dad built together had been installed on a tree near the pond. When Mo and Daisy got to the fork in the path, there was a sign with an arrow pointing that way, and underneath it said UPPER CAIRDEAS POND. On the back of that sign there was also an arrow, under which it said WILL O'WISPS, and then the definition, A BIOLUMINESCENT WATER SPRITE. WARNING: MAY BE DANGEROUS TO FOLLOW!

"When will the owlets come out of the box?" Daisy asked as they got to the deck near the pond. Mo offered Daisy the jelly beans again, but she shook her head, so he popped the last handful into his mouth, crumpled the paper bag, and stuck it in the back pocket of his jeans. Daisy sat on the bench near the rail, and Mo plopped down in his usual spot, feet under the rail and hanging over the edge of the deck.

"That's hard to know too," Mo said. "We don't know exactly when the mom laid the eggs or when exactly they hatched."

"I hate not knowing when stuff is going to happen," Daisy said. She picked her feet up and wrapped her arms around her knees, looking out over the pond. There were yellow irises here and there and pink azaleas blooming everywhere. Looking over the rail into the water, she could see the carp swimming around.

"No kidding," Mo said. "This year has been so much not knowing. It gives me a stomachache sometimes."

"Me too," Daisy said.

He took a deep breath and let it out. He kicked his feet back and forth, and the shadow of his Vans danced on the water.

"So, I started bar mitzvah tutoring last week, and my mom's been planning the party," he said.

"Is it going to be big?" Daisy asked.

"Bigger than anything I've ever had, that's for sure," Mo said. "But not like that girl Anna's was."

"Yeah," Daisy said, "but Anna's was so nice. The flowers were so pretty."

"I don't remember the flowers, but the cupcakes were really good," Mo said. "We're doing the party here. At the mansion at the preserve."

"That's cool. Mine's going to be small," Daisy said. "My mom said we'll just have a brunch thing at the synagogue and then take a family trip to Italy next summer."

"Italy?" Mo said. "Not Israel?"

"My mom's got some kind of Jewish heritage tour of Italy she wants us to do." Daisy shrugged. "I'd rather do that than have a fancy party that would be over in a few hours."

"I'm kind of looking forward to a fancy party," Mo laughed. "It feels like a pretty big thing for me to become a bar mitzvah." He nodded. "And it's like celebrating everything, you know?"

Daisy knew he meant his mom's health. She nodded too.

"Let's go look at the owl box," Mo said. "We won't see anything, but I like to go check anyway."

As they stepped off the deck and started walking

down the path together, Mo's shoulder bumped into Daisy by accident. So, she bumped him back on purpose. They both laughed, then started jogging toward the owl box.

It was weird. For as long as Daisy could remember being a kid, Ruby had been her friend. But Ruby would never *not* be a kid. She'd had that thought before, and every time she did, she got *so* sad. Part of growing up and getting older is exactly that, *growing up and getting older*. She remembered when she and Ruby were talking about *like* liking boys or girls, about getting boy crazy or girl crazy, and how neither of them was even close to ready to think about that. It was less than a year later now. If Ruby were still here, she'd be turning thirteen this August, in just a few months. Even the thought of that made Daisy's eyes tear up. Daisy would be starting bat mitzvah tutoring in the fall, even though she didn't turn thirteen until February. Ugh. Ruby wouldn't be at her bat mitzvah, either. She hadn't even begun thinking about her bat mitzvah before Ruby died. She was only twelve now, but in the past year she felt like she'd grown up a lot more than just one year.

When she and Avery talked about liking boys or

girls, Avery said she thought she could *like* like either. As they sat on the stone wall, looking out at the sound, Avery handed Daisy a box of raisins. She opened the box in her hand, counted out three, and popped them into her mouth.

"Every time I think about that bookish girl, Kristin, who's in my social studies class, my stomach gets kind of fluttery," Avery said. Daisy was listening and eating her raisins one by one, chewing thoughtfully as Avery talked. "She's so smart!"

"I don't really know her," Daisy said. "I think she went to the other Roosevelt Cove elementary school."

"But my stomach also gets fluttery when I think about that boy Garrett, who's in advanced math with me."

Daisy knew Garrett. He was on the soccer team with Mo.

"I just can't tell if it's Garrett or advanced math that makes my stomach feel fluttery," Avery said.

Daisy laughed. "Oh, Avery," she said.

Then Avery Googled *How do you know if you have a crush on somebody?* Of course she did.

"Apparently some of the symptoms are butterflies in your stomach and giddy laughter."

"It says that?" Daisy said.

"Yep," Avery answered.

They sat quietly for a minute, looking out at the water. Then Daisy began to laugh. Which made Avery laugh. Until they were both sitting there, giggling.

Then Daisy said, "Oh my god, are we giddy?"

Avery said, "I mean, it's funny, but on a scale of one to ten, I'd rate it a one for giddy."

Daisy laughed again and said, "I'd rate it a one too!"

"I love you, Daisy," Avery said, "but I don't *like* like you. Sorry."

Daisy smiled and said, "Me neither! I mean I don't *like* like you either."

She stopped smiling and swallowed. Her eyebrows drew together. Avery had just said *I love you* to her, so matter-of-factly. Like it was no big deal. Like *of course* Avery loved Daisy. Daisy had never thought about whether she loved Avery. That wasn't something she and Ruby had ever said to each other. They did, of course, love each other. Had loved each other.

"What's wrong?" Avery said, her smile fading. Daisy swiped at her eyes.

"I love you too, Avery," Daisy said. Avery put her arm around Daisy's shoulders.

"Why's that make you sad, though?" Avery asked.

"I don't remember ever telling Ruby I love her. I mean, *loved* her," Daisy said, wiping tears off her cheeks.

"I don't even remember the last thing I said to her, like if it was something important or stupid or whatever."

"Hey, I never knew Ruby," Avery said, "but from everything you've told me, and knowing you, I would say there's a ninety-nine percent chance she knew how much you loved her."

Daisy put her head on Avery's shoulder. "I don't know what I'd do without you, Ave," Daisy said.

"I know, right?" Avery said. "You'd have to listen to Mo talking and talking and talking about his owls and his bar mitzvah one-hundred-percent by yourself!" They both laughed.

"I mean it," Daisy said.

"I know," Avery replied. "Same for me."

Creating Magic

*D*aisy climbed through the top branches of the tree bridge. A twig pulled at her T-shirt, and she flicked it off and kept climbing. She stood atop the trunk for a second, then made her way over to the fence. It was hard to even remember that this used to feel dangerous or difficult. She stopped, as she always did, before leaving her property and entering the preserve. She scanned the sky, and there was the osprey, riding a thermal. In a few weeks it would be a year since Ruby died. Just thinking about that gave Daisy an ache under her ribs. It felt like forever ago and also like yesterday. She took a deep breath and kept going. On the other side she jumped down, and the satisfying thud of her sneakers landed on the soft forest floor. Her phone dinged. She slid it from the outside pocket of her backpack and saw the new message. Meet us at the gazebo, it said. She wrote back, On my way.

As she always did when she walked past the underside of the fallen oak, she looked over her shoulder where the fairy window had once been, just in case. The sun shone through the lacy spaces in the dirt, the rays of light looking almost solid against the bits of soil that clung to the roots. It looked like she could reach out and touch the golden beams, just like that first day. But there wasn't anything sparkly to be seen through the other side. Nothing glittered or fluttered. Nothing flitted, bird or insect or tiny magical flying personlike being, through the opening. No fairy.

She hitched her backpack up on her shoulders and walked toward the path. She passed one of her signs. On one side of the sign was an arrow pointing toward the bench. It said ANGELO VITALI BENCH. The other side of the sign also pointed to the bench, but it said GOOD PLACE TO REST, WISH, PRAY, THINK.

It was warm for the end of June, and she'd forgotten to put on deodorant. She sniffed under her arm to make sure she didn't stink. Not that either Mo or Avery would notice, or care if she did. If anything, Avery would probably explain the mechanism of sweating and what the chemical makeup of perspiration is, and suggest doing an experiment to compare whose sweat was smelliest. She smiled, thinking about it.

"What are you so smiley about?" Mo asked as Daisy approached the gazebo. He was sitting on the ledge, his beat-up Vans kicking against the lattice below him.

"Just thinking," Daisy said, sitting down and shrugging off her backpack.

"Thinking about what?" Avery asked as she rummaged through her string bag.

"Body odor," Daisy said. Mo and Avery looked at her, and nobody said anything for a minute. Then they all giggled. Daisy took three apples out of her backpack, and in unison they bit into them.

"Body odor?" Mo said around a mouthful of apple. He shook his head. "I thought I was supposed to be the weirdo."

Avery swallowed the enormous bite she'd been chewing. "I'm pretty sure all three of us are the weirdo," she said.

Daisy took a tidy bite of her apple.

When they finished, they all threw the cores toward the tree line. Mo's went farthest, and he grinned and wiggled his eyebrows at them behind his glasses.

"Whatever," Avery said.

Daisy laughed.

Then Mo adjusted his glasses on his nose. Avery was holding a blue bandanna, twisting it and untwisting it. Mo said, "So, we kind of have a surprise for you, Daisy."

"I don't like surprises," Daisy said. "What kind of surprise?"

"It's a good surprise," Avery said. "It's a hakuna matata surprise."

Mo rolled his eyes. "It's not funny, Ave."

"It's a little funny," Avery said.

"She means it's a tikkun olam kind of surprise," he said.

"You're surprising me by . . . repairing the world?" Daisy said. "I don't get it."

"Well, we can't repair the whole world all at once," Mo said. "So I told Ave we should start with one person at a time, you know? Tikkun olam can be giving a friend a surprise."

Avery added, "And besides, surprises are fun. But we have to do it correctly for it to work." Daisy looked down at the bandanna. Avery said. "The correct procedure for surprising someone includes a blindfold. So here." She handed it to Daisy.

"Seriously?" Daisy said. She looked at Mo.

He shrugged. "It's a nice surprise," he said. "You won't be disappointed. Promise."

So she took the bandanna, folded it, and tied it around her head, covering her eyes. It was soft and smelled like the lavender detergent all of Avery's clothing smelled like now that Melania wasn't doing the laundry, which made it not as bad to put on.

"Okay," Daisy said. "Surprise me."

She heard Mo jump down from the ledge. Avery grabbed her left hand. Mo took her right hand, which made her stomach do something weird. She was pretty sure she'd never held his hand before. She hoped this didn't mean she was going to start to get boy crazy. She still didn't feel ready to *like* like anybody. Even Mo.

"Careful going down the step," Mo said.

It was strange, walking blindfolded over the grass. The sun warmed her face, but she couldn't tell which way they were going, because she'd forgotten to pay attention when they first started walking. Gravel crunched under her feet, and Avery gave her hand a squeeze.

"We're almost there," Mo said.

"You can take the blindfold off, for the maximum surprise effect, when we get there," Avery said.

Daisy tried to think where the gravel path led from the gazebo, and where they might be taking her.

"Are you getting excited?" Avery said. "I thought walking blindfolded would increase the anticipation for your surprise. And that would make it even better."

Daisy chuckled. Avery was so Avery. "Well, my eyelids are sweating behind the bandanna," Daisy said. "So I'm looking forward to taking it off. Do sweating eyelids count as increased anticipation?"

She lost her footing for a second and stumbled when there was a shallow dip in the gravel. Avery grabbed her elbow.

"I'm all right," Daisy said, and they kept walking.

"Careful," Mo said as they started walking on grass again.

"Are we almost there?" Daisy asked.

"We're here," Mo and Avery said together.

"Can I take this thing off?" Daisy asked, reaching for the bandanna.

Mo cleared his throat. Avery said, "Yes."

She slid the bandanna off her head, and the knot pulled at her hair, catching in one of the curls. Avery helped her untangle it. They were standing at the edge of a copse of trees.

"What's the surprise?" Daisy said.

"Look in the trees," Mo said, his voice catching in his throat. But she looked at him instead. He took off his glasses and wiped at his eyes with the back of his hand.

"Mo?" Daisy said.

"He's okay," Avery said, putting her arm around him and giving him a half side hug. "Right, Mo?"

"I'm okay," he said.

Daisy scanned the trees but didn't see anything in particular. She took a few steps closer, looking up and squinting.

"It's not up," he said. "Look down." His voice sounded hoarse.

She took another step closer to the tree line, and then she saw it. Near the bottom of a big evergreen tree, almost where the trunk met the ground, was a small triangular green wooden door set into the tree. In the middle of the door was painted a white-and-yellow daisy. There was a small brass doorknob and a little window in the top part of the triangle. Next to the door was a miniature bell. Daisy knelt down and touched it with her finger and heard a teeny-tiny *ding*.

She looked at Avery, who was smiling. "Open the door," Avery said.

She looked at Mo, who was wiping at his eyes again.

"Did you do this? Did you make this?" she asked him. He looked away.

Daisy gently tugged at the brass knob. The door swung open perfectly on miniature hinges. She looked at her friends, and Avery was beaming. She nodded at Daisy to keep going. Daisy peered into the space beyond the door, and there was a small pale green envelope inside. She took it out, and on it, in tiny, very precise handwriting, it said *Open Me*.

"Open it," Avery said.

"What is this?" Daisy said. "Why did you guys do this?"

"Read what it says," Avery said. Avery still had her arm around Mo, who looked like he needed it.

Daisy took the tiny piece of paper out of the little envelope and had to squint to read it, it was written so small. It was clearly Avery's handwriting, and Daisy knew that Mo had built the fairy door.

She couldn't figure out what she'd done to deserve friends like Mo and Avery. It was a miracle.

She would never ever stop being sad about Ruby's death or stop missing her. She was so lucky, though. Mo and Avery had shown up when she was so sad and broken and lost that she didn't think she could ever make another friend. They had let her be awful when

she needed to be awful, and then let her come back and
be their friend again. She looked down at the tiny note.

It said . . .

Dear human,
Don't stop looking.
Magic is everywhere.
Friendship is forever.
Your friends,
The fairies

Something caught the light in the trees above them.

Daisy, Avery, and Mo looked up at the same time. In
the branches of the tree above them, there was something
sparkly, maybe even magical. And they saw it together.

Dear Readers

I know from personal experience how devastating it can feel to lose someone you love. It's not something we ever forget, even when we grow up. It changes us. When someone we care about dies, or leaves in other ways, sometimes it's hard to imagine a path through our sadness. But we can and do eventually move forward. Sometimes it's a friend—an old one or a new one—that helps us. Sometimes it's a thing that seems impossible or improbable or maybe even maybe magical.

For those of you who are grieving, I want you to know: I see you. Imagine me tossing a sprinkle of healing fairy dust out to you, sparkling and shimmering, like a prayer on the wind. Try to keep your heart open to receiving it, even when it's difficult. Keep looking for magic in the world.

Acknowledgments

There are so many people I want to thank, who have made a difference for me as I wrote this book. The first person I must acknowledge is my agent, Rena Rossner, who understood what was at the heart of my story and championed it into the world—I am very grateful for her support and partnership. Thank you to my editor Kristin Gilson, who took such care and kindness helping me express the nuances of grieving and healing, and cried every time she read and re-read the manuscript.

To Peijin Yang, who captured the emotions of my story and created the most dreamy cover to reflect them, and art director Heather Palisi, who designed such a beautiful interior. To Rebecca Vitkus and Elizabeth Mims, whose comprehensive copyediting included correcting this Marvel fan's mistakes (thank you!); the rest of the team at Aladdin/Simon & Schuster, Valerie Garfield, Sara Berko, Olivia Ritchie, Amy Beaudoin, Lisa Quach, and Nadia Almahdi.

To my New School ladies—you know who you are— for being there from the very beginning; Jill Santopolo for helping me see that there was a place for my story out in the world, when it was barely a germ of an idea. To Edward Einhorn at Gotham Writer's Workshop, for making me plot, when pantsing left me with a saggy middle; my childhood friend Dr. Cori Bussolari for vetting my questions about grief early on in the life of this story.

To my book coven—Amber McBride, Ally Malinenko, and Kath Rothschild—for their friendship and encouragement; my clients, who help make me be a better writer and call me to be a better person; Sarah Aroeste, for being my Berkshires guardian angel.

To my ECLA family—Mandy Hubbard, Garrett Alwert, Caitlin White, and D. Ann Williams—for woohooing me on my journey to publication; my beloved doodles, for lending place-saver names that stuck; James Morrison, for the coziest writing space in which to finish; George Brown and everyone at the Highlights Foundation for providing me the time, space, and place to put words on the page.

Rabbi Lee Friedlander, Rabbi Jodie Siff, Cantor Eric Schulmiller, and the Reconstructionist Synagogue of the North Shore community, for informing and transforming my relationship with Judaism.

To Wendy Paisner and Jamie McCormack for asking me all the right questions with compassion and humor.

To Karen Fisher, Toby Helfenstein, Robin Arzt, Jenny deBeer Charno, Tracy Frierman, and Cynthia Rosen—for always being there to share the good times, and holding my hand to walk me through the bad ones, until I could walk myself—I couldn't have better best friends; my dear friend Alison Green Myers for being a critique partner and writing buddy without equal—our friendship is bashert and this book wouldn't be in the world without her.

To Judi Epstein for her witchy magic and big love; Christi Nelsen-Epstein for unwavering support and confidence in me; David Nelsen-Epstein for everything (Yes, *everything!*); Stewart Weingord, for his strength, dependability, and belief in me.

Thank you to my children—Anna, Rayna, and Spencer—for their steadfast love and faith in my ability (I adore you with all my heart, my loves).

And lastly, thank you to my parents, who didn't live to see this book published, but who always encouraged me to live a creative life and see the magic around me. They would have been so proud.